S0-AYV-077

STEP BY STEP

As he rode, Cedric countered the effects of his aches and pains by thinking of the times he had been happiest recently, the times he had spent with Jane. He relived their kisses. Each one of them—and there had been far too few—had seared itself into his head and heart.

The first kisses in the garden, between the rows of yews, had been perfect. Eager, yet tentative. Warm, yet unskilled. Innocent, yet carrying an undercurrent of excitement. The rush of a first encounter, the initial step toward passion. She had not pushed him away or ordered him to stop. . . .

Other Books by Victoria Hinshaw

The Fontainebleau Fan

The Eligible Miss Elliott

Miss Parker's Ponies

Miss Milford's Mistake

Cordelia's Corinthian

An Ideal Match

Least Likely Lovers
(Coming in September 2005)

Published by Zebra

ASK JANE

Victoria Hinshaw

ZEBRA BOOKS
Kensington Publishing Corp.
www.kensingtonbooks.com

ZEBRA BOOKS are published by

Kensington Publishing Corp.
850 Third Avenue
New York, NY 10022

Copyright © 2005 by Victoria Hinshaw

All rights reserved. No part of this book may be reproduced
in any form or by any means without the prior written con-
sent of the Publisher, excepting brief quotes used in reviews.

If you purchased this book without a cover you should be
aware that this book is stolen property. It was reported as "un-
sold and destroyed" to the Publisher and neither the Author
nor the Publisher has received any payment for this "stripped
book."

All Kensington titles, imprints and distributed lines are available at special quantity discounts for bulk purchases for sales
promotion, premiums, fund-raising, educational or institu-
tional use.

Special book excerpts or customized printings can also be created to fit specific needs. For details, write or phone the office
of the Kensington Special Sales Manager: Kensington Publishing Corp., 850 Third Avenue, New York, NY 10022. Attn.
Special Sales Department. Phone: 1-800-221-2647.

Zebra and the Z logo Reg. U.S. Pat. & TM Off.

First Printing: April 2005
10 9 8 7 6 5 4 3 2 1

Printed in the United States of America

With gratitude to the members of The Beau Monde.
Special thanks to Shari, Mary, Denise, Sherrie,
Jo, Margaret, Muna, Donna, Jan, Pam,
and particularly to Ed.

CHAPTER ONE

Cedric Williamson forced a hearty laugh before he drained his tankard and slapped it on the rough table in the noisy taproom.

"Yer awful cheerful fer a man whose new horse came in last in 'er first race." Charlie's voice slurred with drink.

Tom guffawed. "'Specially when ye lost yer skirt . . . ah, shirt."

Charlie almost choked on his cackle. "An' 'is breeches besides!"

Cedric gave an elaborate shrug, hoping his façade of careless indifference convinced the innkeeper as well as his companions. He pushed his chair back and stood, pretending to stagger like a drunkard. "Goin' to the privy . . ."

He stumbled once or twice on the way to the far door, then pushed out of the hot, smoky gloom into the spring chill. As quickly as his skin cooled, he shook off the effects of the meager amount of ale he had actually consumed. The ostlers and stable boys tossed dice at the lighted doorstep of the distant kitchen. Now well past midnight, the yard was silent. No one else seemed to be about.

Trying to keep to the shadows, Cedric crept across the empty yard and cracked open the stable door. He winced at its rusty creak, and held his breath for a moment. No one called out. All he could hear was the rustle of horses from inside.

Inhaling deeply, he edged through the opening and pulled the door shut. Now accustomed to the darkness, he had no trouble finding his saddle horse, Atlas. He let himself into the stall and grabbed his bridle from a peg, whispering softly, hoping the animal would cooperate. Atlas shook his head and backed up, holding his head high and out of reach. Cedric took a piece of sugar from his pocket and held it out.

In a well-practiced move, as the horse reached for the sugar, Cedric slipped the bit between Atlas's teeth and lifted the bridle over his ears. "Ha," he murmured. "Your greed will always win out, old boy."

Cedric tossed his saddle over the horse's back, cinched up the girth, and fastened his saddlebags over Atlas's rump. He swung the stall door open and led the immense black horse down the aisle. The back door opened with another creak, but again no one stirred.

Once into the lane behind the inn, he checked the cinch, then swung up on Atlas, heading him toward a stable near the track that housed that damnable filly. If he were not so cursedly angry, he would never consider breaking in to steal his own property. He had been thoroughly gulled, cheated like a green youth still wet behind the ears. He, Cedric Williamson, a Corinthian of considerable sporting abilities, a London man about town, admired for his skill in the ring and at swordplay, winner of innumerable curricle races with his pair of prize chestnuts.

Yes, he, Cedric Williamson, had been fleeced like the most gullible gapeseed ever to hit the Newmarket racecourse. Swindled out of his last shilling. Left with a stack of debts worth his total quarterly allowances for the next five years.

His only course of action was flight, and the least he could do was take Atlas and that damnable filly with him. Take them to the only place he knew where he could lick his wounds in seclusion. Uphaven, Aunt Amelia's estate, was only a dozen miles away—or was it twenty? Lord, it had been years since he visited, but the place was vast and sure to be signposted from the main road to St. Edmundsbury

It would carry a considerable cost to his self-regard. No

matter what kind of story he concocted for her, his sharp-witted aunt would know the truth before the week was out. As one of the leading inhabitants of Suffolk, she had an indefatigable circle of contacts and correspondents around the county. Nothing happened here that did not come to her eager ears.

He could only take refuge in the truth, however lowering it was. He had nowhere else to go. He was already way behind in paying his shot at that inn, owed half his friends, and had not even a coin or two to toss to a groom if he waited until morning to fetch his pitiful racehorse.

Devil take it, he had been a fool to fall for that swindler's palaver, though the filly had been a beauty, long-legged and deep in the chest, bright of eye and frisky. He had always prided himself on his ability to pick a fine piece of horseflesh and she looked like a sure thing. Like a chuckleheaded stripling, he had fallen for the pitch that fast-talking Josiah Trentworthy delivered. "She is prime. Best bloodlines. Fast breaker. Heavy on endurance."

Why, Cedric recalled with disgust, he had hardly bargained with the rum cove. Hardly even tried to bring down the price. He had fallen for the story that some London dandy had just gone to find his friends before closing the deal. Cedric had been so anxious he practically jammed his money into Trentworthy's waistcoat.

What a greenhead he was. What a bacon-brained puppy. What a simpleminded pigeon. How Trentworthy must have laughed as he substituted another, broken-down animal.

Or dosed the filly with some potion. Something that changed her from an eager runner to a pitiful scrag. On the track she faded by the halfway point and barely cantered home, dead last by many lengths.

Now, after hours as the butt of innumerable jokes, as recipient of manifold insults and abundant abuse delivered with back-slapping laughter, Cedric let his anger bubble forth in a string of invectives hissed into the dark of the night. His jaw ached from gritting his teeth while the abuse raged, his stomach rumbled from lack of food and only two mugs of ale, and his entire body burned with the urge to exact revenge from that devil of a muckworm who had sold him the horse and almost guaranteed she would win.

At the barn near the track where he had left the filly, Cedric tied Atlas and went inside for the young horse. No one stirred in the darkness, but he would not have cared if he had been challenged. After all, he had a bill of sale in his pocket.

The bay stood in the far corner of the stall, head hung low. She looked nothing like the lively head-tossing specimen he had seen before the race, purchased and put all his money on, along with a considerable number of wagers on credit, bets backed by no cash but the guineas he expected to collect after she won.

The more he looked at her, the more he felt certain she had been switched for a ringer. Either that or nobbled. Drugged.

He had no way to prove either a switch or a drugging. On the bill of sale, the report of a bay filly sixteen hands could have described hundreds of horses right here in Newmarket, perhaps thousands in Suffolk alone.

He scowled at the listless animal, half asleep and breathing shallowly. Maybe it was not worth taking her. But he might as well. Perhaps Aunt Amelia had a little cart that needed pulling.

He found a line to fasten to her halter and pulled her from her stall, slowly, as he would a cantankerous donkey. She plodded out the door behind him with no more spirit than Cedric felt himself. Atlas snorted his disapproval of the sorry nag as Cedric mounted again, but they moved off and found the empty road by the light of a pale half-moon.

Now, if she didn't break down completely getting away from Newmarket and to Uphaven, at least he had salvaged something after losing his last farthing. Better than nothing. But only barely.

In the middle of the night, his head was not quite up to

totaling his debts. Paying his shot at that inn was the least of his worries except for the fact that a constable would be quickly on his case if he did not make good on that particular obligation. But by heading out of town without anyone finding out, he would at least escape the immediate shame of being unable to meet his betting obligations on top of being gulled, hoaxed, and thoroughly swindled!

Jane Gabriel dipped her pen in ink and wrote the date, 6 April, 1816, at the top of the page. She bent to her task of summarizing the letter before she was called for breakfast. While Jane had a penchant for rising early, her mother and Lady Stockdale preferred to sleep most of the morning away. Which gave her a few extra hours to work each day.

Her account of the contents took almost an entire page. She quickly looked over the letter to see that she had covered the essentials, replaced it in the velvet box of papers from the last century, and put it in a drawer. If she started working on the next letter, her absorption in its contents might cause her to miss breakfast again, setting Lady Stockdale and her mother to fretting.

She stood and smoothed her dark blue skirt, then glanced in a mirror to straighten her cap and tuck up a few strands of her long gold hair. She wrinkled her nose at her pink lips and clear blue eyes. No matter how she tried to pull back her hair into a tight bun, a few tendrils always escaped to curl around her apple cheeks and give her the baby-faced countenance of a country milkmaid instead of the scholarly and sober look she wished for. She certainly did not look her four and twenty years. Perhaps a pair of spectacles would give her an air of studious intensity.

Why would anyone wish to hire a young chit to pursue a serious study of family history? Jane knew she had the ability to write the story Lady Stockdale wanted, but her mother's dear friend wanted a man for the project. Jane's contribution would be limited to organization, construction of a chronology and notes on the biographies of the artists represented in the Uphaven collection, all material to be turned over to some man to form into a narrative account.

She was perfectly well qualified to write the book. She had been studying for years, though she owed this employment to her mother's friendship with Lady Stockdale, not to her abilities. Nevertheless, she was determined to convince Lady Stockdale that she could accomplish more than any latecomer to the material.

Her hope was that eventually the excellence of her book would bring her new projects. She would sign her name "J. D. Gabriel" and conduct negotiations by post to protect her identity as a female.

Fortunately, from what she was learning about Lady Stockdale's late husband, the sixth Lord Stockdale, and his forebears, the story would be interesting enough to capture the attention of many a potential client looking for a family biographer. Jane knew she was capable of giving the story of the Barons Stockdale of Uphaven and their art collection a life that would resonate with a large audience.

Giving her reflection another frown in the mirror, Jane left Lord Stockdale's library and went outside, taking the time for a quick turn around the early spring garden before she joined her mother and Lady Stockdale in the breakfast room.

At the end of the smoothly trimmed hedges, there was a double perspective. In one direction, the Jacobean house of mellow pink-toned brick was perfectly framed between allées of conical yews. In the opposite direction, an opening cut into the hedge acted as a window to the broad expanse of flat heath stretching to the horizon.

Peering outward, she saw the fields dotted with hundreds, perhaps thousands of sheep, ewes hardly moving, lambs playing hide and seek among their fat mamas cropping at the rich turf. Tall, billowing clouds skimmed across the wide span of bright blue sky, heading west away from the sea. The scene was the perfect image of bucolic English beauty, prosperity, and serenity.

The Suffolk landscape fascinated Jane, so different from the steep wooded hills and narrow valleys of Somersetshire near their home in Bath. She heard an occasional bleat, and sniffed the slightly salty fresh breeze gusting from the distant sea. Beyond was the place she yearned to visit someday, the canals and fields of Holland, subject of so much of the seventeenth-century Dutch art she had studied. Not until she saw the sweep of the Suffolk plain had she realized how much the landscape resembled that of the Low Countries.

The view across the heath told the whole story of the Uphaven art collection. The fortune based on the wool trade, the business conducted in Bruges and Amsterdam, the familial affection for the seventeenth-century Dutch masters. It all added up. No wonder Lord Stockdale, his father, and his grandfather before him had been drawn to the art of van Ruisdael, Cuyp, even Judith Leyster. Discovering the art of a female was the most exciting surprise of her work so far. Jane chastised herself for her unfortunate habit of gazing over the fields and letting her mind wander. She hurried back, the breeze blowing her cap from her head and requiring her to rearrange her hair again before joining the others in the breakfast room.

Amelia, Lady Stockdale, looked up at the opening of the door with a sweet smile. Her pale face was crisscrossed with webs of little wrinkles, making her skin look as though it had been wadded up like thin tissue paper and never successfully smoothed out again. She was comfortably plump and dressed in the same dark colors Jane's mother always wore. Despite her handsome fortune, Lady Stockdale was no haughty termagant. She had been a good friend to Jane's mother for as long as Jane could remember.

Jane's mama, Mrs. Gabriel, was thin and angular where Lady Stockdale was plump and rounded. As soon as she received her stipend from Lady Stockdale, Jane intended to have a gown made for her mama to replace the worn hand-me-downs that Lady Stockdale had re-cut for her best friend. Mrs. Gabriel refused to take charity from anyone, but from time to time, Lady Stockdale managed to make her insistence stick.

Jane dropped a little curtsy to Lady Stockdale and patted her mother's shoulder as she passed behind her to take a seat at the table. "I have been reading the fourth baron's letters from Paris in the 1740s. It was just after the war and he was eager to reestablish his French contacts."

"My, my." Lady Stockdale took a slice of ham from the footman's platter.

"He attended a salon in the studio of an artist and wrote of his regret that he had not purchased a canvas he saw there."

"I do not think there is a single painting of French origin in the house," Lady Stockdale said.

Jane spooned a bit of jam onto her plate. "It makes him seem more real, does it not? To see that he sometimes wondered if he did the right thing to confine his purchases to Dutch art. But that was what he knew . . ."

"Doubts?" Mrs. Gabriel sounded shocked.

Lady Stockdale nodded. "Very human to have doubts. I am not at all surprised."

Jane's mother spoke softly, almost in a whisper. "Perhaps doubts are the luxury of those who have means . . ."

Lady Stockdale nodded again, her chins waggling. "I have doubts from time to time. Especially doubts about the future. I had planned to leave this estate to my nephew but he has never shown much interest. And he gambles more than he can afford."

Jane gave a little sigh. She had hoped to direct the conversation to her ideas for an introductory chapter.

Lady Stockdale, however, had put down her cup and stared out the window. "I hate to think of him selling some of the land or even this house to finance his bad habits. I still have hope he will eventually outgrow his youthful nonsense."

Jane's mother swallowed a bite of ham. "Is there no entail involved?"

"The Uphaven barony became extinct when Lord Stockdale died. Not a single sprout remained on his family tree. He was the last Baron Stockdale of Uphaven. That is one of the primary reasons I want to make the family story known to the world."

Jane quickly finished chewing her toast, eager to exhibit her knowledge of the material.

But Lady Stockdale was too fast for her. "I remember when I came to Uphaven as a bride. We had a lovely ceremony in London. Do you remember the day, Winnie? It was almost thirty-five years ago . . ."

Jane listened with only half an ear as the two reminisced. There was something infinitely sad about Lord Stockdale and Lady Stockdale living here for so many years, wishing to have the house filled with the childish voices of a large brood of little ones. Lady Stockdale had never mentioned her sadness at having no children but Jane's mother had occasionally reflected upon the unfairness of the childless state of her friend's life. Jane knew that her Mama and Papa had almost given up when she had appeared, like the answer to all their prayers, when Mama was two and forty.

Lady Stockdale had not been fortunate enough, Mama said, to have one child, even a daughter, to carry on her line. And now her chosen heir for the estate was proving a disappointment.

She supposed Lady Stockdale referred to Cedric Williamson. Jane remembered him from a visit several years ago in Bath. A young man too charming by half. Too handsome for his own good. Too concerned with cutting a dash to pay much attention to their quiet circle in Bath. He had taken her for a ride in his curricle, a spin, as he called it.

Her best hat had blown off. She could still remember how her hands ached from clutching the seat when his vehicle skidded around corners and nearly collided with other vehicles more than once.

Back at her door, he had laughed and kissed her gloved

hand after he helped her down and felt her trembling. Jane felt a twinge of distaste when she remembered how her heart had skipped a beat. Certainly it had come from the perils of the ride and not her reaction to his well-practiced techniques of flattery.

Cedric was one of the fellows who had turned her against the idea of marriage. Not that she had a passel of eager suitors anyway. Pretty young females of gentle birth and no financial means were both numerous and distinctly inconsequential. Men of fortune looked to alliances that enhanced their wealth, not to penniless gels with equally needy mamas. Further, Jane had never had the opportunity to know an eligible gentleman well enough to assess his character. Only a man of strong morals and even temperament would appeal to her.

Because Jane knew she was unlikely ever to meet such a man, she considered herself quite firmly on the shelf. And as a spinster, it was even more important that she develop an ability to earn a living sufficient to support her mother as well as herself. She simply must convince Lady Stockdale to let her write the book about the barons.

Lady Stockdale continued her homage to Lord Stockdale's early years. "He made sure that Joshua Reynolds painted my portrait. No one else would do . . ."

Jane knew the work well, for a copy of it hung in the Bath residence where Jane and Mrs. Gabriel made their home nowadays. Several years ago, when their money seemed to go less and less far, dear Lady Stockdale insisted they make use of the house as she rarely visited it anymore. Most of the formal rooms remained in dustcovers, but they had a pleasant apartment on the second floor and their maid, Nell, got on well with the servant couple who cared for the place.

The work from Reynold's brush, and not that of his assistants who made the copies, hung above the fireplace in the Green Drawing Room here at Uphaven. Jane loved the way Lady Stockdale's creamy skin and delicately tinted rosy cheeks contrasted with her upswept, lightly powdered hair. She wore a filmy white fichu and had a thoughtful, almost pensive look on her lovely face. Jane wondered whether, so early in their marriage, Lady Stockdale already knew her attempts to have a family would bring only distress and heartbreak.

The thought that her nephew did not have the sense to live up to her expectations made Jane angry and she stabbed at her eggs with unaccustomed vigor, dropping her fork with a clatter.

Her mother twisted toward her. "Jane, are you unwell?"

Jane shook her head. "Pardon me, Lady Stockdale, Mama. I fear I was daydreaming. Thinking about that Reynolds portrait. I shall be more careful."

Lady Stockdale reached over to pat her hand. "Think nothing of it, my dear. I remember the preparation for the sitting. I wanted to wear something much more grand, with a large brimmed hat and ostrich feathers. But Lord Stockdale would have none of it. He wanted me as I was each day. Quite a romantic fellow he was, don't you know?"

Jane smiled at the dreamy expression on Lady Stockdale's face. Jane's case for writing the book herself could wait for another time. And now she had a new idea for a chapter, centering on an anecdote about how a baron who owned a magnificent art collection would allow no one but the realm's finest portraitist to paint his lovely young wife.

CHAPTER TWO

Hours past noontide, Cedric's stomach growled with hunger. He alternately broke out in a sweat and then chilled to the bone as fast-moving cloudbanks passed across the sun. His head throbbed with each plodding hoofbeat of the two horses. The filly stumbled repeatedly, now limping from a near fall, reducing their progress to a snail's pace. Or slower.

Even Atlas trudged along like a ragpicker's nag, his head hanging listlessly and his ears laid back against his head. Only the angry swish of his tail betrayed the rage the big stallion must have been nurturing inside.

They had long ago turned off the main road and lost their way among a maze of quiet lanes. From the pure tedium of the journey, Cedric's own anger had diminished enough to carry the dilemma of dealing with Aunt Amelia to the forefront of his pulsing head. It had been more than a year since he had seen her, a visit cut short because he had left to go fishing at a friend's Dorset estate, right in the middle of her annual stay in London for a taste of the Season.

She had not seemed offended, but he should have delayed his departure and fussed over her for at least another week or two. This year, she had not come to town at all. Unless she had arrived in the last few days, since he left for Newmarket.

Could he be that fortunate? If she were not at home, the Uphaven servants would be more than happy to welcome him. That is, if he was still her favorite. A stab of dread coursed through his veins. Deuce take it, if Aunt Amelia had bequeathed her fortune and estate to someone else, he was even more hopelessly in the suds. His father had adamantly refused ever to pay another of his debts. As had his brothers. Even his friends were out of the running, for he owed most of them the very money he needed to pay off his debts to others.

In fact, the pitiful state of his finances had caused him to risk everything yesterday.

Risked and lost. Lost it all.

Another stab of anxiety pierced his skull. He had nothing to sell, except that miserable filly, worthless as she looked. He had no skills to offer anyone, for all his talents centered on being a Corinthian of the first order, a man of no use to anyone except as a sparring partner or companion in the hunt. No one paid a Corinthian to be a good sport. Instead of cultivating some aptitude for which he might have received monetary compensation, he had frittered his time away in useless endeavors. Who cared now if Cedric Williamson was a fencer *par excellence* or a dab hand at helping a fellow bid on a pair at Tatersall's?

Not that anyone would ever trust his judgment of a piece of horseflesh again after yesterday's debacle. He looked over at the filly and shook his head in disgust, wincing at the rattle the movement gave his aching brainbox.

Pitiful beast that she was, her eyes had a bit more shine and her ears perked up at his little whistle. Perhaps she really had been given some drug, and the effects were wearing off.

Drugged? The Jockey Club did all they could to punish anybody caught tampering with a horse, but Cedric had no proof. He had not even noticed any suspicious behavior, other than the oily weasel who talked him into the purchase. Cedric shivered as the sun hid once more. He reached in his pocket and found the bill of sale, unfolding it and checking the name of the fellow. Josiah Trentworthy. Worthy indeed! Worthy of a sound thrashing. No, more than that. Return of Cedric's money would be a start.

He glanced at the sum he had paid, two hundred guineas,

of which he had only handed over eighty. Trentworthy would be livid when he discovered Cedric had disappeared. Lucky none of his companions in Newmarket knew of his aunt and her estate.

He glanced behind him but saw no riders approaching, only a single farm wagon. No one could have followed his circuitous route anyway. He kept a careful watch for the next signpost and breathed a sigh of relief when it appeared. "Uphaven, 3 miles." He turned Atlas's head to finish off the last leg of the journey.

Jane cut a morsel of her lamb cutlet and chewed slowly. Lady Stockdale kept country hours, and having a large dinner so early still felt uncomfortable. The older ladies always napped afterwards, but Jane wanted to continue her study of the letters for a few more hours.

Lady Stockdale took a sip of her claret. "I am thinking of joining you in Bath next winter, Winnie. Having you and Jane here for the past few weeks makes me realize how lonely I have been."

"Oh, Amelia, my dear, we would love to have you back. Your old doctor, Mr. Pearson, asks about you every time I see him."

Jane wondered if she and her mother would have to find a new residence if Lady Stockdale took over her house once more.

Lady Stockdale smiled. "I rather fancy the treatments Mr. Pearson used to prescribe. Yes, I seem to remember they made my joints considerably more comfortable."

The sun slid behind a cloud again and the room darkened. As if he came to light the candles, the butler entered.

Lady Stockdale looked up in surprise from her turbot fillet. "What is it, Barton?"

Barton's usually sober face was wreathed in smiles. "It is Mr. Cedric, milady. He will be here in just a—"

"Aunt Amelia!" The tall and handsome nephew clapped Barton's shoulder, pushed past him, and strode up to Lady Stockdale, clasping his startled aunt in an eager hug. "It is so good to see you. I declare, you do not age a day. I'd never have guessed the fountain of youth was right here in Suffolk!"

Jane tried to prevent her reaction of strong distaste from showing on her face. So this was what Cedric Williamson had become, a flatterer, a toadeater, a rogue.

He hardly stopped for breath. "I must say the estate looks excellent. I see the fields quite full of, er, of baby sheep. Hardy looking little things. Now, I apologize for showing up in all my dirt, but I have met with the most peculiar misfortunes. And I must throw myself upon your good nature, dear Aunt Amelia, for I have acquired a young filly who needs attention—"

Lady Stockdale held up her hand to stop him. "I assume this filly is of the equine variety?"

He drew back, eyes wide with a look of exaggerated outrage. Jane smothered a giggle at his over-acting.

He placed a hand on his heart. "Why, obviously, she is a horse. Why would you . . ." He looked around the table, as if noticing Jane and her mother for the first time.

"My dear ladies, please excuse me bursting in upon you. Do I not recall Mrs. Gabriel? How very nice to see you again. It has been much too long indeed."

Jane watched her mother blush, smile and even preen a little at his palaver. No doubt the butler had given him their names before he entered.

"And Jane, Miss Gabriel, is it not? Why I have not had the pleasure of your company for nearly five years, I am sure. You will pardon me for having the audacity to observe that you are in the very best of looks, Miss Gabriel."

Jane wished she could smack his handsome face. Or at the least tell him exactly what she thought of his kind of nonsensical nattering. But she had to confine herself to a mere inclination of her head and a look she hoped told him of her opinion.

But he was cheerily immune to anything as subtle as a reproving look. When Lady Stockdale, waving away his feeble protests, invited him to sit down and partake of the meal, he again made bows to all three of them and, continuing his dissent, immediately sat. As soon as Barton brought him a plate, Cedric filled his mouth with food, thankfully breaking his constant flow of words.

Lady Stockdale wore an affectionate smile, though her tone was less accommodating. "You have not mentioned the circumstances, however peculiar, under which you acquired this filly of yours."

Cedric paused, swallowed, and grinned. "I will not try to embroider this sad tale, dear Aunt Amelia. I was spending a few days in Newmarket, as you no doubt had already presumed."

Unless Jane was entirely mistaken, Lady Stockdale actually rolled her eyes before nodding.

"I, ah, purchased the filly before a race in which she looked to be an easy winner—"

"But she did not succeed." Lady Stockdale's observation was a statement, not a question.

"Indeed, she did not. I regret to say she was . . . she came in last."

Again, Jane had to bite her lip to keep from laughing out loud.

"How is your father these days?" Lady Stockdale apparently had little curiosity about his exploits.

Cedric now smiled broadly. "The earl is sometimes dyspeptic and, on occasion, troubled with gout. But in robust health otherwise. Why did you not come to London as usual this Season, Aunt Amelia?"

"Like Lord Clarke, I have my little ailments to indulge. And perhaps these old eyes have seen all the histrionic theater they need, and my old ears have heard all the caterwauling opera singers they can stand."

Cedric laughed appropriately. "But all your friends! Do you not miss seeing them?"

"A horde of valetudinarians with nothing but complaints about their aches and pains. Only a little conversation worth hearing."

"Now, Aunt Amelia, you know you and your cohorts enjoy dissecting every young buck and silly chit on the dance floor at Almack's."

Lady Stockdale chuckled. "How true. But foregoing that mild pleasure is nothing compared to the discomfort of making the journey. Is that not true, Winifred?"

Jane continued to watch Cedric stow away the food while her mother dissembled.

Mrs. Gabriel coughed, looked from one person to the other and back again, fluttering her hands. "Well, I have . . . ah, I had . . . er, I am not fond of long trips . . . but . . ."

Jane ended her mother's agony. "If trips are taken in easy stages, one can endure the discomforts. A day cooped up in a chaise can be very enervating indeed."

She felt Cedric's eyes on her and looked over to see him chewing, a thoughtful expression on his face.

He leaned over and took his aunt's hand in his. "Next time, my dearest, I shall come for you in father's finest coach with his very best team."

Lady Stockdale raised an eyebrow and regarded her nephew with a little smile. "I declare, Cedric, you seem not to have eaten for a week."

He ducked his head as if in shy embarrassment, tilted his cheek and peered at his aunt as if he were a naughty boy trying to win over an indulgent parent. "I daresay it has been only twenty-four hours, but it felt like a full seven days."

Sunlight flooded the room again, though a quick glance at the windows showed storm clouds gathering in the distance.

Jane studied Cedric and realized, upon closer inspection, that he did not present quite the picture of London elegance she had at first perceived. His nose and cheeks looked reddened by the sun; his neckcloth hung limp and wrinkled; here and there were little patches of whiskers on his jaw, as if he had shaved too hurriedly. No, despite his bravado, he looked less than his best. Not to mention his admission of losses at the races. Was she perhaps witnessing Cedric Williamson getting his well-deserved comeuppance?

Cedric set down his fork and grinned at his aunt. "As always, dearest Aunt Amelia, your table is admirable, rivaling any this side of Carlton House."

To Jane's chagrin, Lady Stockdale smiled warmly. "Do not be silly. My cook is excellent, but hardly on a par with Careme."

"How can you be so sure?" Cedric reached for his aunt's hand again and this time, drew it to his lips. "You deserve the very best, superior in every respect to everyone of my acquaintance."

Jane restrained herself with an effort. How dared he compare Lady Stockdale with the kind of characters he must have associated with at Newmarket?

But her mother was wide-eyed. "Are you acquainted with the Prince Regent, Mr. Williamson?"

Now they were in for a peck of humbug, Jane thought, watching him settle back in his chair and assume a look of self-satisfaction. Too bad he knew exactly how to captivate the old ladies. He probably thought he could enchant young ladies too, but a woman of intelligence would never be taken in by such transparent drivel.

"Mrs. Gabriel, I cannot claim a close association, but I have dined at Carlton House a few times, so I can also attest to the superiority of my aunt's kitchen. To tell the truth, though it should be an honor to be invited to attend royalty, the actual events are usually insufferable—too crowded, too noisy, too hot and a dead bore."

Lady Stockdale took the last sip in her glass. "Well, I accept your commendation of my cook, Cedric. As for London Society, I do believe the standards of our day continue to be undermined. But that does not surprise us, Winnie, does it?"

Jane's mother nodded, then shook her head, obviously unsure how to agree.

Lady Stockdale placed her napkin on the table. "I believe I am ready for my rest, or nearly so. Jane, I suppose you are anxious to get back to your work?"

Jane tried to wipe any trace of her scorn for Cedric Williamson from her smile, keeping her tone as even as possible when she would rather have shared just what she thought of his fawning conceit. "Yes, I have many things to do."

Cedric turned his dazzling smile on her. "And what is the work that occupies your time, Miss Gabriel?"

Her return smile contained no cheery feelings. "I am doing a project for Lady Stockdale."

He inclined his head toward his aunt. "And might I ask what it is all about, Aunt Amelia?"

"The barons' papers. Jane can explain it better than I. You will have to ask her. Can you help me to my boudoir now?"

Cedric rose and helped his aunt from her chair. "I am at your service for anything you desire, Aunt Amelia."

Jane breathed a little sign of relief. The very last thing she wanted was for Cedric to stick his nose into her project.

When Aunt Amelia tucked her arm into the crook of his elbow, Cedric placed his hand over hers. She held a cane on her other side, but deigned to lean upon it.

Cedric felt certain that once they reached her room, she would have some well-chosen words for him. There had been surprisingly few questions from her, and no admonitions whatsoever at the dining table. But he knew they were coming.

Mrs. Gabriel followed in their wake, mumbling about delicious fish and succulent lamb. She was the kind of henwit he could not abide, silly and useless, fluttery and scatterbrained. Her daughter Jane had turned into an unattractive antidote with her tight little bun and proper ape leader's cap. It was a pity, for once she had been a pretty gel. Now she seemed to be resigned to unappealing spinsterhood. Few words, but a sour expression.

In fact, he mused as they approached the staircase, her eyes had held the glitter of anger when she looked at him. What possible reason could she have for feeling rage toward him? They'd not met for years.

Cedric helped Aunt Amelia up the steps one at a time while she dismissed Mrs. Gabriel's effusive thanks. It seemed to be a ritual they had repeated many times.

Jane would not provide much diversion for him at Uphaven. Too bad she was not a livelier female, for he had not indulged in a light flirtation for many months.

But wait! Could Jane be here to dangle after Aunt Amelia's fortune? Had he not heard that both Gabriels lived in his aunt's house in Bath? Everyone in his family knew that Mrs. Gabriel and Aunt Amelia had been friends forever.

When they reached the landing, he led his aunt to the great window overlooking the south parterre. "Look at that vista! Is that not a scene of nature's beauty at its finest?"

"You can cut line now, Cedric." His aunt spoke in an ironic tone. "Mrs. Gabriel has scurried to her room. I think she anticipated my need to talk with you alone."

"Why by all means. I am eager to have a good talk with you as well." His heart sank lower and lower.

"But not here. What I have to say to you is not for the ears of anyone else, particularly the servants." She cast him a sly look, wiggled her eyebrows into a half-frown, and started up the remaining steps without his arm, her voice dropping to an undertone.

Could he believe his ears? Had she truly muttered something about a worthless wretch? What the devil! He had landed himself in a dreadful coil, all right.

An angry aunt, a pair of her needy and grasping friends, and that damnable filly. And until he raised a bit of cash, he dared not set foot off Uphaven's premises.

Aunt Amelia settled onto a sofa and waved him to a seat facing her.

Before he sat, he picked up a shawl and offered it to her.

She shook her head. "No need to play the gallant with me, Cedric. I am immune to your fiddle-faddle. Now, sit down and listen."

Cedric sat and hung his head in what he hoped was a contrite manner.

"In front of Mrs. Gabriel and Jane, I did not wish to embarrass you further than you yourself already had. But I must say I am very disappointed in you, Cedric."

"I cannot say I deserve better, Aunt Amelia. I was thoroughly gulled by a fellow I had absolutely no business even talking to—"

"That is not quite what I mean, Cedric. Associating with fellows of low quality is only a small part of what I see as your problem."

He had no argument with that point!

She pursed her lips and stared into his eyes. "You have a facile tongue, Cedric. Though no qualifications whatsoever to be of use to Society. I do not think you are deficient in character; indeed your family's accomplishments are exceptional."

"Yes, ma'am."

"Your father should be ashamed of himself for letting his son drift so. I cannot blame my sister, for she has her hands full guiding the girls. It is Lord Clarke's responsibility to see that his sons are a credit to their family."

Cedric could not help squirming. "George did well in the army, though he hasn't much to do lately. Sidney, my youngest brother, will soon be taking orders. He has himself a living somewhere in Hampshire, I believe."

"And Charles is assisting his father in running the estates?"

He nodded.

"So you are saying you are the only one of the four boys who has not found his niche in the world?"

"Why, no, of course not." Though that did seem quite obviously to be the case, Cedric thought.

Aunt Amelia had a way of lifting one eyebrow to show the skepticism with which she met most of his remarks.

He sat up straighter. "Here is what happened. I went to Newmarket with some friends to watch the races. A fast-talking fellow offered me a filly, and I fell for his sales pitch. The horse is a loser and so was I. That is the bare truth of the matter, Aunt Amelia."

"So you are entirely without funds?"

He nodded.

"How old are you Cedric, six and twenty?

"Yes. Until September."

Aunt Amelia pursed her lips. "And you have no means of supporting yourself, other than your quarterly allowance from your father?"

He tried to suppress another fit of wriggling. "I, ah . . . er, yes."

"I believe you tried a diplomatic post at one time?"

Cedric groaned. "I nearly froze in St. Petersburg. I had no facility for the language. In other words, I was a failure."

Aunt Amelia's glittering eyes bore into him. "Well, I have more than one word for you, Cedric. You need to grow up. In your very own terms, you are a loser and a failure. Instead of gambling and cavorting at races—and do not annoy me by cataloging the other useless activities of your set—you need to make something of your life, something worthy of your family. I expect more of you than fribbling away your youth."

Cedric could think of no response, for she was entirely correct.

She went on. "I must say you do not look your usual dapper self. In fact, you look like you have been up all night."

"Yes, ma'am, I have."

"But you must have had lodgings in Newmarket." Her face took on a shocked expression. "Cedric, do not tell me you ran off without settling your bills!"

"I fear that is the case. But if I could borrow a few guineas from you, Aunt Amelia, I shall see that—"

"Be still! Because, and only because I will not have county merchants cheated by my kin, I will send a man to Newmarket to pay that innkeeper. The Silver Fox, I imagine?"

"Yes, ma'am."

"And do you owe any other of the local shops?"

Even if Josiah Trentworthy was a Newmarket man, Cedric had no intention of paying him the rest of the money for the filly. "Not a penny, Aunt Amelia. And I certainly appreciate your generosity—" He started to rise from his chair.

"Be still, I said. If there is any brain matter in that handsome head of yours, you will sit here and listen to the rest of my flogging without further comment!"

Cedric sank back without uttering a sound. He wished he could have a real beating rather than listen to this litany of his faults, flaws and defects.

"I should have had this talk with you five or six years ago, or better yet, your father should have done so. Is there a respectable gel in your life?"

His jaw dropped open and he peered at his aunt with care. Was she teasing him?

But she now watched her fingers play with the fringe on a satin pillow as she spoke. "Some men have been known to seek out young ladies who have their own fortunes."

He could not believe his ears.

She wound a strand around her finger. "In my day, families saw to it that such things were arranged. You are of an age to be married."

He watched her nod to herself. He could not begin to fathom where her thoughts were heading. Did she have some grand-niece of the baron's to settle?

Abruptly she dropped the fringe and met his eyes. "What do you know about breeding anyway?"

He gulped in surprise. Breeding? What was she talking

about? "Ah, well. That is, I understand the process, that is, I know how, er . . ."

"I daresay you do. After all, you are a handsome devil. Too good-looking by half and too much charm. Might get you in many boudoirs, Cedric, but hardly in a position of comfort. Unless, that is, you find yourself a rich widow . . ."

"Aunt Amelia!" He could not stop another squirm of embarrassment.

"So your tastes do not run in that direction?"

"Most certainly not."

"Good. But, do you know anything about choosing sires and matching traits to reinforce certain strengths and overcome weaknesses in offspring . . ."

"Well, I, ah, er . . ."

"As I suspected. You have no idea what I am talking about. Though I assume you know something about breeding racehorses."

"The filly has good bloodlines and might be a good broodmare. After she has won a few races."

"I am talking about farm animals. Cattle, not racehorses. I am talking about the livelihood of Uphaven, not the playthings of the wealthy."

He had a miserable racehorse that was no good even as a plaything. But he took her point.

She lifted an eyebrow again. "As you well know, I have long had a soft spot in my heart for you, vulnerable as I am to rascals and rogues."

Oh, he thought, if only that were true!

"But if you think I am going to hand over this place to a know-nothing, think again. You will start with sheep husbandry."

A shepherd! She wanted him to become a shepherd?

"Since you have no means to go elsewhere, I suggest you make yourself at home here at Uphaven for a few months. See what you can learn about sheep farming."

Good Lord, talk about wasting time! "Yes, Aunt Amelia."

"Sutton is my steward. He worked for Lord Stockdale and he now manages everything. I shall tell him to expect you tomorrow morning."

"Yes, ma'am."

"Know this, Cedric. Uphaven must go to someone who will continue its heritage. And I am not at all sure you are up to the job."

Cedric had no defense. He knew nothing of country life, nor did he much want to know, though he dared not say so aloud.

She was not finished. "You need to know more than just how the crops are planted and harvested, how the sheep are raised and shorn."

Worse and worse. With difficulty, he kept from groaning.

"You also need to learn the wool business."

More likely, he should just give up and bawl.

"Wool has been the foundation of the Stockdale fortune for centuries. Ask Jane. She is sorting the letters and preparing the family papers for a biography of Lord Stockdale and his predecessors. Learn about it in those letters. Learn what generations of barons did to build their fortune."

Devil take it, now she wanted him to study. He might as well go back to Eton. Or try a term at Cambridge. His skills as a student were pitifully meager.

She peered at him without the hint of a smile. "Perhaps you can make yourself useful to Jane and assist her along the way. If you do, I might consider advancing you a few guineas, which I assume you need to pay off any local gambling debts, is that not so?"

"Yes, a few local fellows . . ."

"You will pay those off first, Cedric, before you try to settle with any of those useless London characters you call your friends. You must give me your word."

"Aunt Amelia, I will not pretend to make excuses for my manifold shortcomings. I appreciate your patience and your generosity in giving me another chance to make something of myself." What the deuce, he could hardly bear to listen to his own gibberish.

"I am certain I will be entertained daily at the dinner table by accounts of your progress, Cedric."

He went to her and kissed her forehead, then drew her hand to his lips again. "Thank you, Aunt Amelia. I shall do my best."

As he was leaving, she spoke once more, this time with a little grin. "By the way, you handsome devil, those baby sheep you saw in the fields? They are called lambs!"

CHAPTER THREE

Jane drummed her fingers on the library table and fumed at her lack of self-control. Yes, it was decidedly unfair to have her plans interfered with by Cedric Williamson, that imbecilic cad. But why was she so agitated? He was unlikely to seek her out, and this book-lined haven was the last place in the house he would want to occupy.

She should not have crept close to the staircase to overhear Lady Stockdale begin ringing a peal over his head. She had yearned to sneak upstairs to listen at the boudoir door. Quite odious to eavesdrop, but nonetheless, she would have listened if she had any courage at all. But even standing well out of their sight a floor below, her heart pounded so loudly in her ears she could hardly make out their words, and her nerves had failed her as they went on from the landing to the floor above.

Now, fully half an hour later, she should be able to direct her concentration to the work at hand, instead of fussing about how Mr. Williamson's presence might upset her campaign to write the book. She gazed at the velvet box that held the letters and willed her mind back to the days of the fourth baron's visit to Paris. She squeezed her eyes shut and tried to remember the words of his last letter. Instead, Williamson's empty babble echoed in her ears.

She walked over to the small painting in the corner and tried to place herself within the serene view of placid cows beside a tree-lined canal. All she envisioned was the crooked

grin and teasing manner of that practiced flirt, as he toyed
with his aunt and her mother.

How fervently she hoped Lady Stockdale was sending her
feckless nephew on his way back to London. As unmerited as
it was, Jane hoped Lady Stockdale would give him enough
money to keep him far from Uphaven for the next few
months. If he stayed here, his presence would be like a handful of gravel in one's shoes, a constant irritation, needing to
be disposed of at every turn.

Oh, it was hopeless. She might as well admit that she
would not recover her attentiveness while the thought of
Cedric Williamson spoiling everything held sway in her head.
Perhaps a walk in the herb garden might clear her thoughts.

In lieu of going upstairs again and risking an encounter
with him, she took a cotton sunbonnet from the stillroom and
headed through the kitchen garden to the walled plot of herbs.
The lavender was coming into bloom, filling the air with its
fragrance, certainly one of her favorites. She stopped to run
her hands through the stems, inhaling deeply.

She sat on a little bench and let the sun warm her back. But
even here wretched thoughts intruded. If Mr. Williamson
spent most of his time at the stable, her opportunities to ride
would be fewer. She had not the slightest wish to expose her
lack of equestrian expertise to his disapprobation. In recent
years, she had few chances to hone her skills in the saddle, so
she had welcomed Lady Stockdale's invitation to ride the
quiet cob she no longer used. Though Jane had loved riding
many years ago when her father was alive, she and her mother
could no longer afford horses. No carriage, not even a donkey cart. Once they moved to Bath, vigorous walks had to
replace Jane's youthful hours on horseback.

Now her brief return to riding would be ending, at least as
long as Mr. Williamson stayed at Uphaven. Unless she could
ride very early, before he was up. London men rarely rose before noon, or so she heard. She could try tomorrow and at the

same time catch a glimpse of his horse, the one that had sent him up the River Tick, to use his own expression.

It could have been worse, much worse. Cedric entered his bedchamber, closed the door and leaned back against the linen-fold panels.

But Aunt Amelia's scold had been bad enough. Difficult to endure. Because he knew she was correct in her very low estimation of him. A life of little consequence. Indeed, a life that counted for little, that few would miss. He knew she was right, and however he despised the thought, he was going to have to knuckle down. Probably too much of a stretch to think he would actually make much of himself, but it appeared he had no choice but to try. At the moment, even mucking out after the pigs could be no worse than the situation in which he had landed himself.

At least Aunt Amelia had not decided to leave the estate to someone else. Like Jane Gabriel.

How unfortunate that a gel with such potential a few years ago had become a stuffy bluestocking. And so very unattractive, as if she worked at making herself as plain as possible. Why would a young lady do such a thing?

He gazed at his bed, thinking he would like to crawl in and go to sleep. But it was covered with the few clothes he had spirited out of the inn and stuffed in his saddlebags. Bless Barton and the rest of Aunt Amelia's efficient staff. His coat of dark blue superfine was brushed and pressed, his shirt ironed, a handful of neckcloths starched beside them. His newest Hessians, polished to a glowing shine, stood beside the bed, and his shaving things sat on the washstand beside two cans of hot water swathed in towels.

He had only a few more things left behind at the Silver Fox, but as long as Aunt Amelia was going to pay his shot, he could send someone to collect them later. Charlie and Tom, the men he had come with from London, were probably heading home by now. He could send them a letter later in the week, though he doubted any explanations were really needed. Once they sobered up, they would not be surprised that he had taken a powder.

Charlie would not be on his way back to London, come to think of it. Had he not said something about visiting his bride-to-be? Someplace in this region? Cedric remembered he had agreed to attend the wedding in a month or two. No telling what else he had promised his good friend, Mr. Charles Ferris Venable.

He squeezed his eyes shut and tried to remember. The betrothed was a pretty blond creature. But were not most of them blue-eyed with a mop of gold ringlets? Was she one of the dozens of Carolines or Charlottes? No, but she was the daughter of a viscount, that much he remembered. What was the girl's name? Some unlikely virtue or other . . . Prudence . . . Charity . . . Mercy . . . Patience! That was it. Patience Sewell. Her father's estate was not far from Uphaven, in the direction of Ipswich.

He would have to get busy and write Charles a letter. Men who prided themselves on being Corinthians—no matter that their relatives intended to make them into shepherds—always fulfilled their promises. And at least honoring his word to Charlie would not cost him much blunt.

For the moment, he needed to shave and have a good wash to make up for the half-hearted job he had done in the stable with the groom's gear. Once he looked his best, he was prepared to seek out Jane Gabriel. Perhaps he would pick some flowers for her first. He needed her as an ally, not an adversary. And he needed to know what she was up to regarding Aunt Amelia's property!

When Jane stepped into the library, she was amazed to see Mr. Williamson reading one of the letters. How dare he walk into Lady Stockdale's library and inspect the table where she worked? Without a by-your-leave, he had opened the storage box and now held one of the letters in his hand, tilting it to catch the light from the window. She wanted to lunge across the room and grab it but forced herself to appear unruffled by his snooping. After all, it was his aunt's house, her library, and her papers. Nevertheless, exasperation washed over her, seeing his free and easy handling of papers she considered so precious.

By clenching her hands into firm fists, she managed to keep her voice composed. "Mr. Williamson, I assume you know that is one of the letters Lady Stockdale has entrusted to my care."

He turned slowly, a crooked grin on his face. "Ah, Miss Gabriel. I wonder if you could spare a few moments for me."

She resisted the temptation to send him away immediately. "Yes, if it is just for a few moments."

He sketched a bow to her and gestured to a vase of roses. "I hope these flowers meet your approval."

She nodded. "Very pretty."

"My aunt tells me you are sorting the letters of her late husband and his forebears."

"Yes, I am." He could not possibly be interested in these letters. What could he be up to? Flowers? Questions about her work? She went to her usual chair at the long library table and sat down, hiding her tight fists in her lap.

He pulled a chair close to the other side of the table and lowered himself into it in one graceful movement. "How far back do they go?"

"Oh, there are a few letters from more than a hundred years ago." The fragrance of the roses threatened to gentle her nerves.

Again, he gave her a wide smile. "And what do the various Lord Stockdales write about? Or do some of the letters precede the barony?"

"Yes, but not many. Mr. Stock, as he was in 1662 before he was honored by Charles II, wrote to his wife, asking about her well-being, that of his children.

"Nothing about the, ah, farm? The sheep?"

"He asked about weather conditions, the health of the flocks, other ordinary things."

"I see. And where had he gone that he had to write home? To London?"

She met his eyes and refused to look away. "No, he was in Bruges. He accompanied a shipment of fleeces he was selling to a wool merchant."

"Ah!" He cocked an eyebrow at her, then glanced away, seeming to stare at the shelves of books. "Was that the beginning of the family trade?"

"I daresay the family's wool business was centuries old by that Mr. Stock's time. I could not say for certain, but I plan to do more research on just when the family began to sell wool in Flanders. The business had been going on between the east of England and the Low Countries since the Middle Ages, perhaps even earlier."

Jane stopped talking. Why was she saying these things, showing off in a quite unladylike way, exhibiting her superior knowledge? Trying to make him think she had special knowledge? He would not be impressed anyway. In fact, there was probably nothing she could do that would impress him.

She opened her fists and placed her hands flat upon the table. "May I inquire why you are asking?"

"I am interested in anything that has to do with Aunt Amelia."

Aunt Amelia's money, perhaps. "Of course you are." She smiled in her most artificial manner. He would not know the difference between unaffectedness and complete insincerity.

He looked at the letter in his hand. "This one is dated . . . let me see, 1735."

She held out her hand and to her astonishment, he put the letter in it. "The Lord Stockdale in this letter was the fourth baron."

"It has been many years since I studied history, but I suppose we can assume the first baron was a supporter of the monarchy in the Civil War."

She nodded, refusing to let her surprise show on her face. Not that such knowledge was anything remarkable for a young man such as he. Something must have rubbed off on him while he put in his time at Eton. "That appears to be the case."

He leaned back in his chair and tilted his head. "So, after Charles II regained the throne, he rewarded his father's friends. I suppose it didn't hurt that Mr. Stock was a very prosperous man."

She gritted her teeth to avoid mentioning Mr. Williamson's lack of funds. Just a little nudge would have been so satisfying, she thought, a mere pinprick to his inflated self-estimation. But again, her efforts at restraint won out. She did not wish to discuss anything remotely personal with him.

When she began to rise to dismiss him, he was already walking to the bookshelves. She allowed herself to wrinkle her nose in disgust at his back. "May I help you find something to read, Mr. Williamson?"

He shrugged. "I am just studying these titles. *A Treatise on Ovine Diseases and Their Prevention.* That one looks to be very old." He ran his fingers over the spines of more books. "Here is a newer one. *The Appropriation and Inclosure of Commonable and Intermixed Lands.* Do you suppose my uncle actually read these tomes?"

"Perhaps I could find you a novel, if you want some reading material. Do you like adventure stories or something historical, by Mr. Scott, perhaps?"

"Don't think I have ever read a novel." He removed a volume bound in red leather. "*Plan for an Undertaking for the Improvement of Husbandry.* I think this one might do."

Jane almost laughed out loud. Cedric Williamson, reading a work like that, certain to be as dull as a dark day in December?

Her surprise must have shown on her face, for he immediately sent her another of his little grins, the kind that made his eyes twinkle. She found those looks far too disconcerting indeed.

"Do you have a better suggestion? I am looking for something about breeding."

She sat down abruptly.

His grin widened. "I mean, breeding sheep. Finding the desirable males to, ah . . . I suppose this is not quite your area of primary interest? Pardon me for trespassing into the realm of restricted topics of conversation."

She pretended to rearrange her notes. "Do not be concerned, Mr. Williamson. I am not easily offended by the processes of nature." She kept her face bent toward the papers as she was certain he would read the warm flush in her cheeks to mean exactly the opposite of her words.

He turned back to the shelves. "But, wait. Here are bound issues of *Farmer's Magazine*. Perhaps I might find what I need here, the most modern ideas, the newest techniques."

She peeked up to see him leafing through a brown volume. No doubt, the shorter articles with smaller words would be more to his liking.

He brought three to the table and placed them beside the husbandry text. "Will I disturb you if I just sit here and look these over? I promise to be absolutely silent."

Jane bit back her exasperation. "Please make yourself at home." After all, it was his aunt's house, his late uncle's library. What right had she to send him away, no matter how much she wished him to go?

"Thank you, Miss Gabriel." He settled down and opened the first of his stack of books.

She bent back to her notes, reshuffling them into the correct order. As she opened the storage box to retrieve the next letter, she inadvertently let the lid slam against the table, like a shot in the quiet room.

"I am sorry, Mr. Williamson." How had she been so clumsy?

He only smiled that gorgeous smile again and turned a page.

Taking great care, she lifted out the letter and began to

read. She could see him out of the corner of her eye as he stifled a yawn. He said he had been up all night. Then why was he not taking advantage of this time to take a rest before they had tea?

Obviously, he had changed clothes before he came down here. And shaved. She had not noticed until now that he was dressed in a fresh jacket, and his cravat was tied in a complicated display that would have pleased the most fastidious gentlemen of her acquaintance. Not that her friends in Bath made much show of sartorial splendor. But she knew a well-dressed man when she saw one, especially one with such a pleasing countenance. Not only pleasing, she corrected herself. Downright magnificent.

After all, she could appreciate good looks in a person, just as she appreciated masterful drawings or fine paintings. Or beautiful horses. It was all the same thing, grasping the symmetry of line, the elegance of proportion, the value of color. Mr. Williamson's cheeks, for example. Smooth and tinged with a hint of bronze, as if he enjoyed the outdoors.

Good heavens, what was she thinking? She forced her attention to the letter. Lord Stockdale was indeed writing from London. She wondered if Mr. Williamson had read much of the text. She read a few more sentences. Though he was being very quiet, she could not help but hear the whisper of the pages as he turned them. Rather quickly, she thought. Even if he was only skimming, he could not possibly absorb anything that fast.

She read another sentence of Lord Stockdale's. He had attended a court levee, and there followed a long list of men in attendance. She picked up a quill and dipped it in the inkwell. Just below the last entry in her notes, she printed the date of the letter and its subject matter. The scratching of her pen sounded loud in the quiet of the room, but as she tried not to press so hard, the pen slipped and she made a blot on her notes. Just a small one, but untidy nevertheless.

She reached out and met Mr. Williamson's fingers on the

blotter, then snatched hers back. How mortifying! He had been watching her ineptness.

"Thank you." She took the blotter from him and tried to pick up a little of the stray ink.

"I think you need a better point." He took the quill and examined it closely. With the penknife, he trimmed a bit from the edges to sharpen the tip. "There. That may help a little."

Why did he not go away and leave her alone with her work? "I am sure it will be much better. Again, you have my thanks."

She simply ought to stand up and ask him to find another spot for his reading. But she could not risk letting him know how much his presence disturbed her. Cedric Williamson seemed like the kind of fellow who would, if he knew how much he bothered her, make himself into a constant pest.

She brushed back a strand of hair that tickled her ear as she tried again to read the letter. Where had all her powers of concentration gone? Usually she could quickly peruse the content of the letter and summarize it in her notes in a matter of minutes. This afternoon she could hardly make out a sentence.

The back of the letter seemed blurry and she realized a film of frustrated tears had marred her vision. If she was going to be so silly, she might as well go to her room and leave him to his books.

She turned her attention to replacing the letter in the box and closing it without a sound. As she did, she noticed the ink stains on her fingers. How could she have been so careless? She felt for a handkerchief in her sleeve, but could not find one.

"Miss Gabriel, please take mine." Mr. Williamson held out a neatly folded square of snowy white linen.

"Oh, no, thank you. I could not spoil your handkerchief with my dirty hands. I shall go and wash, for I am sure we will have our tea shortly." She pushed back her chair and rose.

He stood and stepped around the table, so close she could feel his breath on her forehead. He gave off a faint exotic scent, like no cologne she had ever before encountered. Her heart hammered like a blacksmith at his anvil.

He pressed the handkerchief to his mouth, then carefully touched her cheek. "You have a little ink on your face, Miss Gabriel."

She almost flinched at the slight moisture, but caught herself in time. This was no moment to let her wobbly knees betray her.

He bent over her and dabbed again at her cheek. "I think that will do it. You have very long eyelashes, quite exquisite."

What could she say to that? It was exactly the kind of fatuous flattery she expected from him. So why did it make her legs shake even more and her heart skip a beat? She knew he was an out-and-out rake, well skilled in his guile. He had years and years of practice in the most stylish ballrooms of London. How could a female like her, with only one partial London Season, unsuccessful in the extreme, and many years of avoiding the dance floors of Bath—how could she be expected to handle a man like him? By fighting fire with fire?

She pulled back, opening her eyes wide and staring into his. "Why, Mr. Williamson, your eyelashes are rather long too. And quite thick. I do believe any gel would be proud to have their like."

He gave a deep rumbling chuckle. "I shall take that as a compliment rather than an insult, Miss Gabriel, though I am not sure quite how you intended it."

She tried to make her smile as enigmatic as possible.

He took her hand, again touched the handkerchief to the tip of his tongue, and rubbed away the inkstain. Jane could not move, could not breathe. He captured her eyes with his sparkling gaze.

Barton opened the door, breaking the moment. Jane sighed in relief when he announced that tea was being served, then bowed his way out.

She hurried to the mirror and tucked a drooping strand of

hair behind her ear. A few more wisps had curled up around her face and she tried to smooth them into place.

Mr. Williamson offered his arm, and she took it reluctantly. She ought to go upstairs and deal with her wayward locks, but she decided to let them be. She had already revealed her loss of composure. To let Mr. Williamson think he had any additional effect on her equanimity was beyond enough.

As they entered the Green Drawing Room, Lady Stockdale waved them both to the sofa. "Well, Jane, do you think Cedric can be of any help to you?"

Jane pressed herself against the arm of the sofa. "Pardon me, Lady Stockdale. I fear I did not quite catch your question."

Cedric turned toward her, almost touching her knees with his. "Aunt Amelia asked me to see how I can assist you with the letters and papers, Miss Gabriel. But I am afraid I got so involved in the husbandry text, I completely forgot to ask."

The air in the drawing room felt too thick to breathe, pressing on Jane's chest and hissing in her ears. Cedric Williamson, sticking his nose into her papers? Spoiling her plans for the book?

Never! She started to speak, but realized she had no words to express her dismay. Jane kept her gaze on the tea as Lady Stockdale poured a cup for Jane's mother. *I can not concentrate when he sits across the table.*

When she said nothing after a moment, Cedric spoke in his smooth, deep baritone. "Miss Gabriel and I will make a prime team, I am certain."

She could not help glancing at him, taking in the affable tilt of his head, the ample smile, the vivid cobalt of his eyes. She felt even more tongue-tied.

Lady Stockdale handed her a saucer and cup. "I am glad to hear you will work together."

"Oh, yes," Jane's mother chimed in. "Indeed, you will be able to finish much faster with two persons dividing up the work."

Every muscle in Jane's body tensed. She could feel three

sets of eyes on her, all waiting for her response, and she wished she could disappear, simply vanish from the room. Forcing a smile to her lips, she met Lady Stockdale's gaze. "I am sure we shall work together quite agreeably." She almost expected a bolt of lighting to strike her for voicing such a formidable untruth.

Instead, Cedric leaned toward her and gave just a hint of a wink. Her heart lurched in her chest, but she prevented her teacup from rattling for more than an instant, and pretended she did not notice him.

CHAPTER FOUR

Jane strode toward the kitchen where she hoped to find a slice of bread to stave off her hunger and a few carrots for the horses. This morning, she had slept much later than she usually did, all attributable to Mr. Williamson and the way he had charmed her mother and his aunt last night after supper. Over the whist table, he had the two old ladies simpering like a pair of schoolroom chits. Perfectly ridiculous, to Jane's eye, and the performance went on for long past their usual time to retire.

She had played along, pasting a smile on her face while inside she fumed, determined not to allow anyone to suspect the depth of her chagrin. Odious Cedric Williamson, pawing about in those valuable letters, letters she intended to be the foundation on which she would support her mother and herself for the rest of her life. The thought of him interfering was positively abhorrent.

She slowed her steps when she heard voices coming from the kitchen and caught the words "Mister Cedric." The speaker sounded like Sam, head groom of Lady Stockdale's stable. Jane stopped outside the room to listen.

"That black devil of his is more'n a handful."

Between his words, Jane heard the slap of a wooden spoon against a bowl. Mrs. Peters stirred batter, no doubt. Perhaps griddle cakes for the maids.

The cook beat away at her task. "I hope he's come to stay a while."

"Don't know 'bout that. But m'lady would like him to stay, I spect."

"Milady loves him, though we all know he's somethun of a rascal. But smart, she sez. Mebbe too smart."

Sam gave a snort of laughter. "How's that?"

"Left all his schoolmates behind, she sez. Never took t' book learning 'cause he was smarter'n the rest. He found more fun in making trouble, she sez. Never buckled down."

"Mebbe he shudda' gone in the army."

"Had a brother in Spain. His father wouldn't hear of another of his sons going. M'lady told me all bout it once."

The groom took a noisy slurp of his drink. "Well, 'e knows 'is horses, even though that filly he brung yesterday barely staggered to the finish line, he sez."

"That don't sound like she's a pip."

"She'da been drugged, Mister Cedric said, and she bunged herself up a little, but she's already looking better and she'll be fine in a day or two."

"What d'ya mean, drugged? Who'd give drugs to a horse?"

Jane leaned against the corridor wall. She had exactly the same question. Drugging a horse? The poor thing!

Sam spoke without hesitation. "I figger some scoundrel who intends a horse to lose. Ain't no telling what some'll do to fix a race. A sleeping draught or such. Or so I've heard."

"Don't sound fair t' me."

"That's the whole point, don't ya see?"

Jane felt a pang of pity for the poor, helpless filly. Anyone who would hurt a vulnerable animal was far worse than a scoundrel. She gathered up the long skirt of her habit, silently retraced her steps and went out the front way. No matter the tempting fragrance of newly baked bread, she wanted to go immediately to see that filly. Perhaps she could help the pitiful thing recover.

When she entered the stable, she heard only the rustle of horses moving, chomping on their hay. She passed the carriage horses and stopped at Sandy, the cob she usually rode.

He pressed his nose against the bars of his stall and she patted it gently. "I'll be with you in a moment, old boy."

The next horse, a huge black presence, tossed his head, stamped nervously, and snorted. This was a stranger, obviously belonging to Cedric, but definitely not suffering from the aftereffects of any drugs.

After two empty stalls, the last one held a tall, long-legged bay, rump toward her, with a short black tail. The horse looked around and pointed its ears in Jane's direction.

"Good day, Miss Gabriel." Cedric Williamson, in his shirt-sleeves, stepped out from behind the filly, a brush in his hand.

Jane almost clapped her hand over her heart in surprise but instead buried her hands in her voluminous skirt. His shirt was open at the neck, showing a wide vee of skin. His shoulders were naturally broad. No padding needed in his coats, she thought as she stared. With his sleeves rolled to his elbows, she could see the color of his strong forearms and long-fingered hands proved he was often outdoors.

She struggled to recover her aplomb, hearing her voice as an unfamiliar croak. "Good morning, Mr. Williamson. I am surprised to see you so early."

He gave a little bow. "Please excuse my dress. I wanted to see how Sibyl fared overnight. I did not expect to encounter any ladies other than females of the equine persuasion."

She forced a smile and tried to drag her gaze from his chest to the filly. "She is called Sybil?" Her question sounded so inane she wanted to bite her tongue. What else would he be talking of as he stood ankle deep in straw, grooming his horse?

He put the brush on the edge of the manger and slicked a hand over the filly's long neck. "She is by Sorcerer, the leading sire of racehorses in the last two or three years. Or so it says on the papers I have, not that the scoundrel who sold her to me could not have forged all that." He grinned, cocked an eyebrow, and shook his head, sending locks of his brown hair falling across his forehead. He raked his hand through the wayward waves, brushing them back into place.

Jane drew a deep breath and willed her heart to mute its thunder. "Yesterday you said she finished last in her race."

"She did indeed. Lost all her energy." He stepped closer to the stall door.

"Is she better now?"

"Yes, but not like she was when I bought her. She was alert, head high, eyes bright, full of spirit. After the race, she could barely keep herself on her feet when we started out from Newmarket. I had to rest her every mile or so, and she managed to stumble, kick herself and almost fall down three or four times."

Jane peered into the stall and saw a few dark red gashes on the filly's legs. "I have some salve that will help those cuts. I will go get it right away." When she looked back at him, he was only inches away, separated from her only by the bars of the stall.

"That would be excellent, and—"

Before he finished, she whirled and nearly ran out of the stable, holding up her skirts as she jogged along. What had come over her, nearly to fall in a faint at the sight of a man's exposed arms? To have a peek at his chest? How ridiculous she was, like an elderly spinster needing a shot of hartshorn after passing a pair of half-naked pugilists. Certainly she was made of stronger stuff.

Giving a cheery hello to Mrs. Peters and Sam, still talking at the kitchen table, Jane bustled into the stillroom and found the jar of ointment she'd made up last week from the first batch of freshly picked comfrey and feverfew. It would help anything heal—a cut, a burn, a scrape. Lady Stockdale had given her the receipt, one she had sworn by for decades.

Jar in hand, she went back through the kitchen, the shortest route toward the stable.

"Miss Gabriel, I will come along and saddle Sandy for you." Sam pushed his chair back from the table.

Mrs. Peters held out a plate holding thick slices of fragrant bread. "Here, now Miss Gabriel, take a piece."

Jane stopped. "Thank you, Mrs. Peters, but I think I will decline your kind offer. Mr. Williamson is in the stable, waiting for this salve."

"Well, then, just a moment." Mrs. Peters hustled to the larder and brought back a saucer of butter and a pot of gooseberry jam. She wrapped six slices of the bread in a square of linen and placed everything in a basket. "You take this along to Mr. Cedric. I know he did not stop here for a bite before he went out."

"Thank you, Mrs. Peters. I am sure Mr. Williamson will be most grateful."

"Now, you eat something too, young lady." The plump cook wiped her hands on her apron and nodded at Jane.

"I shall. Thank you." Jane went through the door held open by Sam and walked beside the groom towards the stable. How very typical, she thought. A plain slice of bread would have been fine for her. But for Cedric, Mrs. Peters sent along her special jam and rich butter to enhance the flavor. That man's effect on women was entirely laughable, quite outside any explanation except the silliest impulse of a female to coddle a good-looking lad sporting a disarming grin.

Absolutely beyond logic or good sense. But even a person like herself felt her pulse pounding and her fingertips tingling when she recalled his dark eyes meeting hers.

Half an hour later, Sam tossed her up onto Sandy's saddle. Mr. Williamson, who had donned his coat and cravat by the time she returned to the stable with his breakfast, came outdoors and put a hand on his hip.

"Miss Gabriel, you do not mean to ride alone, do you?" He held a slab of bread generously spread with butter and jam.

"I usually do, Mr. Williamson. I do not go far, just down to the stream and back, all within the park."

"But surely you should not be without an escort."

Jane stiffened her back. "I go this familiar route several times a week. I do not require any assistance."

He frowned and cocked his head to one side, twisting his mouth in an expression of disapproval. "Is that right, Sam?"

"Mr. Cedric, I did not want to let her go by herself, but there's jest me most days and she does insist . . ."

Mr. Williamson gave Jane another look of censure. "I'll finish dressing the filly's legs. Please saddle Atlas, Sam. He needs a run anyway."

"I assure you, I never gallop Sandy," Jane began, then thought better of bothering to remain here embroiled in an argument. She steered Sandy's head toward the lane and urged him forward. As she turned toward the park, she looked back. Sam had walked into the stable, but Mr. Williamson stood, legs wide, arms akimbo, glowering darkly in her direction.

Her feeling of satisfaction did not last. Not ten minutes into her ride, she could hear hoofbeats rapidly overtaking her. She guided her horse to the side and tightened his reins, not wishing to have Mr. Williamson on Atlas gallop by and perhaps tempt Sandy to increase his pace suddenly. But to her surprise, the approaching hoofbeats slowed to a trot. Atlas carrying Mr. Williamson fell in beside her at a sedate walk.

The black stallion was much taller than her chestnut gelding, and Mr. Williamson leaned down to speak. "You knew I would catch up with you, Miss Gabriel."

"I knew you could if you chose to, but I certainly do not consider the presence of an escort to be necessary."

"Is it not a matter of propriety for a lady to be attended on her rides?"

She knew he was correct and hearing him point out her *faux pas* smarted. "Perhaps in the wilds of London, Mr. Williamson, but it hardly seems necessary here at Uphaven." She kept her eyes straight ahead, looking exactly between Sandy's ears, now swiveled toward the big black beside him.

"Nevertheless, will you accept my company for a while? Perhaps you can help me recall the pleasures of my aunt's estate. It has been a long time since I toured its farthest reaches."

Gritting her teeth, she nodded. "I accept your gracious

offer to accompany me, Mr. Williamson, but I am far from acquainted with the many farms and tenants on the estate."

His voice was wearyingly cheerful. "Perhaps we can discover them together."

Why did he insist on keeping her company? She must be the farthest thing from his taste in feminine companionship. Yet, she dared not make an enemy of him, for Lady Stockdale appeared to dote on him. "I know there is a small cluster of houses beyond that next rise, where the road crosses the stream. I believe it is a hamlet known as Uphaven Common, the closest of several on Lady Stockdale's property."

"Then I suggest we head in that direction."

"Very well." Jane wished she could think of a way to tell him she was not an experienced rider, but anything she thought to say sounded either too disparaging of her abilities—or not disparaging enough. How very lowering that she should even have to worry about explaining herself.

Mr. Williamson spoke before she could come up with an adequate explanation.

"How long have you and your mother been visiting Aunt Amelia?"

"We came a few weeks ago."

"I see."

She let a hint of sarcasm tinge her words. "And you are wondering how long we plan to stay, Mr. Williamson?"

"Why, no, that is none of my concern."

"Nevertheless, I will tell you we plan to be here for some months, for I believe my work will take a long time."

"Even with my help?"

She refrained from laughing. "As you will soon see, there are many letters and a number of paintings to catalogue."

"Again, I will reveal my ignorance, Miss Gabriel, but I am curious. Are any of the paintings valuable?"

"Why yes, some are quite valuable. But I could not venture to estimate their price if they were sent to auction. Perhaps the demand for such works is not exceedingly high, for the moment." There, she thought, do not think of trying to convince your aunt to sell any of them.

With Atlas a few steps in the lead, they trotted back along the lane from the arched stone bridge where four cottages stood beside a wheelwright's shop and the blacksmith's. Several children had waved at them as they passed and one lady curtsied as she pegged out her wash on a line stretched between two apple trees about to break into bloom.

"Rather a comfortable little spot." Cedric twisted in his saddle to look back at Jane.

She was not paying much attention to the road; instead she watched him sit his restless black. No matter how the animal danced and tossed his head, Cedric rode with ease, even with grace. "Ah, y-yes," Jane stuttered. What was he talking about? Oh yes, the tenants. "Lady Stockdale is quite attentive to her dependents. She cares for their welfare."

He reined up, Atlas sidling to the edge of the brush. "Do they appreciate her kindness?"

"As far as I can tell, they do. She is planning a big party when the sheepshearing is completed in just a few weeks."

Atlas shook his head and half reared. Cedric laughed. "Whoa, boy. I know you want a run and in a few minutes, I'll give you your head." He grinned at Jane. "This horse has had enough lollygagging for the last two days. He's ready to fly, so as soon as the stable is in sight, do you mind heading in while I turn him loose in the fields?"

"Not at all. I warned you, Mr. Williamson, I never gallop and rarely canter. My equestrian skills are quite rusty."

"I think you sit that cob very prettily. And you look like royalty in that habit. Very fine indeed."

Jane felt a blush rising to her cheeks. He probably thought she had been angling for compliments. In fact, she knew she looked better in this trim jacket and sweeping skirt than in the gray kerseymere or any of her tired old muslins. The little dark hat with a trio of pheasant feathers was uncommonly becoming, even to her critical eye. She moistened her lips and acknowledged his remarks with a tip of her head. "Thank you. Please feel free to give him a run any time now. The stable is just beyond the bend."

But he stayed beside her, keeping his massive stallion to a jittery walk.

"Mr. Williamson, tell me about this animal. How did you acquire him?"

"I hesitate to tell you. I, er, I won him at cards, I am embarrassed to admit."

"At cards? Do men often wager their cattle?" She tried to keep her voice light, not succumbing to the amazed disapproval she felt.

"I would not say it is the usual thing, but from time to time, I have heard of other instances. In this case, I got a great deal more than I bargained for. He was a bad-tempered fellow and more or less untrained as a saddle horse. When I decided to ride him to Newmarket from London, I had no idea what a trial I was providing myself."

"What do you mean?"

"He despised a sedate pace and seemed to glory in disturbing other travelers. He almost tore apart a stall at one inn with his kicking. But he has greatly improved and with the right kind of treatment, he will eventually learn his manners."

"What made him so unruly?"

"I asked the fellow I won him from, but he had no idea. Seems likely he was badly mistreated."

"How very sad. I cannot abide persons who abuse animals." Jane waited for a moment, hoping he would tell her about the filly and how he suspected she had been drugged. But he said nothing further.

They rounded the curve and the stable was in full view. "I will see you in an hour or so in the library, Miss Gabriel. It has been a pleasure this morning." With a little salute, he swung Atlas across a shallow ditch into a field and sat forward as the big black struck off at a lope, lengthening into a full gallop, his long tail flowing behind him.

To Jane's way of thinking, it was a beautiful view, man and horse moving together in harmony. With part envy, part admiration, she stopped Sandy and simply watched for a few moments until he almost reached the far line of trees. She forced herself to shift away from the sight and continue to the stable.

Cedric Williamson was a charming fellow, and it would be easy for her to have her head turned. Either that or she might end up screeching at him like a fishwife if he spoiled her project.

Why had he not mentioned the drugs she had overheard Mrs. Peters and Sam talking about? Cedric would not have doped his own horse. So who had? And why had he refrained from mentioning it to his aunt?

She sighed, trying to suppress a wave of irritation. What did she expect? He prided himself on being of the Corinthian set, a sportsman of the first stare. He would not share his concerns with a mere female, no matter how sensible she seemed.

Mr. Williamson would not wish to spend much time in the library. At least, that was her fervent hope. She wondered if he would even carry through on his obligation to Lady Stockdale. If he asked to help her today, Jane would give him some of his uncle's rambling letters to read. Meanwhile, she could proceed as she wished with the first baron's papers.

Cedric gloried in the feeling of strong horseflesh between his knees. Atlas galloped once around the large field, his shiny black mane whipping at Cedric's chest. At first, the stallion stayed far from the sheep, but with his reins loosened, the horse suddenly swung towards a group of inattentive, fuzzy white blobs, as if he wanted to see them scatter before him. Cedric slowed the black and guided him around the small flock. Only two or three bothered to trot a little farther off, their bland faces looking at the huge horse with only a modicum of unease.

A shepherd indeed! How could Aunt Amelia think he

could learn about sheep? How could he make himself care about a clump of wool with four feet? He had always heard sheep were among the stupidest of God's creatures.

But useful little buggers, the foundation of the Stockdale fortune, not to mention dozens, nay, hundreds of other great estates all over the realm. Since the Middle Ages, according to Miss Gabriel. Though he had no recollection of anything he had learned from those days, beyond knights in armor riding about the landscape rescuing maidens in distress, he had no reason to doubt her knowledge. Perhaps if he thought of the beasts as mutton and wool on the hoof, he would have a better chance of success at learning how Uphaven operated.

He kept Atlas galloping near the edges of the field, making a second circuit of its perimeter. Of course, the Uphaven estate was far more than sheep. Workers on the home farm were only the beginning. Those villages provided laborers for the farms run by the tenants, growing all sorts of cattle and crops. Just like his father's properties, which would someday belong to his eldest brother, Uphaven formed a complex pattern of interlocking parts. Cedric knew he had a lot to learn, but somehow he found the idea of fitting together all the pieces of this puzzle quite appealing, even comfortable. How his old friends in the Quorn Quartet would laugh if they heard such a plumper! First, they would have howled themselves senseless at his gullible purchase of Sybil and then they would split their sides over Cedric turning serious. They would never believe it would last. He was not so sure that he would not wake up one morning and decide to chuck the whole scheme.

When Atlas began to slow on his third circuit, Cedric let him drop off to a brisk trot. Miss Gabriel had looked her former self in her riding habit, pretty and fresh, instead of dull and staid. Nevertheless, he expected to see her in shapeless gray again this afternoon. He wondered what she would wear tonight, when Aunt Amelia said the neighboring squire was bringing his family to dinner.

Which reminded him, he felt certain the squire's son was

one of those he owed from Newmarket. He hated to ask Aunt Amelia for money, but she had been quite adamant that he pay off his local debts. He had no choice in the matter.

His good mood sinking, he turned Atlas toward the stable.

CHAPTER FIVE

Cedric entered the Green Drawing Room and patted the pocket in his jacket, sure the bank notes were secure. Aunt Amelia had parted with the money with only a lifted eyebrow. He was more than grateful, for she could have used the opportunity to reiterate her formidable list of the unsympathetic qualities he possessed, her opinion of his reprehensible behavior, and her judgment of his innumerable imperfections. Instead she had touched his shoulder and, with a bark of laughter, told him to exercise his charms upon the ladies of the Walker family.

No one else had yet arrived and he strolled around the room, looking closely at the paintings. Other than the portrait of his aunt and the long gallery full of Lord Stockdale's ancestors, he had never paid the least attention to the pictures in the house. As far as he was concerned, they were simply part of the decorations, like gilded sconces and marble fireplace surrounds.

Over a silk damask sofa hung the largest canvas in the room, a landscape of a flat plain, with boats on the water in the distance. It was a pretty picture, he thought. Perhaps it did take talent to swirl tints of light blue, pale gray and white about to represent a stormy sky. But to him, it did not look like it would be so difficult.

On the other hand, he thought, the elaborate display of flowers in a picture above a marble-topped console showed real skill. Each petal was painted with lifelike veracity and he almost felt he could touch the velvety petals of the tulips. But what was this? He peered more closely and found a variety of insects, even a lizard, in the painting. What kind of a painter would spoil his pretty flowers with such distasteful creatures?

"Good evening, Mr. Williamson."

He turned to find a very different Jane Gabriel than the scholarly lady he had sat with an hour ago in the library. She looked quite lovely. "Miss Gabriel." He bowed to her.

She curtsied in return. The bodice of her unadorned gown of creamy white was considerably lower than the neck-hugging gray she had worn earlier, bringing a definite improvement to her appearance. A dainty concoction of lace topped her hair, which was dressed in a pile of curls instead of her usual tight bun. He caught a trace of a sweet fragrance, like flowers. Of what variety he could not say, but he liked the scent.

He gestured to the painting. "Before the others arrive, can you explain this painting to me?"

"I shall try." She stepped closer. "It is a very lovely picture of flowers, by a Flemish painter called Jan de Heem. Very realistic. And full of symbolism."

He glanced from her to the picture. "How so?"

"Look closely. You will see many varieties of flowers, many of which could not bloom at the same time."

He leaned over the table, his head quite close to hers. "Why, yes. But I see that lizard and the bugs around the bottom. Why include such things with the pretty flowers?"

She spoke softly, and he looked more at her than at the subject of their conversation.

"The spiders and ants, the snail and the salamander represent death. But look at the top of the bouquet. There is a white poppy and a butterfly, representing re-birth."

Cedric shrugged. "I would have said it was quite straightforward, just a bouquet."

"Oh, paintings often have quite subtle meanings."

He took her hand and led her to another picture, this one

smaller. "This one is surely just a picture of some fellows outside of a tavern, drinking tankards of ale."

Jane smiled, her face glowing, eyes bright. "Mr. Williamson, look at the darkness of the colors of the tavern-front and the clothing of the drinkers. Then note the lightness of the sky, with the church steeples against the clouds. The stork is in her nest near the chimney. This shows a strong contrast between the low life and the higher values of their world. Would you not say so?"

He gazed into her eyes, but the arrival of his aunt and Mrs. Gabriel interrupted their momentary intimacy. He turned and bowed to the ladies. "Aunt Amelia, you look charming, as always. And Mrs. Gabriel, may I compliment you on the shade of your gown? It is almost the precise color of your eyes."

Aunt Amelia sat on the sofa and patted the place beside her. "Come, Jane, sit with me."

Jane followed her suggestion, while her mother settled in a nearby chair.

Cedric stood back and looked from one to another. "What a charming tableau you ladies make. Aunt Amelia, can I fetch you a footstool?"

"Yes, if you please. But, nephew dear, do not waste your charm on us. You have promised to be all that is gallant to our guests, and you may find it a bit of a challenge."

Not until the five Walkers crossed the threshold did he appreciate the necessity for such an admonition. He had been about to express his admiration for Miss Gabriel's appearance when the Walkers were announced and crowded the drawing room with their presence.

The squire, a florid, beefy figure, had a hearty laugh to accompany his loud voice. Mrs. Walker, as bony and lean as her husband was plump, spoke in a nasal whine that made Cedric want to wince and cover his ears. Miss Walker, whose ample bosom strained the fabric of her bodice, and Miss Flora Walker, who had inherited her mother's scrawniness, bobbed up and down in curtsy after curtsy. Striking a pose of infinite *ennui* by lounging against the edge of the door, Mr.

Oswald Walker, a young man in his early twenties, waited until his mother and sisters were seated to saunter across the room and make his leg to Lady Stockdale, Mrs. Gabriel, and Miss Gabriel. Cedric watched him carefully, to make sure Oswald was one of the fellows to whom he owed money. His waistcoat, a glowing shade of lime green that indicated his pretensions of dandyism, made Cedric blink in astonishment. The fellow did seem to linger over Jane's hand for an excessively long time.

Cedric made quite sure he himself was not frowning when Jane spoke to the fellow with a demure smile on her face. He felt his aunt's eye on him, and he acknowledged her lifted eyebrow with a little wave of his hand, a gesture meant to convey his grasp of the task she had set for him. Her smirk told him she understood perfectly.

"Miss Walker?" He smiled broadly at the eldest of the sisters. "Did I not see you in London a few months ago at Almack's?"

The force of her giggle made her chest heave, and he pasted his eyes on her face in order to avoid the spectacle of her dress giving way.

She shook her head, making her mass of ringlets jiggle in the air. "Oh, my, no, Mr. Williamson. I have never had that honor." Thankfully, her bodice remained intact.

Cedric swallowed his aversion to absolute falsehoods. "I was certain you were the young lady that so captivated the cream of the city's beaus."

This time her high-pitched giggles were echoed by her mother's nasal yelps of glee. "No, Helena has all she can do to keep track of her admirers from nearby. She has yet to conquer the balls of London."

Cedric nodded sympathetically, hoping Miss Walker would not assume his outrageous lies meant she ought to have a go at the *ton*. If she did, he knew she would be quite disappointed. Just imagining Miss Walker confronting Lady Jersey made his smile of amusement quite genuine.

But it was going to be a very long dinner.

An hour later, when Cedric had delivered his entire repertoire of fatuous flattery and fawning comments, relying on repetition and shameful exaggeration to an extent that stretched his considerable abilities at sycophancy, and even brought himself to the point of embarrassment, Lady Stockdale at last led the ladies from the dining room. Cedric poured Squire Walker and Oswald a glass of port, then filled his own goblet.

Instead of the recent meet at Newmarket which Cedric expected to discuss, Squire Walker patted his ample stomach and talked of sheep. "I will say one thing for an exceptional cold winter. The fleeces 're as thick as I ever seen. Gonna be a good year in that regard."

Cedric could do nothing but agree. He had no idea the wool business was affected by the weather. "Yes, indeed. Thick. Ah . . . yes, very thick. And dense."

He glanced at Oswald, who seemed to be studying the flame of a candle through the ruby wine. Yes, Cedric thought, seeing him in that pose made his recollection whole. He certainly owed Oswald Walker a bundle, just as he thought. But, Cedric observed, Walker bided his time, probably uneasy about mentioning his gambling activities before his father.

The squire drained his glass and held it out for more. "I been following Coke's scheme for rotating the plantings in each field, just as I've advised Lady Stockdale to do. You take to that program, Mr. Williamson?"

Cedric shifted in his chair. This was as bad as keeping the ladies aquiver. Perhaps worse. "Seems useful, for the most part." If the squire advocated whatever the scheme was, it must be workable.

"Yes, so I'd say, too. Hard to tell what would happen if you kept to the old ways, but Coke swears he makes his fields more fertile every year."

"That he does." Cedric promised himself to check those magazines tomorrow for the name Coke. He knew he'd seen it somewhere. "What's the size of your holdings, Squire?"

Cedric breathed a little sigh of relief as Walker began to survey his estates, enumerating the size and contents of his fields, his flocks, the number of his tenants. He paused only to refill his glass. When he finished his fourth, he set the glass down with a thud. "Here I am, runnin' on, tongue loosened by that Uphaven cellar, I s'pose."

"Are we ready to join the ladies?" Though he sensed no enthusiasm from either of them, Cedric rose, and they left the dining room. As they entered the drawing room, he caught Oswald's sleeve. "I need to have a few words with you, alone, at an opportune time."

Oswald Walker nodded with a wink. "Tomorrow? At the Ramshead in Higdon Stile?"

"I'll be there at three." Cedric relied on Sam to know the way.

He took a chair next to Mrs. Walker and spoke softly to her. "I understand you are quite the prime supporter of the church." It was a stab in the dark, but he had run out of sure topics.

"Oh, oh, yes." Her laugh was more of a series of snorts.

He drew a careful breath. He feared her bray would haunt his sleep all night long.

She clapped her hands to her flat chest and rolled her eyes toward heaven. "I really do so little, but I think it is important. The flowers, I mean. They make people think of heaven's gifts, although I do rely on my garden most of the time. To find the flowers in the fields is so very time-consuming, don't you know? And I do think that wildflowers wilt so easily . . ."

Cedric let his mind wander as she prosed on. Unless he had misunderstood entirely, Squire Walker said he had quite a few fields full of turnips, for which he had the highest praise. Cedric had never developed a taste for the wretched roots. But apparently there was no end to the information about agriculture he did not possess. More than enough to learn in a lifetime.

***

The next morning, Jane hurried back from the stable and changed into her gray gown. She hoped to have at least an hour alone in the library before Mr. Williamson came back.

Yesterday she had given him two letters of recent origin and now she wanted to inspect his notes and see if he had summarized them accurately. Once in the library, she felt quite like a thief in the night, sneaking a look at his work. He had placed the folder of letters on top of his notepad. Would he notice if she moved it? Carefully she noted the exact placement, set the folder aside, and read the first page of notes.

After perusing the first few lines, she choked back a gulp of surprise. He had concocted a very succinct and complete summary of each letter, composed in a neat script, quite the contrary of what she had anticipated. In just a short time, he had captured the thrust of the letters and noted their most important substance. She closed the notepad and replaced the folder atop it.

Why was she surprised? Though he assumed a mantle of self-deprecation and unconcern regarding his scholarship, he obviously had a head on his shoulders.

Last night Cedric Williamson had been exceptionally polite and kind to the Walker ladies. The kind of social patina that apparently came so easily to him, which she usually despised, had seemed considerate and charitable to the two young ladies. Neither had an iota of polish themselves, not even the moderate ability to carry on an amiable conversation. Yet he had made them feel good, and their mother even better.

Mr. Williamson seemed a gentleman of many incongruities. She did not understand him at all. But if she was to accomplish anything this day, she had better get busy before he returned.

Yesterday's task had been an easy one for him. But now, she had a more demanding assignment, one she sincerely hoped he would not complete. Jane placed the oldest of the letters in a pile for Mr. Williamson to sort and read. They were the most difficult to decipher, the hardest to read, the most challenging to interpret. She had spent hours on them, writing careful summaries of each.

Cedric Williamson, she felt sure, would not have the patience to figure out the unfamiliar spelling and old-fashioned script, much less deduce their meaning. She allowed herself a private smile. The sooner he gave up on the assignment, the sooner he left Uphaven, the better for her. Then she could fulfill her intention to talk Lady Stockdale into letting her write the book.

Yet her intentional and unscrupulous deceit seemed hard to justify. Especially after last evening, when Mr. Williamson had been so very polite and amiable to Mrs. Walker and her unlovely daughters. Any good looks that the Walker children received had gone to the brother, Oswald. His appearance was not bad at all, compared to the lack of attractiveness of both sisters.

Of course, she thought, idly running her fingers over the velvet box of the remaining letters, Oswald Walker was not half so handsome as Mr. Williamson.

Which did not solve her immediate problem. How would she survive the next few hours, sitting across from him and trying to concentrate? She hoped he would not last long at the desk. Men like him were not used to working hard. The set of early letters would be a challenge to anyone. Certainly she had found them so, all written before spelling was standardized. He would find them complicated, very hard to make out.

Yes, if she gave him the first few, he could never last long. Meanwhile, she could proceed as she wished without regard to what Mr. Williamson did or did not do.

Painstakingly, she set out her pens and paper. She had to make it look like she had started with the latest letters and worked backwards. Then, if he asked, she could suggest she chose the latest set of letters to work on. She would pretend their work would meet in the middle. But she could hardly start today with the last letter of Baron Stockdale's, could she? It would appear as though she had done nothing for the last weeks, if he happened to check.

What trouble it was to concoct a deception! She felt entirely out of her element shuffling the letters around in this fashion, but she needed to discourage him.

Jane thumbed through the letters and counted out the last thirty. She could start there, even if it would be difficult to pick up the thread. But remember, she reminded herself, her goal was to drive him away and the later letters, two of which he had read yesterday, were obviously too easy for him. She wanted him to be bored to tears, annoyed, thwarted. She simply wanted him to go away.

She had no more than settled herself with the thirty-first letter, when Mr. Williamson arrived, smiling and begging her pardon for disturbing her deliberations. "I took the liberty of cutting a few more roses. The old ones were drooping this morning." He set a vase of pink blooms on the table.

Jane murmured her thanks.

"I shall put myself at your service, Miss Gabriel. What can I do that would be of the most value to you?"

She was amazed at how easily she dissembled. "I have been reading backwards from the last letter of Lady Stockdale's late husband. So if you start with the very first of the letters, the earliest ones, that would be most appreciated."

He looked surprised. "You are reading the letters backwards? I would have thought that counterproductive, Miss Gabriel. But then, I do not understand your methodology."

She cast about for a valid reason. "I am interested in the most recent years, as a beginning of my familiarity with the family."

"I see."

He sounded unconvinced, and to be fair, she thought her reasoning quite dubious. She tried again. "I thought I could take advantage of many of Lady Stockdale's recollections."

"Oh, yes, that makes sense."

She breathed deeply and pushed the velvet box of the oldest

letters across the table. "I hope you will not mind beginning at the beginning."

"Whatever is helpful to you, I shall be glad to attempt." He opened the box and took out a letter, written on a heavy parchment-like paper. He glanced at it, then held it closer to his eyes.

She could not help watching him, waiting to hear his reaction.

"Is there a magnifying glass?" he asked.

"In the drawer in the desk." It was the one Jane had used to read that exact letter.

He stood and went to the desk. She tore her gaze away. How could he sit in such snug-fitting inexpressibles?

Blushing at the thought, Jane fastened her eyes on the letter before her, placing her hands at each side of her face to blot out all peripheral vision.

My dearest Amelia. The meeting with Mr. Borland was not as useful as I had forecast.

She grabbed her notes and wrote the name of Borland, beginning a list of persons she would have to identify as she read through the pile of letters.

But removing her hand from her face allowed a sideways glimpse of Mr. Williamson squinting through the glass at the letter. She almost wanted to help him, but restrained the urge. Was not this attitude of puzzlement exactly what she wanted?

She let herself peek at the hand that held the glass. He wore a large gold signet ring, and she wondered what his seal looked like. As the son of an earl, would he wear a family crest, or was it something he had made up for himself?

She jerked her gaze back to the letter. It was going to be a very long and rather warm afternoon. Her inattention had nothing to do with Cedric Williamson. She was simply distracted by the fragrance of the roses.

***

Cedric excused himself from the library with only a twinge
of regret. Miss Gabriel had looked up with an expression that
spoke of her satisfaction that he did not linger very long over
his task. As much as he loathed meeting her expectation, for
it was more than obvious she wished him to the devil, he was
glad to leave.

He had hardly made out the handwriting on a single old
letter, even with the help of a magnifying glass. And the exe-
crable spelling had entirely garbled the meaning of the lines.
The two hours of toil in the library left him praying for relief.
The letter he read wandered from subject to subject, and he
was hard-pressed to sort out the worthwhile information from
the accounts of visits to the theater or gossip about a party the
writer had attended.

With relief, he went to the stable and mounted the stallion
for the short ride to his meeting.

When he rode Atlas into the small yard at the Ramshead
Inn, no ostler appeared, only a small boy who quickly ran
away when Cedric dismounted and the stallion danced and
blew like a dragon. Shrugging, Cedric pushed open a door
to a dark stable, which appeared empty. Atlas obviously did
not care for the smells, and only with great effort and a well-
placed slap on the rump did Cedric wrestle the horse inside.
At least the stalls appeared sturdy enough to hold him if Atlas
took a notion to kick his way out. When Cedric was almost
done removing the bridle and loosening the girth of the saddle, a man ambled in.

"Boy said someun' came in. You Mr. Wilumson?"

Cedric squinted at him, but could hardly make out his
shape in the shadows. "Yes. I hope it is all right to leave my
horse here."

"Yessir. Mr. Walker's waiting fer ya."

The thought of dredging up the memories of his trouncing,
his utter humiliation at Newmarket, made Cedric shudder,
wishing he could get back on Atlas and retreat. But he could
not. He needed to settle his wagering debt with Oswald

Walker. And he wanted to know more about Trentworthy. Perhaps enough to crush his schemes.

The man took the coin Cedric handed him. "I'll give the horse some water."

"Thanks. He's a bit of a handful, so don't turn your back on him."

"Right."

Cedric blinked in the bright sunshine until his eyes adjusted to the glare, but when he stepped into the inn, he was again plunged into near darkness. He barely missed rapping his head on the low beam above the door, ducking just in time. The smell was almost as raw as the odor of the stable. The taproom reeked of malty brew, unwashed bodies, and the lingering aroma of fried fat.

"Over here, in the corner, Williamson," Oswald Walker called. "Draw my friend a tankard, if you please, Higdon."

Gradually Cedric became accustomed to the gloom, even to the smell. He slid onto a bench at Walker's table in the otherwise empty taproom.

The barkeep set a foaming mug before him. "Thanks."

The man disappeared through a side door and pushed it shut behind him.

Cedric took a sip of his ale. "This doesn't look like your kind of haunt, Walker, but this brew is tasty."

"It's the one place I can be sure my father won't come. He's tried to get this place shut down and cleared for years, but it's a freehold and Higdon won't sell. Makes the pater apoplectic every time he thinks of it."

Cedric chuckled. Higdon was no doubt delighted to take young Walker's money and thumb his nose at the squire.

Oswald leaned back and grinned at Cedric. "You put the spring in my mama's step last night, Williamson. Had both m' sisters still in spasms this morning. I admire your technique, especially since neither of them has much to offer the eye of a connoisseur, far too much in one case, not near enough in the other."

Cedric saw no reason to abuse the young ladies. "I found them both quite charming."

"Get out! Neither has an ounce of town bronze, and Father refuses to spew enough rhino to send them to school or to some poverty-stricken gentlewoman in London who'd teach 'm to behave proper."

Cedric just nodded. He prayed he would not have to spend another evening in their company.

Oswald pursed his lips and narrowed his eyes. "You had a fine dust-up in Newmarket a few days ago, Williamson."

"True. I cannot fathom what came over me. To buy a horse just before a race. I must have been demented." Cedric felt his anger building, a knot at the pit of his gut. He wanted to get back at Trentworthy, prove he wasn't the kind of fool the damn swindler thought he was. He wished he could pound out his fury on the table but instead he wrapped his hands around the mug of ale and held them rigid.

Oswald gave a derisive snort. "Your man likely had the same kind of silver tongue as the rat who rooked my friend Ben Frey at York."

Cedric leaned into the table. "He bought a horse just before a race?"

"A fast-talking cove snagged him and managed to convince Ben to part with his blunt, lots of blunt. You ain't the first and won't be the last."

"Which does not give me any consolation, that's a fact. What was the fast-talker's name?"

"No idea. I been trying to remember. But it was not Trentworthy, that I know for sure."

"What did he look like?"

Oswald made a dismissive gesture. "My height. Ordinary. Not a fancy dresser."

"Had you seen him before?"

"Naw. Not that I would have noticed. It was just his line of rubbish that set him apart."

Cedric sighed. Probably Trentworthy with a different name. "Does this kind of thing happen at every meet?"

"Don't know. It could. I saw it one other time, at Doncaster. In both cases, the rogue bought back the horse, at a very great loss to the dupe, naturally."

Cedric pondered for a moment. Could it be possible that Sybil, whose papers were probably not genuine, could have been sold and resold? She had no distinctive markings, just a coat of the most ordinary dark bay. "Would it be with the same horse? Or a different one?"

"Who knows?"

"Can you remember what those horses looked like?"

Oswald squeezed his eyes shut for a moment. "Nothing that sticks in my mind."

"But how do they get away with it? Can't the Jockey Club do something about it?"

Oswald shook his head and pulled a face. "They'd have no grounds. Anyone can buy and sell a horse. Those sellers did nothing wrong, at least nothing you could prove."

Cedric clenched his jaw, but tried to give an offhand shrug. "No, and making fools out of green striplings is a crime only to those of us who fall into the snare. I still cannot believe I was so easily gulled."

Oswald wiped a fleck of foam from his lip. "You hardly seem the type, Williamson."

"Thanks, I think. I s'pose those scoundrels have a knack for finding fellows who'd be susceptible." As Cedric knew he'd been, showing off and bragging. Flaunting his supposed talents at picking winners for those newly acquired friends. And his sapskull idiocy only made him angrier. "Tell me about your friend who got bubbled at York. What happened?"

"Ben and I went up to the races with friends. In the morning, we walked around, looking over the horses, choosing some good bets, naturally. This fellow invited us to take a look at his horse, one he was trying to sell for a friend, he said. It was due to run that afternoon. Looked prime, healthy and frisky. The fellow said it was a sure winner. After a fair bit of jawing about it, Ben decided to take the fellow up on his offer."

Seeing himself in Ben's place, Cedric promised himself for the hundredth time to keep his anger under control.

Oswald downed another gulp of ale. "Ben was cocksure that horse was a winner. Got us all to bet. Heavily."

Cedric nodded, clamping his hands around his tankard. Getting all the fellows to bet, just as he had done last week, making a big profit for somebody, probably quite a few collaborators of Trentworthy's.

"Just like your horse, Williamson, that one brought up the rear. Acted like it never ran that far in its life."

"Then what?" Cedric practically spat the words.

"We all had money on that horse, lots of money. Ben was mighty irritated, but we all ribbed him, just like your friends must'a done."

"They did indeed." Cedric seethed inside, almost welcomed the jabs of rage that made his heart twist and his gut coil in a tight knot.

"Late that night, when we were all well foxed, the fellow found Ben and offered to buy back that horse. Said he knew it wasn't worth much any more, after such a bad showing, but he knew a place that worked with sure losers and mebbe they could make something of it."

"So Ben sold it back?"

"Ben had no use for it, just another mouth to feed. First I thought he was gonna tear the dirty dog apart, but he could hardly stand, much less take a swing. Pretty soon, the swindler got him to sign some papers and gave Ben a fistful of money."

Cedric's head spun. Was it possible he'd bought the very same horse? "Do you remember what that horse looked like? Young?"

"Jest a two-year-old, they said."

"Colt or filly?"

"Well, can't say I remember, Williamson, but I can ask Ben."

"What about color?"

"Nothing special. Bay, dark, black mane and tale, same as a thousand horses."

Figured, Cedric thought. It seemed so obvious now, even to his rage-charged brainbox. If the horse had a distinctive color, or a white stocking or a star or blaze on its face, that would be too memorable for the kind of fiddle he assumed Trentworthy was working on gullible young men—men who drank too much, wanted to show off for their friends, and had no sense whatsoever. It galled him that he had been picked as such a gull, for he had long prided himself on his shrewdness.

"Did Ben talk to the jockey about what happened to the horse?"

"Naw, the jockey knew nothing. Said that horse must'a been too tired from traveling to the meet."

"Did you believe that?"

"Seemed possible, but didn't act like it before the race, in fact, it looked fit to run like a breeze, not nervous or frightened, but full of vigor."

"So it wasted all its energy before the race."

"Seems so."

"But after the swindler bought it back, you and Ben never saw the horse again."

Oswald gave a snort of laughter. "I'll say we didn't. Ben never wanted to see it, ever!"

"And you never wondered why the horse couldn't run as expected?"

Oswald drank, then set his tankard on the table. "I've been going to race meets since I was knee-high, first with Father, now with my friends. I've heard plenty of stories about how races are fixed, jockeys paid off, horses' feed laced with drugs, even the kind of switches you talk of."

"I've been to a meet or two in my day as well." Dozens, if the truth be told, he thought. "I never figured I would do something as demented as buy a horse and take on all bets, but I fell for Trentworthy's line. I could blame the grape or even blue ruin, but what's the use? I was gammoned, and now I intend to pay off my debts."

He peeled off a few bills and handed them to Oswald. "I would like to meet your friend Ben. Perhaps we could commiserate together."

"We can go into St. Edmundsbury some night soon. There's usually a game at the Angel for those who care to wager an evening away."

"Fine. Send word to me, and I'll ride over with you sometime soon." The very last thing Cedric needed was any more gambling, but perhaps he could strip Ben away from the group and get his impression of what his horse had looked like.

Anger built again and he shivered it away as he put a few coins on the table and stood. "Until then, Walker."

Oswald lifted a hand as a wave good-bye.

Cedric remembered to duck again as he went out.

CHAPTER SIX

Jane handed Sandy's reins to a young groom and turned to watch Cedric mount Sybil. For the past few days, he had taken the bay out for exercise following their morning ride. The filly's legs were almost completely healed, the result of her salve, Jane was sure. Cedric declared the young mare seemed to have returned to her promising level of liveliness.

Sybil seemed eager to be off, sidling from side to side almost as Cedric's stallion Atlas did, but not from nervousness or bad temper. The bay filly seemed eager to run, to revel in lengthening her stride and stretching her neck into the wind. In a few more days, Cedric said he was going to let her go full speed, but now he would hold her back a little, keep her from straining too hard before she was entirely restored to full health.

Cedric gave a wave, turned the filly's head toward the fields, and urged her forward. Jane admired her dark coat, now smooth and shining, unlike her ragged, worn-out condition on that first morning. Cedric had grown in his concern for the filly. He must have been quite disgusted with her at first, but now he was sincerely involved in bringing Sybil to full recovery. Perhaps he only wanted to win races with her, but whatever his incentive, he was considerate of the horse's welfare.

She watched them canter toward the distant line of trees that marked the edge of the field. Cedric had showed his resolve to follow his aunt's directives in the afternoons they worked in the library. In fact, Jane was genuinely surprised at his determination to read each of those early letters. His notes, when she saw them, were careful and thorough, far better than she had expected from a man who did not try to deny his reputation for indolence and foolish behavior. He might be making a genuine attempt to make something of himself. Perhaps he only pretended to be slothful.

And thinking of indolence, Jane gathered her long skirt and strode back to the house, eager to read a few of the most recent letters before Cedric arrived in the library.

By this morning, the fourth day he would spend in the library with her, they had established a little routine, rising early and riding together, she on Sandy, he on Atlas. Then while he rode Sybil, she changed and went to the library, hurrying through the newer letters, starting from the last written by Lady Stockdale's husband only a few weeks before his death, and going backward. When Cedric arrived, he set to work on the earliest letters, those she had secretly finished.

She thought for a moment of how he looked when he burst through the door each morning, his face eager, his manner so engagingly deferential. His hair was often still damp, his jaw smooth, and his scent the spicy touch of bay rum. He always looked every inch the exemplary Corinthian, perfectly groomed and far more handsome than any man she had ever known, much less sat across a table from day after day. Underneath the polished veneer he presented, she sensed a core of power and strength that only occasionally peeked through. And on top of everything was a layer of amused cynicism, a way of looking at the world with a grin and a shrug, a willingness to march off for a lark or a prank at any moment.

Good heavens, she wondered, as she hung her riding skirt in her clothes press, what am I doing? Mooning over a London dandy, while I don this gray dress with its associated gray demeanor, so very opposite of the attitude of Mr. Williamson? It was not him but his aunt she was obligated to please with her work.

She slipped the drab gown over her head and gave herself

a stern stare in the cheval mirror. *You, my dear Miss Gabriel, are acting like the veriest peagoose!*

In just under an hour alone in the library, Jane finished reading three letters, set them aside with her summaries, and spread out her notes on Aelbert Cuyp, painter of two fine oils acquired by the third baron. One, temporarily removed from the Green Drawing Room, now stood on the easel in the corner. Just as she rose to stand before it, Mr. Williamson surged through the door, wearing his usual wide smile and carrying a fresh bouquet.

"Please excuse me, Miss Gabriel. I did not intend to startle you." He set the roses in their usual place.

Jane waved a hand in the air. "You did not, sir. I was just getting up to study that painting."

He stepped over to look at it and stood beside her. He brushed back his hair and shook his head. A lock fell onto his forehead. "This needs more light. Can I move it nearer the window?"

"Yes, please, Mr. Williamson. That would be most helpful."

He held the frame in one hand and lifted the easel with the other, placing it out of the shadows. "There, that is much better. Look how the colors gleam now."

"Thank you. I agree, it is much better. The clouds are almost silvery against the blue sky, and the water reflecting the boats sparkles, does it not?"

"I think we should recommend that Aunt Amelia place this in a room with more light. It deserves to be seen."

Jane nodded, trying not to let her eyes stray to the way his admiration made his eyes sparkle too.

After a moment of silence in which they both gazed at the painting, he gave a little sigh, sat down at his usual spot at the table, and reached for the box of letters and his folder of notes. "From the brilliant brush strokes of a great painter to the deplorable penmanship of the first baron."

Jane remained at the painting, but took a little pity on him. "Perhaps you could skip a few of the earlier letters and move ahead." After all, she had done those letters already and had her notes on them finished.

"Oh, no, Miss Gabriel. I am learning a great deal from these letters. He lists the exact weights and amounts of money received for the fleeces. I am finding out how the wool business evolved. They may be difficult to make out, but the effort is worthwhile."

Jane looked at him in surprise, too late realizing her astonishment might show on her face.

He laughed out loud. "So you do not believe me?"

Jane felt her cheeks warm. "It is just that, ah, I know you want to . . ." She let her voice trail off.

"Please do not be embarrassed. I myself am amazed I find it interesting. And some of the articles I have read in *The Farmer*. I never thought much about how all the sheep get fed and moved around, shorn for wool and slaughtered for mutton. I had never thought beyond what I put on my back and eat off my plate."

"One takes so many things for granted."

"I grew up on an estate where we had many tenants and a large home farm. I played all over the property with my brothers, riding and fishing, shooting in the fall. We even had a sheepdog for a while and spent hours throwing sticks for him to chase. I suppose I never gave a thought to what those dogs were trained to do until I began to watch them work here at Uphaven."

Jane nodded, her embarrassment giving way toward the pleasure of seeing his sense of discovery.

"Mr. Richards, the home farm manager, says the best dogs come from the highlands, up in Scotland. There they have to search all over the terrain for the sheep. Here in flat old Suffolk, they just have to keep the flocks together when they move from one patch of pasture to another. Well, here I am, blathering on and keeping you from your work."

"Not at all. I am pleased to see you finding satisfaction in your reading."

"And I shall get back to it right away. I cannot spend much time here in the library today, because I am going to St. Edmundsbury later with Oswald Walker. Now I shall be quiet as a mouse."

Jane said nothing and turned her gaze again to the painting. Just when she had grown so impressed with Mr. Williamson's hard work, he was leaving early. Whatever business he had with Mr. Walker she could not imagine. But then, what they did with their time was no affair of hers.

She gave a little sniff and picked up a tape to measure the painting. It was thirty-six inches wide, and she noted the figure on her pad. Twenty-six inches high. She glanced at it again, and somehow the silvery clouds looked darker, the water a bit less brilliant.

Jane sank into her chair and pulled a large volume toward her, paging through until she found the section on Aelbert Cuyp. She peeked at Mr. Williamson, whose forehead wrinkled as he squinted at the letter. A dangerous man, at least dangerous to her.

He was far too attractive. She did not dare to let her thoughts wander into forbidden territory. He might never amount to much, probably far more interested in his horses and his wagers than in his belated concern with agriculture. Not that it should matter to her.

He, a man of the fashionable London set, would never be interested in plain Jane Gabriel, who aspired to the status of a bluestocking author of family biographies.

She tried to concentrate on the reference work. Cuyp was born in 1620, almost two hundred years ago.

Mr. Williamson carried his letter to the window, holding it up to the light. "Sorry to disturb you again, Miss Gabriel, but sometimes this writing is very difficult."

She looked up and met his eyes. "Do not be concerned. I am merely jotting down a few facts about the artist."

He returned his attention to the sheet of paper before him, and again his forehead creased in concentration.

Jane watched as he bent his head. Another small curl fell forward, then a few more strands followed. In the bright light, the waves of his dark hair were tipped with gleaming copper. *Jane, you henwit, get back to work!*

Cedric left the library feeling as though a gust of wintry wind propelled him from the room. Jane Gabriel's disapproval of his early finish to the day's tasks was obvious, no matter how she tried to hide it behind a smile, a smile that did not engage her usually expressive eyes.

It could not be helped, he thought, heading to the stables. Aunt Amelia had told him to enjoy himself, even handed him a purse of money in case he encountered any more of the local fellows to whom he owed debts of honor. Of course, Aunt Amelia had many years of experience beyond Jane's, whose life must have been quite sheltered. Or perhaps Miss Gabriel's disapproval had been more disappointment than censure. She had been all smiles when he told her of his growing interest in the routines of the home farm and the cycle of yearly production.

It was, to be honest, rather a surprise to him. He had expected to find the workings of the estate farms to be tedious in the extreme. Instead, he enjoyed his tours of inspection with Mr. Sutton, the steward, and the hours he spent with the manager of the home farm, Mr. Richards. What could explain it? He admitted he had no idea. He was completely stumped by the situation. He had wasted not a moment wondering what was happening back in London, what capers his friends were planning, what mills they were attending or what house parties they were gracing with their presence. It was probably just the summer doldrums, a natural lull in the year's pace.

Then there was the influence of his aunt, who seemed in good spirits, and the presence of Jane. He still harbored some suspicions about her motives for doing so much hard work for Aunt Amelia, but he could not reconcile his suspicions with her behavior. Anyway, if Aunt Amelia gave her one of the paintings as a reward for the admirable way she was arranging the material, it would be completely justifiable.

Now, he would have to work even harder to restore Jane's esteem, increase it, even. Jane's companionship, so very different from his usual encounters with young ladies, brought him a curious satisfaction, even enjoyment. He truly desired her good opinion of himself.

But this trip with Walker was more than a pleasure jaunt to St. Edmundsbury. If he was to get to the bottom of Trentworthy's schemes, he needed to talk to Ben. Because, Cedric mused, he might be able to think of a way to put Trentworthy out of business permanently.

By late afternoon, Cedric and Oswald left their horses in the yard at The Angel and strolled around the narrow streets of the old town toward the ruined towers of the old abbey. At one time, centuries ago, the abbey of St. Edmund was one of the most influential and wealthy monasteries in England, a shrine to the ninth-century English King Edmund. Obviously, Cedric thought, there was not much left of the religious order, but anyone who saw these massive towers could not doubt the power that once centered here. Now, around the old precincts of the monks, the streets were filled with monuments to the English propensity for commerce. Shops of all sizes, the market square, breweries, manufactories, hotels, even a new theater, filled the busy town.

Once they were seated in The Angel's dining room, Oswald gestured to a young man in the doorway, who immediately came to their table.

"Here's Ben Frey." He slapped Ben's arm and nodded towards Cedric. "Meet Cedric Williamson."

They exchanged greetings, and Ben joined them.

"So I suppose I will have to suffer through a complete version of how each of you ended up a gull!" Oswald laughed out loud.

Cedric and Ben exchanged rueful grins, but no laughter.

Cedric gestured to the waiter. "I suggest we postpone our chat until after we eat. Don't want to upset the digestion, don't you know?"

This time, Ben gave a genuine laugh, however small. "Fine with me."

Over their fish, the men talked of upcoming races at Doncaster, switching to the program at York over the second remove.

When at last they were drinking port, Cedric leaned towards Oswald. "Walker, why don't we join you upstairs in a while. You can get a feel for the game and let us know how things are proceeding before we open our pockets."

"Don't mind if I do," Oswald said. "I'll leave you to your sad stories, and you can commiserate together."

When he was gone, Cedric eyed Ben, and offered to tell his tale first. The humiliating details poured out of him, helped by Ben's sympathetic nods. But Cedric stopped short of mentioning his suspicion of drugs. He did not want to influence Ben's tale.

"And so," Cedric finished, "she simply slowed down and fell back to last place. By the time we got her back to the stall, she could hardly hold up her head."

Ben's faced looked like a thunderstorm. "Much the same happened to my horse. Well, not mine for long. Only owned it for a few hours. He was young but vigorous, and that fellow I bought him from said he was fast as lightning. I did the same darn fool thing you did, plunked down a pretty penny for that nag. Put my money on him, got all my pals to bet. The rest of the field looked mundane, just a bunch of youngsters. The fellow said they were losers . . . but what does it matter what that crooked bastard said? Everything was a dammed lie."

Cedric nodded ruefully. "You said it right, my friend. What was the fellow's name, the one who sold you the horse?"

"Treadwell. George Treadwell."

"An average looking man? Medium height, medium build, on the dark side of brown hair, thinning and wispy?"

"Yes, nothing much to set him apart."

"Exactly, neither young nor old. A man quite perfectly turned out for his profession of cheat, thief, and felon."

Ben grimaced, as if the memory caused him physical pain. "You are correct."

Cedric went on, hardly able to keep his voice from rising. "Probably the same fellow I know as Trentworthy. He is so average, so ordinary, he would blend easily into a crowd. Nothing memorable, nothing obvious to set him apart. No doubt he has a number of names, changed whenever he edges into potential conflict with the law."

"The thought of him makes me livid. I'd like to plant him a facer."

Cedric wondered how far Ben's anger and loss of dignity would carry him. Far enough to be of help in trying to stop Trentworthy? "We were taken for fools. And fools we were, as a matter of fact."

"I could take him down without breaking into a sweat."

Ben was a tall fellow, not exactly slender, but far from stout. "What if Trentworthy punched you back?" Cedric asked.

Ben's face grew redder. "I'd give him everything I've got, and I've gone a few rounds here and there. Not worth bragging about, but I think I'd more than hold my own with that cove."

"And if he had partners, henchmen?"

Ben frowned and his mouth opened, then closed. Obviously he had not thought much about exacting revenge on Trentworthy.

Cedric leaned close to him. "Walker heard of a similar case at Doncaster. Mine was at Newmarket, yours at York. I don't think it is possible for one man to run this kind of a crime alone. He needs a gang of men to find the horses, bring them to the meets, help find a gullible victim."

Ben winced.

Cedric went on. "Then they have to do something that

causes the horse to come in last. Neither yours nor mine went lame, although that is a fiddle I've heard is common in horseracing. So I figure either they switched the horse for a ringer or they used drugs."

"Drugs. What kind of drugs, Williamson? How would you give a horse drugs?"

"There are ways to give drugs—in feed or in the water would be simplest. But I have not figured out what it would be. Enough laudanum to affect a horse would be a packet of powder as big as a loaf of bread. Or a pailful of laudanum drops. Neither would be easy to get down a horse's throat."

"You are just conjecturing—"

"Yes, it's all guesswork. But look at it this way, Ben. If we don't put a stop to their game, who will?"

"But how can we find out more? I tell you, Williamson, if we could stop him, I'd do anything."

"So let's see what we need to know. I've checked in Newmarket. Trentworthy, or whatever his name is, has been there before, several times. Often has a horse to run, sometimes sells it. Has been known to buy it back. Nobody checks up much on sales like that. We can surmise that he, or someone uncannily like him, also works the York meets. And perhaps at Doncaster. We don't know how many accomplices he has, but there must be a half dozen. Can you ask around, see what you can pick up?"

Ben's mouth had a grim set and his voice was hard. "I will help any way I can, Williamson." He scribbled on the back of his card. "You can reach me here, any time. My father has some plans for me, beginning next week when we take in the early hay. I consider myself fortunate that he didn't wring my neck. Though I don't suppose I'll care much for the kind of farmhand labor he will put me to."

"I will be in contact, Ben. Do not worry. You will survive your father's punishment. And eventually, we shall have our revenge."

"Let's get upstairs to the game. This may be my last opportunity for a long time."

Nearing sunrise, as he fell into his bed, groggy with fatigue, Cedric wore a sardonic smile. He and Ben had managed to deprive the other players of most of their ready. In his pockets, Cedric had at least three times the amount he had started with.

CHAPTER SEVEN

Jane placed the ten pages of her draft for the introduction of the book about the barons Stockdale on the table and closed her eyes for a moment. Was she satisfied with the document? Did she want to add another page or two? Or was it better to be succinct?

She almost wished she had not been struck by inspiration yesterday after Mr. Williamson left. Yes, something had driven her to sit down, uninterrupted, and spell out exactly what the book was designed to accomplish.

Now, of course, he was back with all his disruptive ways. Over breakfast he had announced his purchase of tickets for all of them to attend the new theater in St. Edmundsbury in a few nights. They would stay at The Angel after the performance, taking the better part of two days from her tasks. She would have welcomed the opportunity to attend the theater more wholeheartedly if she and her mother would be a less shabby addition to the box Mr. Williamson had secured. Perhaps if she kept the gold satin-lined cape around her shoulders, she would look respectable enough for a provincial gathering.

She sighed, wishing Mr. Williamson to perdition. Lady Stockdale and her mother were thrilled, as she could have expected. Even Hayes, Lady Stockdale's personal maid, bragged to Mrs. Peters about her inclusion in the party, or so it had sounded when Jane had gone to the stillroom to mix more salve for the filly's legs.

She turned her attention back to the introduction. Mr.

Williamson would be here any minute, and then her head might muddle up again. Especially if he brought more of those sweet-smelling roses.

Would it be better to write an introduction once the entire book was completed? There could be important points she had not yet discovered, yet she felt the material was neatly covered, point by point, laying out the sequence of chapters she would write, from the earliest foundations of the Uphaven estate, to the continual expansion of the operation and its diversification into wool production and other enterprises, combined with the activities of the men who developed it. That would fill three chapters. Next would come the circumstances of the creation of the barony, then lives of each early baron, his service to the crown, his family, his travels, and his ventures into collecting art. After the first three barons, she would write a chapter on the collection and the principal artists. The final chapters would cover the last three barons in more detail. The final chapter would be a summary of the accomplishments and honors of the family.

The introduction spelled out the outline. If nothing else, she thought, it would provide her a guide for the chapters, and if she needed to alter the plan or change the order of the topics, she could always change the introduction later.

Jane thumbed through the pages. She was tempted to show them to Lady Stockdale. Perhaps if she saw how nicely Jane had laid out the sequence of chapters, she would agree to have Jane write a chapter or two. But there was also the possibility she would simply keep the pages and show them to some other writer she wanted to hire.

Jane stood and went to the window, staring out at the garden. Why was she now having this failure of nerve? Slowly she scanned the flowers, gently nodding in a light breeze under a sunny sky. The white of the daisies showed clear and stark against the dark green of the yews, almost as though they were glowing with silver highlights.

She was so lost in thought she hardly heard the door open

and close. When she turned around, she started in surprise. Cedric Williamson stood at the table, roses in hand, leaning over and reading her pages.

"What are you doing?" Her voice sounded like she was strangling.

He set down the vase, picked up a sheet of paper, and smiled at her. "This is very good, Miss Gabriel." He replaced the page and picked up another, scanning it quickly. "You have a very succinct style and every thought is expressed clearly."

Jane's heart leaped into her throat and though she opened her mouth to speak, no words came forth. This was not the way she meant to have things go. Not in the slightest.

He read a third page, then a fourth and a fifth while she stood voiceless and shaking.

"I am most impressed." He perused the final page while she struggled to find the words to express her frustration, her anger, her sense of violation.

At last she cleared her throat and fought back the lump. "Mr. Williamson, those pages were not meant for your eyes. Or those of anyone else—"

"But why not? They are very good. Aunt Amelia would be delighted to see how well you have organized the tasks."

"But I did not mean for anyone to read that. At least not yet. That is to say, I am sure there will be many revisions . . ." Her voice failed her again.

He straightened the pages and sat down in his usual chair. "Why are you concerned about revising this introduction already? Are you planning to write the chapters yourself?"

She sank onto a chair and cast her eyes on the stack of books in front of her. "I was hoping to write them, yes."

"I thought we were to sort the letters, summarize them, and catalog the collection for an established writer to put into a volume, someone who had experience with this sort of project."

"Since you have asked, I shall tell you what I want to do." Her anger bubbled to the surface, strong enough that she could blurt out almost anything. "Until you arrived on the scene, I had thought I would do all those preliminary tasks myself. I had hoped I could finish a few chapters and give them to Lady Stockdale, let her read my work. I had hoped she would let me proceed on the basis of what I had already accomplished."

"But did she not want to find a writer who had experience to polish the final version?"

"That is what she said when she asked me to get started. But I want to do the whole book myself. I think I can do this book and do it well." Jane realized her voice had shrunk to a tiny sound, almost like a child's voice.

"You mean that you want to . . . to publish this book in your name?"

"In the name of J. D. Gabriel."

"That is most admirable, Miss Gabriel. I did not realize you intended to try to complete the project by yourself."

Jane sat for a moment. Now that he knew part of the story, he might as well know the rest. "I will be honest with you, Mr. Williamson."

"Cedric."

"My mother and I have few resources. No resources, if the truth be known. We live on less than one hundred pounds a year, drawn from a fund that has little hope of lasting for very long. Truthfully, we subsist on the good will and generosity of Lady Stockdale."

"I see."

"When she wrote to Mother last winter and told her of her desire to have her husband's family memorialized in a volume such as this, I volunteered to help out, thinking I could repay her for the many favors she had done for us. I had thought she could have the letters brought to me in Bath, but instead she sent her equippage for us and installed us here at Uphaven. And she is insisting on paying me for my work, though I tried to decline her generosity. Tried, but did not have any success."

"But I am sure she wants only to compensate you for your time."

"That is what she says. But to be frank, I am hoping this project will do more for me. With or without payment, I want to write the book. If it is successful, if it fulfills Lady Stockdale's wishes, I hope to secure more such commissions as J. D. Gabriel. Eventually, I might be able to earn enough money to support Mama and me, enough to pay our expenses and perhaps even save a little for the future."

She stopped when she saw a frown cloud his brow.

He stroked his chin. "So you are using this project to establish a reputation, to aim at a position elsewhere?"

"When you say it that way, my purpose sounds crass and exploitive."

"That was not precisely what I intended, Jane. Actually, I applaud your resourcefulness. But I wonder whether . . ."

"If I am up to the task?"

"Now you make *me* sound crass."

Jane reached for her pages and aligned the edges of the papers. "We seem to be talking at cross-purposes, do we not? I am trying to be straightforward. I told Lady Stockdale I wished to write the book, but she thinks of me as a mere child. I am sure she does not believe me capable. But she does not want to hurt my feelings either."

"And you are, er, you are a female."

"What does that have to do with it?"

He looked confused. "I merely meant that, well, not many women write such, ah, such biographies."

"You mean that women do not do learned work, research, analysis, that sort of thing?" With difficulty, she kept renewed anger out of her voice.

"Well, yes, I suppose so."

"I can assure you that many women are capable, entirely capable, and even qualified for such work, Mr. Williamson."

"Er, yes, I do not doubt it. But would it not be better for

you to simply find an amiable husband if you are looking for security?"

"And then what?" Again, she tried to tamp down the hostility in her tone. "Live with a man I do not care for in order to provide for my mother and myself?" She pushed the roses farther away.

"Perhaps that does not sound very . . . ah, amiable. But surely you could find a gentleman with whom you could be comfortable. That seems to be what most ladies do."

"It is not how I wish to live my life."

"So you do not care for men?"

She gave him a tight-lipped grin. "On the contrary, I care too much for men to burden one with a wife who does not enjoy his company."

"I had not thought of it in those terms."

"No, Mr. Williamson, I do not think you thought of it at all. But while we are discussing these very personal topics, may I inquire why you have no wife?"

Again he stepped back and averted his eyes. "The married state does not appeal to me."

"Exactly. That is my position."

"But surely, Jane, having a husband would alleviate your financial problems."

"I doubt it. Many men I am acquainted with have no means to support themselves or seem to gamble away any resources they have."

"Ouch!"

She said nothing to temper her words, just realigned her pages once more.

He cleared his throat and opened the box, picking up a letter in one hand and the magnifying glass in the other. "Jane, I do not mean to disparage your work. If I can help convince Aunt Amelia to have you write the book, I shall do so."

She sat back in her chair, a sudden lump rising in her throat. "Thank you, Mr. Williamson," she managed to say.

"I do wish you would call me Cedric, though I confess it is not the most melodious of names."

She smiled, no longer trusting her voice. That he would plead her case was unimaginable.

He set down the letter and gestured with the glass. "As one of several brothers, I have always thought my parents had to cast far and wide to find a name for me. My mother said there was a great chieftain by the name of Cedric somewhere, but I think the story is humbug. It has had one advantage, however. Few others of the name are around and about. When the master at Eton spoke of George or Frederick, he could have been referring to any one of a dozen like-named boys. Not so when he spoke of Cedric. I knew exactly who was in deep trouble!"

Jane swallowed and spoke lightly, grateful to have the subject altered. "My name is exactly the opposite of yours, as common as Anne or Mary. But I think it suits me, as I am rather an ordinary kind of person."

"Oh no, my dear. You are far from ordinary. I find you quite delightfully unique, exactly as I want you."

Jane sat unmoving. He had the power to leave her entirely speechless, her brain awash with disordered notions. The longer she knew him, the more confusing she found his company. But if she was to make the best of his offer, she had better get used to his presence.

He moved the old letter into a patch of sunlight. "Now I shall keep quiet and let you get back to work while I see if I can tell how much this fellow Stock wanted for his sheep in, ah, the year 1636."

Jane met his eyes and gave a brief nod, then bent to her work. The fragrance of the roses seemed suddenly comforting.

Cedric thought about Jane's aspirations to support herself and her mother with considerable sympathy, far more than he had revealed to her. He could not help but compare her situation to his own state of affairs. He had never thought before about a woman needing to earn money. That had always seemed to him the realm of male endeavor. And yet what did impoverished ladies do? Did not most females wheedle their ways into the purses of a gentleman? He remembered that a lady he had known once had declared her intention to become a governess or a companion, though she ended up marrying one of his closest friends. That, he had assumed, had been more her real goal. But perhaps he had been wrong then. And wrong now.

He needed to learn more about Jane's background, and he knew just the person who would tell him what he needed to know. The next morning, he timed his appearance at the breakfast table to follow Jane's and Aunt Amelia's departure.

Mrs. Gabriel sat alone, stirring her teacup. It was practically sugar syrup, he could tell, because she always put several heaping spoons of sugar in it.

This was the chance he needed, to turn the full glare of his charm on Jane's mother.

"Good morning, Mrs. Gabriel. I hope you had a good night's sleep."

She smiled and nodded at him. "It was fair, Mr. Williamson. A fair night."

"It looks like a lovely day. Perhaps you will have a nice walk through the garden."

"Yes. Perhaps I will."

"Are you a gardener, Mrs. Gabriel?"

"Not any more."

Extracting words from Mrs. Gabriel was a chore. "I find Aunt Amelia's roses to be particularly lovely."

"I agree."

"I believe you live in Bath, where I have heard there are also lovely roses, good country for roses."

"Oh, quite so."

"Where in Bath do you live?" He pretended he did not know.

"We reside in rooms in your aunt's house, where she kindly allows us to stay."

"How gracious of her."

"Indeed it is. I do appreciate her generosity."

As well you should, he thought. "Have you lived there long?"

"Just a year."

"And where did you reside before that?"

"In Charlotte Street."

"If I may be so bold as to inquire, Mrs. Gabriel, is that where your daughter spent her childhood?"

"No. When Mr. Gabriel was alive, we had a small property in Devon."

"I do not mean to pry, but I am interested in how you ended up in Bath."

"Mr. Williamson, it has been a long time since I reviewed the sad decline in my fortunes, but since you ask, I . . . you see, I was born into a gentleman's family in Devon, not far from Exeter, though somewhat closer to Ottery St. Mary. Our property was small, but my father was asked by his cousin, the Earl of Talaton, to oversee his local estates, and serve as a magistrate. My mother was not Devon-born, but came from . . ."

Now that he finally had her talking, she apparently did not plan to stop anytime soon. Cedric drew a deep breath and gave an encouraging nod. Mrs. Gabriel's account was bound to be rather drawn out, he feared.

Her soft voice droned on. ". . . my sister was three years younger . . ."

Cedric knew she was a good-hearted woman, and he wanted to know more about Jane. He tried to listen, but as Mrs. Gabriel related the story of her childhood, his mind kept wandering. Did the filly really run as fast as he thought, or was he deluding himself? She seemed as fast as any horse he'd ever watched, but he had little to measure her against, just his own instinct.

Mrs. Gabriel looked away, staring into the distance as she spoke. "My mother was a good teacher . . ."

If, Cedric mused, he took Sybil over to Oswald's, he might

run her against one of Walker's string. That apparently was
the one strong area of agreement between father and son:
their racehorses.

Mrs. Gabriel's voice had quieted almost to a murmur. "So
when I married Mr. Gabriel, I was only nineteen . . ."

Cedric leaned forward, for she was coming to the part he
most wanted to know about. But her meandering account
soon veered off into trivia again, and his mind wandered once
more. He wondered how the new ram he'd bought would fare
in the eyes of Mr. Richards, who had been only mildly interested in bringing a merino to try out with a small flock of
their native Suffolks. Not everyone, he had read, was enthu-
siastic about interbreeding, but one of the articles in a recent
journal had extolled the new mixed lambs as having a superior softness to their fleeces.

Mrs. Gabriel was hunting for something, probably a handkerchief. ". . . and we were so thrilled to have a baby girl. Our
Jane was perfect . . ."

Cedric took a snowy square of linen from his pocket and
handed it to her, just in time to catch a tear rolling down her
cheek. "I hope my questions have not brought you uncomfortable memories."

"Oh no, Mr. Williamson. Not uncomfortable, rather they are
joyous memories. The discomfort came only a few years later,
when Mr. Gabriel succumbed to the effects of a chill. Then we
were left alone. Quite alone." Her tears flowed afresh.

Cedric let his thoughts return to his purchase of a new ram.
Mr. Richards and the tenant farmers at Uphaven might think
him an upstart and far out of his element, but to Cedric, the
experiments were worth undertaking, if only with a limited
number of ewes. When he had stopped by the market in St.
Edmundsbury on the morning after he had won so much at
cards, he had put a little of his take into a fine young ram. He
hoped it would arrive today, brought by the farmer who was
glad to take an extra guinea for the delivery.

Mrs. Gabriel talked on. "The school kept her for several years to help with the younger girls, but sadly, their enrollment declined after the war ended and the hard times came. She has busied herself with her studies and with helping several families in worse straits then we are, and I am sad to say I think she considers herself firmly on the shelf."

This was precisely the information he had been fishing for. Why had Mr. Gabriel left his wife and child near poverty? "How old was Jane when your husband . . . er . . . went to his reward?"

She sniffled and wiped her nose. "Jane was barely twelve. The school agreed to keep her there, even without her monthly stipend. Poor Mr. Gabriel, he had no head for figures. He had some investments, but nothing went well. Just another form of gambling, he said, and like a gambler, he ended up with nothing."

"How very unfortunate." That might explain Jane's dislike of wagering.

"Our home was lost, mortgaged, they said. We moved to Bath at the suggestion of Lord Stockdale. With many economies in our way of living, we were able to survive."

"It sounds like a difficult life for you and Jane."

"Oh, indeed so, Mr. Williamson. It is my greatest regret that Jane has never had more than a few weeks in London. She never had a serious suitor, other than a few gentlemen of advanced years, quite unsuitable for a young lady. Oh, there once was a young man who danced with her frequently, but when he found she was without a dowry, he disappeared."

Poor Jane, he thought. No wonder she sought an undertaking that could bring her some income. "Very distressing to both of you, I am sure."

"Oh, I have run on far too long. Forgive me. I must admit, it has done me good to tell you, however, Mr. Williamson. I fear I have kept you too long from your assignments. And I have my needlework waiting for me."

"You have my best wishes, Mrs. Gabriel."

She rose and gave him a sad little smile as she went out of the room.

He sat back in his chair and thought again of Jane. She was a talented lady, one who would not appreciate his pity. Nor that of anyone.

"Fresh coffee, sir?" Barton held a steaming pot in his hand.

"Thank you, just what I need."

"My pleasure, Mr. Williamson." He poured the coffee and stood back. "If I could just say a word, sir. I believe that Mr. Snelling, the blacksmith in the village, often goes to Newmarket to assist his cousin, who shoes many of the racehorses. He is well-informed about the horses and the jockeys and others at the course."

"Thank you very much, Barton. His knowledge could be damn useful. I will have a talk with him later."

Barton bowed and left the room, a smile on his usually sober face.

Cedric rode Sybil to the village in the late afternoon. He heard the clang of the hammer on the anvil from the edge of the village. Snelling, worked on the rear hoof of a sturdy chestnut draft horse, holding the foot between his knees and smoothing the hoof with a rasp.

When he looked up, the smith touched his cap. "I'll be with you in a moment, sir."

"No hurry," Cedric said. He dismounted and tied Sybil's reins to a ring on the wall. He felt the heat of the forge, though the flames were lessening now, near the close of the day.

He watched Snelling try the shoe he had just finished, file off a bit more on one edge of the hoof, then fit the shoe and nail it into place. He checked it with care, then set it down and slapped the chestnut's broad rump. "There y'are, my fine old girl." He untied the mare and led her away. When he returned, he nodded to Sybil. "She throw a shoe?"

"No, she is fine. I just want to ask you some questions about your work in Newmarket."

"Oh, Mr. Williamson, Lady Stockdale tells me I can do that—"

"No, no, Snelling. Your work there is not a problem. Do not be alarmed. Lady Stockdale is not in the least concerned."

Snelling took out a well-used handkerchief and wiped the perspiration from his brow. "I'm glad to know that, sir."

"This is the filly I bought at the last meet in Newmarket—"

"Yessir, I thought so."

"You must know the whole sad story. It seems everyone here does."

"Yessir."

"Stories like mine, where a fellow is well and truly swindled—those stories travel far and fast."

Probably trying to hide his grin, Snelling took off his heavy leather apron and hung it near the anvil. "True, very true."

"Tell me, Mr. Snelling, had you ever seen this filly before that meet?"

The blacksmith looked her over. "Can't say one way or t'other. She looks like just about any other dark bay. I might have shoed her, but I doubt it." He walked over, picked up each of her feet, and looked at them. "I reckon these are Rusty's work. That's my cousin."

"Do you know the man I bought her from, Josiah Trentworthy, he called himself?"

"Can't say that I do. But I don't know the names of many of the horse owners, just the lads who bring in the nags for us to work on."

"And would you say that most of the lads in Newmarket are honest?" Cedric asked.

Snelling rubbed his jaw. "Well, Mr. Williamson, that's hard to say. Those lads and grooms who have steady work probably are on the up and up. But there's a passel of them who work only during the meets, maybe pick up the odd job now and then. They have too much idle time, if you ask me. Lots of schemes can come to a man who does not keep busy."

"Yes, I see what you mean."

"Some are hard up from time to time. Racecourses bring all sorts. Just as bees drawn to a patch of blooming clover, men who want to make things go their own route can't stay away."

"Indeed, the honest sportsman and shady lawbreaker both come."

"Lots of folks who want to win bad enough might look for a way to cheat."

"So some of them might try to make a horse run faster or slower, give themselves an edge to wager a bit of extra cash?"

"You can depend upon it. More would try if they knew how."

"Not that you would ever do such a thing, but let me ask you, Mr. Snelling. How would you try to stop a horse, keep it from winning?"

"Put on heavy shoes, maybe. Or a smithy could make a horse lame. Wouldn't be right, but that don't stop some."

"Neither of those things happened to Sybil here. I saw her immediately after the race and her shoes were the same ones she has on today. And she was not lame, just exhausted. Hardly able to hold up her head. And it lasted for more than a day. Could you do that to a horse?"

"No way I can think of, sir."

"Do you see it often?" Cedric asked.

"Many horses are tuckered out, but it don't last long once they're cooled down and fed."

His words added to Cedric's suspicion of drugging. "You'll be going there for the next meet, Mr. Snelling?"

"Rusty probably'll need me, so yes, I expect to be there."

"I know you will be busy, but I'd appreciate it if you listen around when you can. If you hear anything, let me know. I'll drop by Rusty's forge from time to time."

"Anything I can do to help, Mr. Williamson. I don't take to folks who'd hurt a horse. No, indeed."

Cedric thanked the blacksmith, mounted Sybil and was on his way with a wave of farewell. Instead of clarifying his thoughts, their conversation had only increased his anxiety. There had to be a way to stop those blackguards. They were a danger to racing itself. Furthermore, if he was going to run Sybil again, he did not want to imperil her.

Jane could hardly stop herself from squirming in frustration as she sat beside her mother in Lady Stockdale's landau on the way to call on Mrs. Walker and her daughters. Another hour in the company of those silly girls! She hated the thought of spending another afternoon away from her work. Later in the week there would be another interruption for a trip to St. Edmundsbury. It was thoughtful of Mr. Williamson to get the theater tickets, which he knew his aunt would appreciate. To include her and her mother was more than kind. She ought not to begrudge his generosity, though where he had found the money, she dared not ask.

She had more work to do, and the summer was upon them. Her mother would certainly wish to return to Bath before the cold weather set in. How had she managed to complicate her tasks so much?

Since she confessed her secret ambition to write the book about the barons Stockdale, Mr. Williamson was even more entwined in her objective. Perhaps of even more concern than whether he would be helpful in convincing his aunt of her abilities, she had revealed far too much to him. Why had she told him of her pathetic-sounding hopes to support herself and her mother?

He was far too polite to denigrate her goals out loud, but what must he think down deep? That she was demented? Certainly he was not the kind of man who admired bluestockings. If she had ever thought he might become interested—oh, what a waste of time to think of such impossibilities. Such foolish dreams!

"Jane." Her mother's voice brought her back to the moment.

"Yes, Mama?"

"Do not frown so and wrinkle your forehead, dear."

"Oh, I did not realize—"

"You need to smile, Jane," Lady Stockdale said. "Do not let the Walkers think we had to drag you away from your books just because that is exactly what was required!"

"I apologize for being absorbed in my thoughts. I promise to attend to the young ladies with all courtesy." The last thing Jane wanted was to become an embarrassment to Lady Stockdale. Where would her plans be then?

Accordingly, she kept a friendly smile on her face as they entered the drawing room and took their places. The girls sat on either side of her and talked, sometimes at the same time, about all manner of subjects, necessitating little more than a smile on Jane's part.

After she had taken only a tiny sip of tea, Miss Walker took her hand and led her to a side room they had fitted up to do silhouettes. Miss Flora hurried along in their wake.

The draperies were drawn, the light dim. A chair stood beside a stand holding a large piece of paper perpendicular to the floor.

"Sit here, please, Miss Gabriel," Miss Walker said. "I will take your silhouette."

Jane sat in the chair and looked at the paper suspended beside her head.

Flora moved in front of her. "Look straight ahead, at the little flower print on the wall."

Jane did as she was told.

Flora lit a candle on the other side of her and then walked around the chair to see the shadow cast on the paper. She returned to set the candle on a book to get the right angle.

"Hold very still," Miss Walker said. "I am going to trace around the shadow."

Jane stared at the flower print and tried to think of anything but the work she had waiting at Uphaven. The filly, for example. She had made time almost every day to go to the stable, or, if the weather was fine, to the paddock. She talked to Sybil, sometimes petted her and rubbed her head, sometimes braided her mane or tied a ribbon in her forelock. The horse seemed to enjoy human companionship more than grazing, affectionate attention more than solitude. And Jane found Sybil a sympathetic listener who never talked back, though like so many females, Sybil seemed quite taken with Mr. Williamson.

"Now, do not leave the chair until we have cut out the black paper version and checked its accuracy." Flora turned up the oil lamp while her sister took down the sheet of white paper and placed it on a sheet of black. Then Flora, carefully following her sister's line, cut through both sheets at once, to form the outline of the shadow cast by Jane's profile.

"That is ingenious, Miss Walker," Jane said. "Very clever indeed."

In moments, they created a faithful silhouette and glued it to another sheet of white paper. Flora held it up for Jane to see. "All ready for framing."

Jane thanked them profusely, quite taken with the ease of the process and the skill they exhibited.

"I did not know you gels had this talent," Lady Stockdale exclaimed when they took the silhouette to the drawing room to show it off.

"May we do one of you, Lady Stockdale, and of Mrs. Gabriel?"

Jane held her breath. The process was not time-consuming, but she hoped they would save it for another visit.

She was relieved when Lady Stockdale declined. "My dears, I would not want to show my triple chins for posterity. But I thank you very much for the offer."

Mrs. Gabriel agreed. "Very kind of you."

"Tell Mr. Williamson we would be very glad to do his silhouette," Miss Walker said.

"Oh, exceedingly happy to take his image. Please give him our highest regards."

Until they were in the landau well beyond the gates of the Walker estate, Jane kept her teeth clamped on her bottom lip. Just the thought of Cedric in that chair with Flora and Helena Walker flitting about him made her want to laugh aloud. Yet hearing the sisters speak of him renewed Jane's determination to guard against his flirtatious ways. And not to succumb to his kindness either.

Between Mr. Williamson and her, all association should be related to their tasks in the service of Lady Stockdale. She might have to summon every iota of her courage to resist falling under his spell, but she knew she was strong enough.

She simply had to be. Losing her heart would be unbearable. Catastrophic.

CHAPTER EIGHT

On Thursday, when Lady Stockdale's coach reached St. Edmundsbury, Cedric left the three ladies at The Angel where they could have tea and rest before going to the play that evening. Aunt Amelia was particularly looking forward to seeing her friends at the play, for she had not attended many events in Bury, as she called it, for the last two seasons. The theater, recently opened, would attract many of her old friends.

Cedric had arranged to meet with a nearby farmer, one who had sold a broken-down colt to someone last year who later won a race with it. Trentworthy—or whatever he called himself at various times—had to acquire the horses somewhere. They had to look promising enough to attract a buyer. Perhaps this farmer was the source of the colt Ben bought.

He hunted in the old streets for the coffeehouse and eventually found it, hurrying inside and looking around at the few customers. One man, in the far corner, raised his head and looked expectantly at Cedric. He went over and nodded to the man. "I am Cedric Williamson, are you Mr. Sperry?"

"Yessir. That's me."

"May I join you?"

"Indeed you can. I got'cher note. What happened to you, if I may be so bold as to request you tell me your story?"

Cedric left out nothing. When he finished relating every detail, he asked for Sperry's help.

"I'll help any way I can," Sperry declared. "I know another farmer over in Norfolk who was cheated, too."

"So do you raise many racing horses?"

"No, just a few. I got three mares suited for prospects, if'n I can find a proper sire nearby. The colt this fella Durward bought was a prime 'un, out of my best mare. I paid plenty to take her to a stallion near Newmarket, a real champ, name of Scobridge, son of Sorcerer."

Cedric thought of how his filly Sybil was supposedly sired by Sorcerer. Was there a connection?

Sperry sipped his coffee and continued. "As a yearling he looked to be turning up a champ. And early in his second year, he was looking so good I thought of taking him to a special trainer in Newmarket, give him a real chance. Suppose I talked him up too much with others, for soon a fellow comes and takes a look at him, sez he'd make a good offer the next day when he brought his friend. Well, by that next day, that colt jest came apart, stumbling and all in a sweat, like he'd took good and sick."

Cedric nodded sympathetically. "Must have been a terrible shock."

"Well, I don't mind saying, I was sick myself, just sick at heart when I saw that colt. When this fellow came with his friend, they were shocked to see it. Argued between themselves for a while. I just stood there and watched that poor colt. Added up what he'd cost me and figgered I was lucky when they said they'd take him off my hands for about that amount. I was afraid the colt had something that might pass to the other horses and my best mare—his mama—had a foal almost as fine as he was."

"Must have been terrible for you, Sperry."

"Yessir, I felt like my heart was broke when they led that poor thing away. And I felt kinda' guilty for them fellows, but I was glad to have their money."

Cedric knew only too well how the colt must have looked: just like Sybil.

"I thought he'd collapse before long and die. But they said maybe they could help him, so I felt a little better then.

"Wasn't but four or five months later that I went to the meet and there was my colt, no doubt about it. Won his race too."

"What did you do?"

"Mr. Williamson, I'm ashamed to say I did nothing. I looked for those fellows who bought the colt, but never saw them. Another cove had the horse. I asked him about the fellows, but he didn't know a thing. That colt was a great runner and I hear he's down south now, runs at Ascot and Sussex Downs. Makes a man pretty gloomy."

"Are you sure it was the same horse?"

"He had no special markings, no white patches on his face or legs, but jest the same, I'd of knowed him anywhere. His ears. The look in his eyes. Nothun' I could prove, but no doubt in my mind."

Cedric wished he had some kind words for Sperry, but he did not.

Sperry shook his head, his face showing pain. "My sons were upset, could not bear losing that colt. Almost like a death in the family. I could never bring myself to tell them about seeing the colt again."

"If it is any consolation to you, Mr. Sperry, you are only one of a number of men who have fallen afoul of this group of swindlers. I hope to put them out of business soon. Can I count on your help?"

Sperry brightened. "Whatever I can do, I'll do it willingly."

They stood and shook hands, parting at the street. Cedric watched him, thinking Sperry stood a little taller, felt at least a ray of hopefulness.

The walls of the new theater were hung with red silk, the oil lamps casting a glow bright enough for identifying friends in the boxes opposite, as Lady Stockdale did. The pit below was full of folks somewhat less rowdy than those of London but noisier than Bath's.

Jane arranged her cape around her shoulders, showing the

shimmery gold lining. Her mother looked quite creditable in
dark blue. Lady Stockdale's gown of deep violet set off her
fine display of the family diamonds at her neck and in her
ears, as well as on both arms. She seemed to recognize and
nod to everyone.

Jane tried not to look at Cedric, whose formal wear made
him the object of much feminine attention. Instead, she
thought about the play, *The Taming of the Shrew*, not one of
her favorites. She promised herself she would concentrate on
the performances of the actors, not upon the words of the
play, some of which she remembered all too well. At one
time, she had thought it hit too close to her own life.

Come to think of it, a reminder of the deceit and duplicity
of Petruchio might be quite apropos as she sat beside Cedric
Williamson in his evening finery.

He turned his attention from his aunt to her. "You are looking very pretty this evening, Miss Gabriel."

She gave him a quick smile before turning back to gaze
around. "Thank you. And you are looking exceptionally dis-
tinguished yourself."

"I am rather surprised at how well this coat fits. I ordered it
from a tailor near The Angel after I bought these tickets.
Thought I needed a new rig to be a worthy escort to Aunt
Amelia. When I stopped in to try it on this afternoon, it proved
to be all the crack. More than I had any right to expect."

"You usually acquire your clothing in London, I presume?"

"Usually. But I find this tailor's skills equal to the best I've
seen. Now are you ready to enjoy the bard?"

"Yes, indeed." To Jane it was much too soon to tangle over
the play.

"I have never been an avid lover of Shakespeare. Too many
reminders of school. One of my masters thought that we all
ought to learn history by reading Shakespeare and comparing
his plays to other authors' versions."

"Requiring students to read any author seems an excellent
way to engender loathing of the work. I remember reading *The*

Canterbury Tales in its difficult version, Middle English or whatever they call it, a real disservice to the story. Perhaps scholars like to study the work in the original. I was surprised how funny it was when I read an adaptation in modern language."

"I must admit I have never tried to read Chaucer."

The play began and Jane could not help but wince at the descriptions of Katherine as an irksome, brawling scold or a wildcat. "Katherine the curst," she was called. It seemed so unfair, while her sister was always known as "the fair Bianca," a biddable lady of beauteous modesty. Jane shifted in her seat. Both her mother and Lady Stockdale looked about the circle of boxes as much as they watched the stage. Mr. Williamson seemed to be staring at his knees, forehead crinkled. Was he even listening?

Petruchio spoke to Katherine's father, telling how two raging fires meeting could consume the things that fed their fury. Jane's recent experiences with Mr. Williamson gave a fresh meaning to the phrases. Yet she had to smile, for the result in the play was to be quite different from the reality of her life. Mr. Williamson was not about to coerce her to the altar, then drag her off to match her stubbornness with his own, as Petruchio did. Nor was she about to succumb to his domineering and arrogant commands. Katherine seemed to change her whole character, something Jane had not the slightest intention of doing.

She looked again at Mr. Williamson. His gaze was on the stage but the expression on his face placed him many miles distant from the theater. A frown creased his forehead and his lips were slightly parted as if he were about to speak. One hand lay on his knee, his forefinger slowly and silently tapping. When the audience laughed, he did not react, did not seem to hear.

What was he thinking of? Jane was certain it was not the antics of the gentlemen competing for the hand of Katherine's sister. No, he had something entirely different on his mind, something that had engaged his entire concentration.

As she watched, he looked up, a frown deepening. His stern expression made her breath catch in her throat. But as quickly as the thundercloud came to his face, it passed away when he looked at her, changing to a little smile and nod. But when the moment faded, Jane remembered his intensity. He had looked troubled.

Between acts, Cedric carried cups of punch for his aunt and several friends who crowded their box, going back for more to serve Jane and himself.

He was perfectly polite, with no trace of his momentary scowls. "Are you enjoying the play, Miss Gabriel?"

"I find the new theater quite delightful. One can hear every word from the stage."

"But do you like the performance?"

"I do not think if I were Kate or Bianca, I would be so eager to have my father decide my future."

"I presumed you might find this play rather dated in its portrayal of marriage."

Jane raised an eyebrow. "Why would I have any view of marriage at all, Mr. Williamson?"

"Perhaps I am misinformed, but when a husband can convince his wife to say the sun is the moon, I . . ." He paused. "I would imagine a lady could make that choice for herself. Do you not think so?"

"I believe the play assumes the primacy of the husband's views over those of his wife. Though I think that what she says and what she really thinks might be very different things."

"Yes, I daresay you are correct. From what I have seen of the married state, a lady is more likely to have her way by persuading her husband with her . . . ah . . . affection."

"How very circumspect you are, Mr. Williamson." Jane's laugh trailed away when she saw his expression turn again to a glower.

"Yes," he said shortly. "Circumspect is precisely what I must be."

Jane winced, but the rising curtain released her from the necessity of a response.

After the play, Lady Stockdale suggested they order a tea tray in their accommodations at The Angel. When they were all happily settled and Lady Stockdale had filled four teacups, Mr. Williamson sought the opinions of all three ladies on the play.

His aunt pursed her lips and sniffed the steam rising from her cup. "I suspect that Mr. Shakespeare put the words in Katherine's mouth that he wished to hear from his own wife. Obedience and tribute from a wife? Pooh! I do not recall those were the qualities Lord Stockdale most desired in me."

Jane's mother wagged her head in agreement. "Nor Mr. Gabriel. Though when I lost him, I . . ."

Jane patted her mother's hand.

"I do think," her mother went on, "men are definitely stronger, particularly in regard to making money. Ladies have so little opportunity . . . and that leaves me . . ."

Lady Stockdale nodded vigorously, setting her tall plumes to shivering. "As I have said to you before, Winifred, your Prosper was a handsome man, but thoughtless of his responsibility to you and Jane. I have often said . . ."

Jane gave an inward sigh. Her mother and Lady Stockdale had discussed her father's shortcomings again and again, and over again. Another round of comments would end with the same conclusions, yet the topic was renewed afresh on frequent occasions.

She stole a glance at Mr. Williamson. As at the theater, he looked preoccupied, by something that bothered him. This time, his whole hand drummed absently against his knee. He looked away from the ladies, his shoulders not quite as straight, his posture not as erect as usual.

She leaned toward him and spoke softly. "Are you worried about something, Mr. Williamson?"

He turned, his face darkly glowering again. "What?"

She drew back quickly, feeling her jaw drop in surprise.

Swiftly his face changed into his usual smile, the frown

erased, the quick anger gone. "I'm sorry, Miss Gabriel," he
murmured. "What did you say? I fear I was woolgathering."

Jane's heart was still pounding with the spurt of alarm his
perplexing countenance had caused. She shook her head and
fluttered a hand. "It was nothing. Nothing at all."

Instead of going to his room and preparing for bed, as he
had told his aunt he was about to do, Cedric went downstairs
to The Angel's taproom.

He slapped a coin on the counter and took the foaming mug
the barkeep handed him to a quiet table at the front of the room.
He wanted to wash away the taste of the tea. And he wanted to
wipe out the vision of Jane's dismay when she caught him
thinking about Trentworthy and his despicable gang.

How could he explain to Jane? She had only the very
briefest of hints about how he was involved with the filly and
her racing defeat. He had not meant to offend her or upset her.
Yet he knew he had. In spite of his first reactions to her, he
wanted to get along. His doubts about her motives regarding
the paintings had now faded. Her integrity was of the highest
caliber imaginable, a thoroughly admirable young lady.

Devil take it, he felt only confusion about what to do. On
the one hand, he wanted to put Trentworthy and his ruffians
out of business. On the other hand, what could he do to stop
the swindler from cheating another young man? Then there
was that farmer, and probably more like him. If Trentworthy
and his cohorts were not stopped, how many more honest
yeomen would he trick out of perfectly good horses?

If only he could think of a scheme to defraud Trentworthy
right back. But how could he?

In the meantime, he needed to apologize to Miss Gabriel.
Or if not exactly apologize, try to explain. And yet what could
he say? "Oh, Miss Gabriel, I was trying to think of a way to
send a swindler to perdition?"

"Oh, Miss Gabriel, can you think of a way to help me

cheat that fellow right back and put him permanently out of business?"

Wait a moment. That is not such a bad idea.

She was an intelligent person. Might she have some ideas? But how would she take the question?

He had not confided any of his concerns to her, probably because he was coming to value her good opinion. He was still ashamed of himself, humiliated at falling into the ridiculous trap Trentworthy had set.

But he could apologize to her for his black mood. Usually he had no problem convincing a gel to forgive him.

CHAPTER NINE

"I wish most sincerely to apologize for my very rude behavior after the theater, Miss Gabriel."

Cedric stood alone in his bedchamber and spoke only to his mirror. He did not care for the sound of his words. Too formal. Too stuffy. Too artificial.

"Miss Gabriel, I hope you will forgive me for my hasty words after the play. I confess I was lost in thought, preoccupied by . . ." By what? By the obsession with the racing fiasco Jane had advised him to overcome? By the dilemma of a farmer who had a hard enough time making a go of it without being cheated by some wicked swindler who was not above poisoning horses?

Forget that last part about being lost in thought, he told himself. Make do with an apology for the hasty words. Hope she was not deeply offended anyway.

But Cedric waited in vain for Jane at the stable. Apparently, he concluded, she did not have time to ride this morning, for she had not appeared even after he had ridden both Atlas and Sybil for more than an hour.

His apologies would have to wait until later in the day, perhaps not until after dinner. They would not meet in the library, probably for the entire week.

Everyone had been assigned tasks. Uphaven bustled with preparations for the annual sheepshearing days and the festival on Friday night and Saturday, the culmination of a week of intense activity. The ladies, Aunt Amelia informed him, would be busy overseeing the various contests and preparing for the ball on Saturday.

Already the scissors grinder was in the neighborhood doing a brisk business from cottage to cottage before he set up his cart near the shearing shed to ensure sharp blades for the scissors. Outside the poultry pen, Cedric had seen no fewer than six ladies plucking the feathers from turkeys and chickens to prepare for the many meals they would serve to the dozens of herdsmen, shepherds, shearers, and all the neighborhood folk who came to help.

He followed Mr. Richards, the home farm manager, to watch the workers wash the sheep. The shepherds and their dogs had already begun to drive the sheep into the creek.

Richards stopped on the bank and surveyed the flock. "It's a little tricky. You start with the first dozen or so downstream and slowly work your way through the flock, moving upstream. That keeps the turbulence low. The mud kicked up from the bottom and the debris picked off the sheep wash away in the current. Then, we have to keep them penned in a dry pasture for the several days needed for drying."

Bathing the sheep, Cedric observed, was a matter of the dogs nipping at their hooves until they finally stepped into the water. The men, standing in the shallows, rubbed their fingers into the wool and saturated it with water, ridding it of leaves and grass, sticks and clots of dirt. The cleaner the fleece, the better the price, Mr. Richards had said.

The wily little dogs watched each animal with care, barking only rarely, though the sheep made quite a commotion, bleating continually.

"They seem particularly noisy." Cedric peered at the closely packed animals, their woolly brows covered with long strands of wool that hung over their eyes, effectively blindfolding them, or so it seemed.

Richards nodded and pushed his broad-brimmed hat to the back of his head. "They cry out like that because we separate out the lambs. It's a fast way to wean them, if they can't find their mamas."

Seems heartless, Cedric thought, but like so many other routines on the estate, practical and efficient, the result of many centuries of custom. Cedric stood and watched, feeling both amazement at the docility of the sheep and the poignancy of the lambs' cries. But he could not keep his thoughts from wandering back to the necessity of an apology to Jane Gabriel.

She had been so lovely in the shimmering light of the theater. The diamond earbobs she wore, though he knew them to be from his aunt's jewel case, danced with fire, in competition with the brightness in her eyes. Then he had spoken quite out of turn and immediately regretted it, without any chance to speak to her alone, to ask for forgiveness.

On the return to Uphaven from St. Edmundsbury yesterday afternoon, he sat with the driver, making room inside for Aunt Amelia to elevate her aching leg on the seat. Cedric had assumed he would have at least a half hour of the journey in which to speak to Jane while Mrs. Gabriel and his aunt dozed. But since he was up top, that opportunity had lapsed. Last evening after dinner, when he had thought to accompany her on a stroll on the terrace, Lady Stockdale had required her presence for a discussion of the week's preparations. Now what could have been a simple "I'm sorry" was taking on the proportions of a gigantic confession. He had to turn his mind to other things.

Like the sheepshearing, which was obviously very important to his aunt and to Uphaven. Aunt Amelia had a well-organized mind, he thought. She had, of course, been doing this for decades, but she was leaving no detail to chance.

He had not attended Uphaven's annual shearing since he was a boy of five or six. He had only the faintest memories of men wrestling on the ground with sheep who looked immensely fat, holding them down while they bleated piteously. When the men finally let them stand up, the sheep were skinny and naked. He remembered feeling sorry for them, and how Lord Stockdale had laughed at him.

He was embarrassed to admit to himself that he had no idea how or when the sheep on his father's estate were shorn. There had never been any kind of celebration associated with it, the wool being only a minor part of the operation of the property. Or perhaps it was not so minor, he thought. Since he had been reading the letters, the magazines, and talking to Mr. Richards and other workers, he had learned a great deal about the value of the wool. Not to mention all sorts of things about how the sheep were used for other purposes, for mutton and milk for cheese, for tallow and grease. The guts were used for sausage cases and several medical purposes. The hooves and horns served as containers and the basis for all sorts of carved materials, from simple buttons to magnificent drinking flagons.

After several hours, as the flocks and men, sopping wet, moved farther upstream, Cedric excused himself and went back to the house, remembering his promise to help Aunt Amelia.

The women, she had said, would supervise the placement of the tents and construction of canvas stalls for the market and for the contests and games. Later in the week they would construct a stage for the presentation of prizes and for the musicians who would play for the village dance. Families from miles around would come to the party. The gentry would be entertained in the great house, with a lavish meal and a few sedate country dances. The dancing outside would be of a more boisterous nature, he guessed.

As he rounded the bend near the village, he saw Jane hurrying in his direction.

"Miss Gabriel, just the person I have been looking for."

"I am sorry Mr. Williamson, I cannot stop to talk now. I am going to find Mrs. Cooper, on an errand from Lady Stockdale."

He fell into step with her. "Then let me accompany you. Does she not live just ahead?"

"I believe so."

In mere moments, they reached a small cottage with an abundance of hollyhocks at its gate. Jane let herself into the garden and rapped at the front door.

A plump woman of indeterminate age and a very red face opened the door, wiping her hands on her scarlet-stained apron. He could not hear their words, but the woman curtsied and nodded.

When Jane returned, she wore a smile of satisfaction. "She says she will go to the great house as soon as she takes her jam off the flame and banks the fire."

"Now will you walk with me a little?"

Jane brushed her hands over her skirt. "But I am hardly dressed for a stroll, Mr. Williamson. I ran off without a shawl or a bonnet."

"It is a warm day, and I am not exactly dressed for St. James Street, either."

"Well, for just a few moments, then, on our way back to the house. I promised to help Lady Stockdale with all sorts of tasks."

He tucked her hand under his elbow and began to think of how he could begin his speech. In a few yards, they turned off the lane into a path that led to the bottom of the gardens. It was quiet and peaceful in contrast to the scene at the stream just across two low hills. Only the song of the birds broke the silence until they opened the squeaky gate and entered the formal garden. Halfway to the terrace, he took her hand and drew her into a side allée lined with tall yews.

He stopped and turned to her, his heart pounding quite unaccountably. "I want to speak to you about the night before last, after the theater. I fear I rather snapped at you. You see, I had a rather upsetting encounter that afternoon—"

Jane's eyes widened and she shook her head. "There is no need for your concern, none at all. I was merely surprised. You seemed deep in thought."

"No, Miss Gabriel, I saw your face when you looked at me. You looked quite upset, startled, might be a better way of expressing it. I sincerely did not mean to—"

She held up one hand as if to stop him. "I—"

Before he realized what he was doing, Cedric pulled her close and pressed his lips to hers. Where the impetus came from he did not understand, nor did he care. He only knew that something beyond his consciousness drove him to take her in his arms.

And even more astonishingly, she kissed him back. Her mouth softened under his and she did not even attempt to pull away.

Her hair, many strands loosened from her bun, fluttered around her face.

Slowly they parted. Her face was flushed, her eyes lowered.

"My dear Jane, I do not know what came over me."

When she raised her eyes to his they were wide and bright, glowing in fact. "I do not understand either."

They stood in the grove for a moment, their gazes meeting, then casting away, then meeting again.

He held her hands.

When she stepped back at last he almost tugged her close again, but dared not.

She tucked her loose hair behind her ears. "I really must. Go. Now."

"Yes. I will see you at dinner."

Suddenly she gathered her skirt, whirled and hastened away toward the house.

What the deuce? Now he had to devise another apology. Or, why not another kiss, instead?

Jane walked faster and faster until she almost ran. Her face felt hot, her heart raced, and every muscle in her body trembled, as though she had run a mile, not just the length of the formal garden. At the terrace door she paused and tried to catch her breath.

How had it happened? Certainly there was a moment when she perceived Cedric Williamson's intention to kiss her. Why had she not shoved him away or ducked under his arm like she had done with that pesky Mr. McVeigh last autumn in Bath?

She leaned her shoulder against the wall and looked back down the slope of the garden. No sign of Mr. Williamson. Why pretend? There was no comparison between Mr. McVeigh and Mr. Williamson. She had not wanted McVeigh's attention. Whether she wanted to admit it to herself or not, when Cedric moved closer, she had longed to feel his arms around her, the touch of his lips on hers.

She put her fingertips to her mouth. His lips, soft and gentle at first, were more delicious than the sweetest honey. And when he drew her close, her veins had filled with bubbly champagne and her nerves tickled as though teased by airy ostrich feathers.

Why had she not pulled out of his arms?

What a silly question! She wished he were holding her still, running a thumb again down the curve of her cheek. She longed to feel her breasts flatten against his chest again, feel every breath he took.

But it must have been a mistake. She glanced down at her gown of wrinkled muslin, its once-jaunty sprigged pattern now faded. She only wore it for the most mundane of chores, like the little jobs with which she and her mother helped Lady Stockdale today.

Jane pressed a palm to her chest and the back of her other hand to her forehead. Certainly a man like Cedric Williamson, a pink of the *ton* . . . how could he care for a dowd like her?

Yet he had often surprised her of late. Almost as often as he had disappointed her.

What did she know of London rakehells anyway? Only the gossip of silly old ladies and mindless chits barely out of the schoolroom.

After a few moments, her breathing almost normal and her cheeks no longer burning, Jane went back to find Lady Stockdale and her mother in the stillroom. Mrs. Cooper, the

woman she had found earlier, was pouring a bottle of
rosewater into a bowl.

They were all well occupied, and Jane backed away without
being seen. A large box stood in the morning room and Lady
Stockdale had earlier asked her to sort the contents, before
their attention had been diverted by the need to mix up more
of the Uphaven elixir Lady Stockdale said she always gave to
her houseguests.

Jane sat down in a straight chair and opened the box. It
was filled with brightly colored ribbons, all snarled together
in a tangle, just as they had probably been thrown in, willy-
nilly, at the conclusion of last year's festivities. She found a
paper of pins in her sewing basket behind the sofa, then settled down to hunt for the end of a blue ribbon, carefully
extracting it from the others and rolling it into a tight coil.
When the last of it pulled loose, she pinned it securely and
placed it on the table. It was slow work, but in a half hour
she had all of the ribbons in neat coils, ready to be used
again for whatever decoration Lady Stockdale had in mind.

As she untangled and wound and pinned, her mind kept
bee-lining back to those moments in the garden. To his embrace. To his caresses. To his kisses. Oh, what a fool she was,
first, to be alone with him—though they had sat many hours
in the library without incident. Second, to be so very close—
though with her hand linked through his arm she could hardly
stay far away. Third, to let him halt her and bring her near—
though that was exactly what she had wanted at the moment.

*Oh, stop, Jane! How can you admit your dreadful com-
plicity in those kisses? More the fool, you! How can you deny
it? And after you were so very willing, even eager, he will no
doubt look for more kisses from you!*

What a very heart-stopping thought that was.

A team of traveling sheepshearers supplemented the men
of Uphaven, several of whom were eager to match their skills

again with the experts who went from estate to estate to ply their craft. Dozens had worked at building pens and preparing the sheds, for the wool had to be dry before shearing. Since it took several days to dry completely, the sheep had to be protected from the rain.

Cedric watched as the shearers turned each sheep on its back and began to cut off the fleece over the stomach. They cut quickly, counting on another to help hold the animal as they moved the shears efficiently with the goal of taking off all the wool in one large piece. Some animals struggled more than others, some bleated pitifully, others were stoic. Once shorn, they looked pathetically thin as they eagerly ran off to be herded away into fresh pastures.

"Some of them look quite relieved to be done with all that weight." Cedric and Mr. Richards watched the operations.

"Yes, when the heat comes, particularly, they will be more comfortable. But for the next fortnight we must protect them if the winds come up or the rainfall is hard."

Most of them had black faces and legs, but some were light-colored all over.

"The native Suffolks have the dark faces, but we've brought in some Merinos and a few other types to mix in. The Suffolks are the strongest, I'd say." Richards scratched his head.

"We are soon to be short on rams, I fear. For the last two years, we've not had as many that look good for breeding. Have taken more wethers than usual."

Wethers, Cedric recalled from his reading, were the castrated males. "And how do you decide which to cut and which to, er, preserve?"

"We look for the best of the young males, the largest and strongest, Usually keep half a dozen a year, but we had only four last year and three the year before."

Cedric followed the progress, watching in particular one of the shearers who seemed to work exceptionally fast and yet whose fleeces were among the most carefully cut.

The shearers worked on each sheep for twenty to thirty

minutes. With more than a dozen men cutting, the shearing would obviously run for at least three days. It took a crew of herders with their dogs, assistants to help hold the animals, sweepers to keep the floor as clean as possible, and women to lay out each fleece, pick out the bristly strands and other straw or dirt, cut off any discolored portions, then fold the fleece and put it in a cloth-lined bin.

They all worked together; some talked, others laughed. There was an air of camaraderie and fellowship, as this was, in many ways, the high point of the year. Now he understood why Aunt Amelia and her predecessors at Uphaven celebrated the shearing with a festival for the workers. There was even a bit of flirting going on, or he missed his guess. One of the traveling shearers, a fellow whose arm muscles rippled in his sleeveless jerkin, grabbed another ewe and flipped her gently into position. Several of the girls who trimmed and folded the fleece wore admiring smiles. And they were all well aware of each other.

Cedric grinned to himself. No matter what the activity, the mating game was being played.

By the last day, there were still plenty of sheep left to be shorn, but clearly they would finish. There was a growing undercurrent of fun, more laughter, everyone anticipating the evening's entertainment.

Cedric took up one of his favorite spots for viewing, near Binsley, the expert shearer, the one who could take off a ewe's fleece as smoothly as peeling an orange, all the time flirting with every woman within fifty feet.

Binsley shouted with glee as he righted a ewe and slapped her rump to get her moving. Cedric laughed aloud at the bewildered expression on the sheep's black face before Binsley shouted again, his mouth almost at her ear, and she leaped forward as fast as her spindly legs could take her.

"She doesn't know what to make of herself," Cedric said with a grin.

"Sir, Oi'd say so too. Have a hand at it, sir? You bin watchin'—like to give it a try?"

Cedric shrugged. "Yes, if you don't move far from me, my friend. This will be a first."

Binsley grabbed a leather apron and hung it around Cedric's neck. "Here, sir, keep yer britches clean."

Cedric tied the strings behind his back, thinking he'd never before worn such a garment. Binsley waved for another sheep and helped Cedric turn the creature on its back and move it into position.

"Here now, missy," Binsley growled at the sheep. "Be still for the master."

Cedric gripped the ewe between his knees and took a firm grasp of the shears. The sheep twisted but he held it firmly, then with Binsley's hand on his, reached down and separated the strands of wool and began to cut.

He knew he was slow, pushing the points through the wool, as close to the skin as possible. "It's a devilish hard job, Binsley. You should have warned me. You make it look simple."

Binsley had a hearty laugh. "Oi got twenty years on ya, sir. If I can't make it look easy now, what have Oi bin doing with me life?"

Binsley guided him and Cedric forced the points through the thick growth of the sides and back, showing him how to wiggle the shears just a tiny bit and to keep them from nicking the sheep's skin. Cedric's hand tingled at first, then ached and even throbbed with the effort and the strain. No wonder Binsley's paws were as broad and strong as a bear's.

As they rolled the sheep to its other side, Cedric glanced up to see quite a gathering of spectators, probably come to see the London dandy make an ass of himself.

But he realized he did not care a fig. Neither did he mind that his arms and legs hurt almost as badly as his cutting hand. This was a new experience, one he quite enjoyed, getting as close to the sheep as he could. He laughed out loud as little by little he cut away the fleece, stripping it off until it fell in one entire piece, perhaps a little ragged, but whole.

Binsley clapped him on the back so hard Cedric staggered

to keep his balance. A chorus of voices joined the shearer's to congratulate him.

"Good show, sir."

"Aye, for Mr. Wilumson."

The sheep bounded away, two women picked up the fleece, and Cedric stared at his sweaty hand. A coating of tufts and tendrils of wool could not hide the angry red welts made by his tight grip on the shears. He rubbed it hard, brushed off the wool, and extended it to Binsley.

"I thank you, my man. I enjoyed that, though I don't see how you do it all day, and so fast."

"Aw, it ain't so hard, oncet ye know how."

"My admiration for you and the other shearers has grown by leaps and bounds this afternoon."

Binsley dropped his head, embarrassed, then waved for another sheep.

Cedric patted the man's shoulder. "My sincere thanks, for showing me the ropes. And for not laughing at me."

Binsley touched his forehead. "My pleasure, sir."

Cedric stepped back and watched Binsley move quickly and efficiently, quite unlike the tentative thrusts and meager cuts Cedric had made. But now he knew what it felt like to hold a squirming ewe, to cut through the surprisingly strong fibers of the wool.

To his own immense surprise, he liked the estate. He liked the men who worked here and he had a newfound respect for the jobs they did. And most surprisingly, he found he quite liked the sheep. Brainless though they were, they applied themselves to their occupations, growing wool and making lambs, with a minimum of fuss.

He planted his hands on his hips and watched Binsley's smooth cuts striping the wool from the sheep.

You had better watch out, Williamson. Before you know it, you will be a man of substance, no longer ready and willing to kick up a lark at every opportunity.

CHAPTER TEN

Cedric heard the clamor before he saw its source. When he passed by a tent and faced the roped-off circle of the children's pet show, his anticipation turned to astonishment. Jane stood amidst the most amazing assortment of animals and children he had ever seen. It looked like a Noah's Ark tableau gone mad. Or half of it anyway, since there was only one of most varieties of animal.

At least two dozen boys and girls clustered around her with animals in their arms, on leashes, in cages, or in containers clutched to their chests. Most of the pets were yowling or yapping, cackling or croaking; the children merely talked and laughed, though a few cried, adding to the din. The dogs barked, and the cats hissed back. The donkey brayed, the parrot squawked, the duck quacked, and the cacophony had set Lady Stockdale's peacocks to screeching in the adjacent garden. Beyond the pet show area, many mothers and grandparents, not to mention older brothers and sisters, called out their encouragement to the contestants.

Cedric met his aunt coming from the house.

"Merciful heavens," Lady Stockdale murmured.

"My, my, my," Mrs. Gabriel echoed.

Jane hesitated for only a moment. The fear she had expressed at breakfast that there would be only a handful of children, all with fuzzy puppies, had been turned upside down and inside out. It was a menagerie, thankfully without a giraffe, but a zoological miscellany nonetheless.

How would she think of prizes for all of them? She had declared that every pet would win something. Would she regret suggesting a children's pet show, especially one in which there was to be a reward for the most unusual pet? Obviously, the children and their families had responded to the category with great creativity.

He watched as she leaned down to tickle the ears of one of the several dogs. Over the commotion, he heard her thank the child holding a hen for the fresh egg. She petted the young donkey, a ferret, several rabbits, and smiled at a box of crickets proudly displayed by a little girl with a halo of white-gold curls.

She crouched down to look into a basket holding a frog, but kept her distance from the grass snake coiled up in a jar. When she stood again, Cedric caught her eye, smiled and bowed. She was handling the chaos with amazing aplomb.

The whole point of the pet show, she had declared, was to give the youngest children something to do in addition to the hunt for the colored stones and the three-legged race. She had declared, when she suggested it to Lady Stockdale, that each animal should receive a prize ribbon.

The noise diminished a little when she opened her box of prizes and began to call out the winners. How, he wondered, would she handle a baby hedgehog? Or mice?

"The prize for the most legs goes to the crickets." The little girl holding the box opened her mouth wide enough to swallow the whole kit. With a shout of glee, she came up to take her ribbon.

"For having the fewest legs, to the snake, who has none at all."

Cedric joined in as everyone cheered. Her idea was a big success, at least with the children and their mothers.

The largest pet was the donkey. The smallest, a snail. The prickliest, the hedgehog. The softest, a tie between the two rabbits. The most cuddly, a gray kitten. The bluest eyes, a white one. The biggest ears, to a hound. The whitest feathers, to the hen.

At last she came to the parrot. As a little boy brought it to the prize table, it ceased its loud squawks and tilted its head to one side. Cedric found himself holding his breath. This parrot looked very much like it could speak and who knew what kind of cursing might pour from its beak.

The entire gathering seemed to be waiting for just such a moment.

The parrot looked away, then back at Miss Gabriel. "Madcap. Madcap. Madcap maid." Its voice was loud, drowning out the dogs and the peacocks. "Madcap."

Jane laughed and the crowd laughed too. A man stepped over the rope and headed for the parrot, which turned and set its eye upon him. "Muttonhead. Muttonhead."

The laughter grew as the man took the cage from the boy, tossed a cloth over it, and stomped away.

Jane held out a ribbon rosette to the boy. "For the most outspoken pet."

His response was lost in a round of applause.

Stifling her laughter, Aunt Amelia patted her lips with a handkerchief. "I am certain we can assume that if Mr. Stall had not grabbed that cage, that parrot would have gone further into its vocabulary. I have heard tales of its nautical expressions, and they are certainly not fit for the children. Though I would love to hear them myself."

"Amelia!" Mrs. Gabriel fanned herself vigorously.

Only with great effort did Cedric suppress his sputter of laughter.

Jane was still surrounded by the children and the twittering, snarling and yowling was increasing every second. Madcap maid, indeed, Cedric thought.

He offered an arm to Aunt Amelia and extended his other to Mrs. Gabriel. "May I escort you ladies back to the house? I will come back for Miss Gabriel. For now, she seems to be surrounded."

When he returned, she was waving good-bye to a little girl whose puppy sported a blue rosette on its collar.

He took the box of remaining ribbons from her. "You have done a wonderful thing for those children. I never would have thought to give each one a prize."

"What else could I do? How can one compare a spaniel to a lizard, or a gosling to an insect?"

"Exactly. Was the pet show not your idea? I thought Aunt Amelia said that was so."

"Yes, but when I said there would be a prize for the most unusual pet, I had no idea what lengths the children would go to in order to find a unique animal."

"I must say, Miss Gabriel, I admire your efforts very much. You have made many children very happy."

She blushed and shrugged her shoulders. "I thought they might enjoy having a contest of their own."

"I hope you will reserve a dance for me tonight."

She gave a little laugh. "I think you will be busy with Lady Stockdale and with Mama, for both of them will be counting on you to accompany them in a minuet, I believe."

"Minuet? I have not tried a minuet since my grandmother made me dance with her."

"You'd better prime your dancing shoes, Mr. Williamson. I have it on very good authority that the Walker ladies will also be counting on your attentions."

He groaned, exaggerating only a tiny bit. "My fate is sealed. I may expire from over-exertion. Miss Jane Gabriel, Madcap Maid, I count on you to rescue me before I am swallowed up."

Her eyes sparkled with laughter. "I make no guarantees, sir. I am quite convinced you know how to watch out for yourself."

Before the dancing began, Cedric asked Mr. Paulson, the apothecary, to join him on the terrace.

When they were settled in chairs quite distant from the others, Cedric got directly to the point. "I have a few questions for you, Mr. Paulson. I know you are familiar with many kinds of drugs and potions."

He nodded. "Yes, quite a few."

"If a person wanted to drug a horse, make it slow and stumbly and in a daze, what could one give it?"

"A horse? Why would a person want to give such a potion to a horse?"

"Perhaps a racehorse. To make it lose a race."

His face showed surprise, then a rueful smile. "Ah, yes, I see."

"I think this might have been done to a horse I own. Someone wanted me to bet a great deal of money on that horse and then wanted to be certain it could not win."

"I see. Well, ordinary dosages made up for a man would hardly affect a horse."

"But a larger dose, say five or six times the size of a human dose?"

"Laudanum or a sleeping potion in that great an amount would affect a horse. But how would you make the horse take the drug?"

Cedric shook his head. "I do not know. But perhaps dissolved in a bit of water?"

"I am not sure a horse would drink it. Horses do not like anything bitter. Even the smell might turn a horse away."

"Yes, I see. And forcing anything down a horse's throat would be an arduous undertaking."

"Yes, most difficult. But if you had thought ahead and planned for it, giving a more concentrated dose would be possible."

"What do you mean?" Cedric asked.

"Take laudanum, for example. It is mainly made of greatly diluted opium, diluted with other substances that really have no effect, just a bit of sugar and other tasteless powders. If a person used opium almost undiluted, just a very small amount, a thimbleful or two, would have the same effect as a half dozen doses of laudanum or more."

"Ah! Then it would be much easier to give it to a horse."

"Well, it would still be quite bitter, so a horse would do no more than take a sip. Of course since a horse does not regurgitate—vomit, that is—perhaps a sip would be all that was needed."

"Or a man could disguise it in some way. Split open an apple, or even a large carrot, scrape out the center and sprinkle in the opium."

"Seems possible to me."

"And is opium easily available?"

"Oh, yes, quite, in almost every apothecary shop. But most of us will not sell it in any quantity. People abuse it terribly, you know. Oh, yes, the stories I have heard . . . and the terrible things men will do if they become addicted . . ." He stared into space and shook his head sadly.

Cedric paused and thought a moment. A man like Trentworthy, with the right contacts and tips for the races, and with a big payoff for success, would have no trouble finding a shop to provide him with sufficient quantities of opium. "How reliable would it be, that is, how could you predict what the horse would do?"

The apothecary straightened up and drew himself out of his musings. "Very difficult to predict. It would depend on the potency of the opium, as you can imagine. As for the amount one would give a horse, it could only be a guess, as far as I know. Too little would have almost no effect. Too much could kill a horse, just stop its heart."

"But a ruthless man, one who did not care what happened to the horse, could give a dose and deal with whatever the consequences were. It is not unheard of for a horse to fall down and die on the racecourse. If one did, there would be no way to tell if it had been drugged, I suppose."

"Probably not."

"And if the horse just lollygagged along, lost interest in running, was listless and stumbly for a few days, eventually the drug would wear off, correct?"

"Assuming that the dosage was not great enough to kill it, I suppose so. In a day or two, perhaps three or four, the horse would probably be right as rain again."

"Ah, yes. Thank you, Mr. Paulson."

"Please do not accept what I say as the only answer, Mr. Williamson. I am the first to admit I have never given any drug at all to a horse. I am only speculating as to the effects of opium on a horse. A large dose might kill it. I would not recommend experimenting."

"But you have been very helpful. I think the men who did this are ruthless enough to kill a horse, if they needed to. But do you think this could be done more than once with the same horse?"

"Mr. Williamson, you are asking me to make the wildest speculations. I have no idea. A man might become addicted to a drug, but I do not see how a horse could, unless a person gave it some drugs regularly. Or it decided to eat its way through a field of poppies every day."

"I will take just a few more moments of your time, Mr. Paulson. Take this supposition, this theory. Shortly before a race, one gives a horse a heavy dose of opium or a sleeping potion. It does not start working immediately, but when the horse starts to run, it spreads around and starts to affect the nerves or the brain or whatever opium does. The horse, feeling groggy or sick, slows down and soon can hardly walk, as though it was bosky from drinking a pail of gin. Could that happen?"

"Stands to reason. But I have never heard of giving opium or gin to a horse."

From the ballroom, the sound of the orchestra tuning their instruments pierced the air. Cedric shook Paulson's hand. "I thank you for your patience and your willingness to answer some very speculative questions."

"I am only sorry I have no scientific answers. Now I'd best get back to my wife. She had a mind for joining in the dancing."

Cedric wished him good-bye and good dancing, then sat

again and stared into the sky. Trentworthy must have a whole network of people who worked in various capacities. Some got paid for their work, others got tips on horses. Trentworthy needed men to find farmers who had good young prospects, someone to slip the horses the drug, then go back and negotiate a low price. Next, there had to be a place to stable the horses until they recovered, to train them and even race from time to time. Ben's horse already had one win, or so they said.

Cedric wanted to pound his fists on the table, but skipped his hands in his pockets instead. Right under the noses of the Jockey Club members, that gang must earn thousands, enough to pay all those helpers, whether inadvertent participants or part of the plot. Yet, was there enough money in buying and selling horses? Not at that level, he thought. Perhaps if they were dealing with champions, but not just in the minor races.

He had lost a bundle on Sybil, but he'd made a lot of personal bets, with all his friends, their acquaintances. Yet that was just a fraction of the people at the meet. Many of the others would have wagered with the bookmakers, men who made a living offering odds and taking bets from all comers.

Trentworthy must be in cahoots with a bookmaker. If he could nobble the favorite in a race, a bookmaker could net a large profit.

Yes, that must be it. Again his anger threatened to boil over and he saw a drop of sweat fall from his brow. Somehow he had to stop Trentworthy. But how?

Jane took a seat beside her mother. "Mama, are you enjoying yourself?"

"Indeed, my dear. I've had more dances tonight than in the last two years in Bath. And are you finding the evening agreeable?"

"Yes. The whole week has been remarkable." More extraordinary than her mother would ever know, for Jane had no intention of mentioning the slightest tidbit about her encounter with Mr. Williamson. "I can see why Lady Stockdale makes such careful preparations."

She smiled to see her mother's toe tapping to the music.

Cedric Williamson was dancing, out of her present view, probably masked by the stout body of Mrs. Walker. He'd been stalwart ever since the dancing began, leading out first his aunt, then Mrs. Gabriel, other ladies of the neighborhood, and, of course, all three Walkers.

Oswald Walker found the evening amusing, he had told Jane as they danced. Watching Cedric Williamson operate in this crowd, he said, was like seeing an elegant gateau served amidst hunks of gingerbread. Williamson's style would be long imitated among Oswald's friends.

The figures of the dance brought Mr. Williamson into view, an amiable smile upon his lips. Jane wished she did not find him so attractive, that her heart did not do its own little dance when he looked her way.

When the music ended, he bowed with an élan unmatched by any gentleman on the floor. He escorted Mrs. Walker to her husband, then strolled across the room to Lady Stockdale.

"Would you care to accompany me out for a breath of fresh air, Aunt Amelia?"

"No thank you, Cedric. I am quite comfortable at the moment."

He smiled at Jane's mother. "Mrs. Gabriel?"

"Oh, dear, no. Thank you anyway, but I think I will remain here with Amelia."

"Miss Gabriel, will you deny me the pleasure of feminine company, as these heartless ladies have done?"

She rolled her eyes and rose to her feet. "It would be impossible for me to be so cruel, Mr. Williamson. You may be assured that I will not force you into a lonely ramble in the shrubbery."

He again bowed to his aunt and Mrs. Gabriel and offered his arm to Jane.

When they had moved away from the others, she gave a little sigh. "I could have sent you to the Walker sisters. I am certain they would have been more than pleased to keep you company."

"Never let it be said that I have not been solicitous of those young ladies."

"Yes, you have been all that is kind. I noticed they danced almost every set once you led them out. Do not be surprised if Mrs. Walker soon plans a ball."

"'Oh, what wretched fate I face.' Isn't that Shakespeare?"

"Not that I recall. But never mind. It sounds quite bard-like. Feel free to use that line with Oswald Walker's friends and they will surely think you exceptionally erudite."

"And the advantage of that would be?"

"Merely to polish your already brilliant reputation among the young swains of Suffolk."

"Ah. Devoutly to be desired, I suppose. But rather than that, let us walk over to watch the village celebration. Unless they have all imbibed too much brew, it is bound to be less dull."

They had barely started on the path when they heard the music and laughter, a far more boisterous translation of the sedate celebration they left behind.

The village green was lit by torches, the wooden dancing platform ringed by benches. The music, provided by a pair of fiddlers and some pipers, had most of the non-dancers clapping their hands and swaying, and those on the platform flying in all directions.

They stood in the shadows for a few moments, then moved onto the benches.

"Here now, sir!" Binsley thrust a tankard of ale into Cedric's hand and a smaller mug into Jane's.

Cedric raised his drink to the man. "Thank you, my friend. Miss Gabriel, may I present Mr. Binsley, who taught me a little about shearing a sheep. Mr. Binsley, this is Miss Gabriel, a very close friend of Lady Stockdale."

"Oi'm honored, miss. You're a mighty purty decoration there on Mr. Wilumson's arm."

Jane grinned as Cedric squeezed her hand. "Careful there, Binsley. You and I might see her as a lovely decoration, but I suspect she won't take kindly to the appellation. She's quite the defender of women's rights."

"Well, then, Oi be very sorry, Miss. Oi don't know much 'bout women's rights."

As he spoke a buxom maid grabbed his hand and pulled him up on the dance platform.

"I daresay you don't," Cedric said softly.

Jane giggled. "I heard that. No doubt you're quite correct. I can see why he would easily have his way with any number of girls."

Cedric's head snapped toward her. "What was that? Sounded like the Madcap Maid and not the proper Miss Jane Gabriel I know."

She took another sip of her ale. "With enough of this, I might say anything."

"While I, my dear, have been struck speechless."

She gazed into his eyes where the bright glow of the torches caused glittering points of light to dance. His lips were parted in a slight smile and the usual lock of hair fell forward. Her hand ached to push it back. But she did not move, could not move.

Perhaps it was only a few seconds, perhaps minutes, but eventually they heard the applause and laughter of the dance ending. As one, they turned back toward the stage and watched new figures form.

Suddenly Jane felt herself lifted to her feet. 'Oi'd be much obliged, Miss . . ."

Binsley set her on the platform without formalities, and she noticed his buxom friend had Cedric there, too.

Still under the spell of that long, smoldering look, Jane could hardly catch her breath, but somehow she managed to fling herself into the dance. At one point she caught Cedric's hand and had a fleeting glance of his wide grin. No standing on ceremony with these dancers, she flung herself into the rhythm.

Round and round they went, ever faster, until she felt herself consumed by the music, dizzy with excitement, caught in a merry tangle of whirling bodies. When she was sure she had not an ounce of energy left, she practically fell into Binsley's arms as the music ended.

When she stepped off the platform, Jane wondered that she had the strength left to stand. She was grateful when Cedric put his arm about her waist, and she leaned against him for support.

They talked and laughed with Binsley and the others for a while, then drifted back into the darkness and headed for the house.

"That dancing was vigorous. They work hard, they dance hard, I suppose."

"Lady Stockdale will wonder where we have gone for so long," Jane said.

Cedric took her hand. "Do you fear for your reputation?"

"Should I?"

"Hmmm."

It was very dark under the trees and she shivered, not entirely with the chill in the air. He stopped and took off his jacket, placing it about her shoulders. It was warm with the heat of his body.

"Do you not need this jacket?"

"Jane, just the thought of you keeps me warm."

"An insufferably bad line, Cedric. Certainly no one could believe—"

Her words were smothered in his kiss. Her knees threatened to buckle beneath her, and his arms slid around her waist to hold her close. The jacket dropped from her shoulders.

He pulled away, only to cover her neck and shoulder with little kisses, murmuring in between about how lovely she looked with her face aglow and her hair bouncing around her face, how her eyes burned into his, how he could not help himself. She ran her fingers into his hair and pulled his face to hers.

"Do not talk so much, Cedric."

His deep moan said more than all his words as his lips found hers and tasted her, teased her.

She heard herself panting as if she had run up a hill. But she could not push him away.

Only when they heard voices approaching did they pull apart.

"More couples looking for privacy." Cedric grabbed up his coat, placed it around her again, took her hand and led her toward the house.

Jane felt as if she were floating up the path. Every fiber of her being tingled and her mind seemed locked in a misty cloud, unable to form a coherent thought.

The party at the house was ending; a line of carriages waited to return the guests to their abodes.

Jane felt reality return like a slap to her cheek. "Mr. Williamson, you must go and bid Lady Stockdale's guests good-bye."

"Yes, I should. But Jane—"

She pushed him away. "We have been very reckless. Please go now and do your duty. We must forget our imprudence."

He straightened and gave her a little bow. "Miss Gabriel, I find I must beg your pardon again. I am leaving for a week or two in the morning. I hope that by the time I return, you have been able to put my improper behavior entirely from your mind."

Jane could barely whisper. "If there is blame tonight, I certainly share it, Mr. Williamson. As for erasing our poor conduct from my memory, I shall try."

But as they parted, he to say farewell to the guests, she to go to her room, Jane knew she would never forget his embrace.

Never.

***

After her morning ride on Sandy, Jane lingered in the stable, talking to Sam and petting Sybil through the bars of her stall.

"She is a beautiful horse, isn't she, Sam?"

"She is, Miss. And very fast."

"It is too bad Mr. Williamson could not ride her on his journey to Holkham instead of that bad-tempered stallion."

"Oh, Miss, that Atlas, black devil that he can be, is a horse for traveling. He can go a long distance, that he can. Anyway, this filly needs to build up her energy for racing."

"Mr. Williamson plans to put her in a race again? I thought she came in last." Of course, she thought, there were the drugs he had talked of to Sam. She had almost forgotten about them.

"I s'pose he thinks she should have another chance."

"Yes, I see." Jane reached for Sybil's head and scratched her ears. Cedric had never mentioned the drugs to her at all.

She turned back to Sam. "She is a lovely horse, and she deserves to win this time. When are the races held?"

"Next month. And, Miss, I have to tell you I won't be here for a week or two. Jest before he left for Coke's Clippings, Mr. Williamson asked me to go to Newmarket. Sorta' get the lay of the land."

Jane took a chance. "You mean, find out about the drugs?"

Sam nodded. "That, 'n see what kinda' folks are about. Sniff out what I can."

"I wish you luck, Sam. I am sure you will find out everything there is to know."

"Young Johnny'll take care of you, miss. He ain't the fastest saddler, but if he don't keep Sandy up to snuff, you let me know later and I'll see he gets 'is 'ide tanned."

Jane broke into laughter. "That I shall, Sam. Godspeed!"

As she walked back to the house and changed into her gray gown, Jane's mind spun. Very clever of Cedric to send Sam to

Newmarket. If, as she surmised, Cedric suspected someone of drugging Sybil, Sam could learn a great deal by associating with other grooms and stable lads. The ordinary talk in an ale-house alone, would be more accessible to Sam than to a nob like Cedric. Even if Cedric dressed in a groom's clothing, his hands would give him away. Or if he hid those somehow, all he had to do was open his mouth and the men would know he was out of his element.

Yes, very clever of Cedric. He wanted to take no chances his horse could be drugged again.

She took a last glance in the mirror. She leaned closer. Not a thing was visible on her face, not a sign of those kisses. Not even her mother had noticed a change. But to Jane, it seemed a massive alteration that must show somewhere besides deep in her heart. Not that they had been her very first kisses. There had been a few, but so tentative, so cautious, so un-memorable she could hardly remember who had taken the liberty of trying.

Cedric's kisses had been different. Very different. Warm and soft. Then hot and hard. Heart stopping. Head emptying.

She watched the pink flush rise in her cheeks. What a lucky thing he was gone for the next week or two. She needed that time to control her foolish emotions. To remind herself he was a London Corinthian, dedicated to sport. And about to race his horse, no doubt to wager large sums as well. Not at all the man for her.

She whirled and ran down the stairs and into the library, closing the door firmly. This was where she belonged, here with the books and letters. With paintings to study and pages to compose. In the last few days, with the festival and all the activity on the estate, she had not accomplished anything. Now that she was free of Cedric for a while, she had to get her momentum back. Try to finish the letters before he returned.

How fortunate she was to have many days to herself in the library. No distractions from Cedric Williamson. No divert-ing scent of roses. Yes, she would go back to the letters. If she worked hard, she could complete them; return to the paintings when he returned.

She wondered what he was doing, perhaps still having breakfast at an inn someplace. Or astride Atlas, covering the miles to Holkham. Lady Stockdale was delighted he wanted to go, to associate with the leading agriculturalists in England.

She glanced over at his chair. Well, the chair he usually sat in. It seemed peculiar, facing her, empty. She got up and walked around the table, looking at her own chair from Mr. Williamson's perspective. Then, feeling insanely foolish, she shoved his chair across the carpet to stand against the wall, its original position before he had come onto the scene.

It had been a sennight since they first sat here together. How she had despised him. Now, when she decided he was doing admirable work, had grown to respect him more, their routine had ended. What a week it had been. From an angry outburst to gentle kisses. From shared moments of laughter to a burst of passion. Did she feel different about him now? Or just different about herself?

She gazed at the painting now on the easel, a portrait, thought to be a self-portrait of the oft-dismissed Judith Leyster. Was it not typical that this smiling image had been attributed to her instructor and mentor? But Jane was certain it was truly painted by Judith herself. She could feel the truth emanating from the canvas like an aura of light.

We ladies must stick together, she said in silence to the painting. She would go to the stillroom and mix a mash of molasses and flaxseed and rosemary to give Sybil strength. And then she would come back here and write a chapter on all that was known about Judith Leyster. Even if Lord Stockdale had made the purchase thinking that painting was by Franz Hals, it was an excellent choice. One little by-product of this Stockdale compendium might be renewed interest in the life and work of Judith Leyster.

Further, if she could do anything to see that Sybil won her race, Jane was determined to do it.

CHAPTER ELEVEN

After spending four days and nights at Holkham Hall participating in Mr. Coke's famed clippings, Cedric mounted Atlas for the journey back to Uphaven. Coke's assembly of agricultural experts made the Uphaven festival look like a picnic for two as compared with one of Prinny's Carlton House feasts for hundreds. In fact, the Holkham sheepshearing had almost become a national institution.

Cedric thought his father attended years ago, but since he had never had any interest in agriculture before, Cedric had never considered angling for an invitation. This year was different. Now he knew a little bit about the wool business and a little about farming and raising sheep. Had even tried his hand at shearing, though his efforts were quite sloppy and poor. But his sheep had been almost as bare as the others that struggled to their feet and trotted off shorn of their heavy fleeces.

The morning sparkled, a cool breeze moderating the heat of the sun. Only a few wispy clouds drifted across the sky. Atlas covered the miles swiftly, sometimes in an easy lope, other times at a trot, and only when Cedric was certain the horse must need rest did he slow the big black to a walk, letting Atlas pick up the pace again when the stallion chose to.

Cedric sought the farm of a Mr. Easton, a man who might have had a run-in with Josiah Trentworthy or his minions. Cedric stopped twice to ask directions, once from the driver of a donkey cart coming in the opposite direction, the other from a goatherd, letting his flock of five animals chomp away at the brush along the roadside. When he arrived at Easton Farm, he knew it was the establishment of a racehorse lover by the superb condition of six sleek mares with foals beside them in the pasture. The farmyard was neat enough even for Aunt Amelia's tastes. A child told him his father was in the barn, so Cedric watered Atlas, then tied him securely to a fence, warning the boy not to go near him.

"Mr. Easton?" he called as he entered the barn.

"Over here."

Cedric walked over to a stall where he leaned over a partition and looked at a new foal struggling to its feet.

"Nice looking fellow," he said.

"Yes, I have high hopes for him."

Cedric introduced himself and explained why he had come, giving a quick version of his humiliation at the hands of Trentworthy's gang and his hope to stop them. "How did you get mixed up with them, assuming they are all in it together?"

Mr. Easton shook his head dolefully. "I have a few mares, just like most folks around here, and I gotta admit I'm more taken with racing them than I oughta be. My wife thinks . . . well, I know it's silly, but I do enjoy seeing my stock bring home a prize. Or sell for a good price. And they usually do."

"But last year you had one that did not, I believe."

"True enough. Prettiest mare, rangy, dark, a real spring in her step. Daisy, I called her."

"Do folks often stop by to look at your young horses?"

"Yes, couple a week, sometimes. There's half a dozen of us nearby who dabble in racehorses along with our other cattle."

"What happened to Daisy?"

"She was running good, fit and faster than my two colts. Had several fellows interested in paying plenty for her. But one day she jest took sick. She could hardly stand, wouldn't eat, jest stood and swayed like a gate with a broken hinge, back and forth."

"Her coat was dull and her eyes glassy? Sweated a lot?"

"Yessir. I was worried to see it. Well, one of the fellows

stopped by to look at her again and said he'd seen cases like hers before."

"Yes, I bet he had!"

Easton looked at Cedric with a jaundiced eye, then continued. "Said he knew an old gypsy who had luck helping horses with the same kinda' problems. He offered me a hundred pounds for her and I figgered that was better than nothing if she up and died on me, as I was 'specting her to do any moment."

"And did she have any special markings like a white blaze or white stocking on her legs?"

"No, just a plain brown, neither chestnut nor bay, but all brown. She was rangy, though, and that's what I saw at one meet, a rangy brown mare a few months later, taking a first, and I was mighty sure it was Daisy."

"Did you ask the owner?"

"No," Easton replied. "Felt like a devilish fool, I did. But then I thought them gypsies often have some potent powders that might have cured her."

"Did you ever have any doubts about the man who bought her?"

"Didn't know 'im. But he seemed all right. Paid cash and led her away, more like dragging her."

Cedric knew exactly what he meant. Exactly. "But later, you did have some suspicion?"

"To tell the truth, I was too embarrassed to say anything. Until a month or two ago, when Mr. Sperry, who farms down your way in Suffolk, told me he'd lost a promising colt. When we compared notes, we decided we'd been gulled. Now you're telling me they've pulled this scheme on more'n jest Sperry and me."

"There is one good thing about it, Mr. Easton. I have not heard of anyone being harmed more than once."

Cedric collected a few names of nearby farmers who raised racehorses. "I thank you for your help, Mr. Easton, and if I can put together some sort of plan to stop these fellows, I will send you the details."

"I'd feel much better if I knew this gang was out of business, that's fer sure."

"Thank you for your help, Mr. Easton. I hope to see you at the races one of these days!"

Cedric headed for the closest farm on the list Easton had given him, but it was not until he came to the fourth place on the list that he found trouble. Near mid-afternoon, he arrived at a small farm owned by a man called Poynton, a lanky man who chewed on a blade of straw as he went about his chores.

"Good afternoon, Mr. Poynton," Cedric said. "I have heard that you might have some young racehorses for sale."

Poynton's face showed outright surprise. "Yes. Are you with those other two, the ones who stopped by this morning?"

Cedric's pulse quickened. "No. I am alone. You say you have had other men looking at your horses today?"

"They said they'd be back this afternoon to take a closer look at a bay two-year-old. They were jest checking with a friend before they came back with the money. But—" Poynton paused and looked at his feet.

"But?"

"Well, nothing. You might be interested in a chestnut filly I got."

Cedric's pulse lifted another notch. "Mr. Poynton, we might not have much time. Did one of those men give your colt an apple or a carrot?"

"Seems to me the tall one fed him an apple."

"Tell me, since then, is your bay drooping, looking strange?"

"How'd you know that?"

Cedric could hardly believe his good fortune; he might well have walked into the middle of one of the gang's deals to cheat a farmer. "Let me explain . . ."

Quickly Cedric told him of the other farmers and their loss of good young horses. "You and I are fortunate enough to be able to spoil their plans today. Are you game to try?"

Poynton tossed away his straw. "I am, Mr. Williamson. Indeed I am."

When Cedric saw the colt, he know why Poynton had not wanted to show him off earlier. The bay's head hung low and unmoving, but sweat rolled off of him, and when Poynton led him from the stable he weaved from side to side and stumbled over his own feet. As Cedric had guessed, he was of a common dark color with no white markings, as indistinguishable as Sybil from a multitude of horses.

In barely a quarter hour, they had set up their plan, hiding the drugged colt in a shed behind the dairy. Whether it worked or not, at least Cedric would get a look at two of the conspirators. When all was in readiness, he sat in the shade of an old beech and watched the bees buzzing around Mrs. Poynton's roses, hoping he would see Trentworthy arrive soon.

When Cedric thought about Trentworthy and could assuage his anger enough to consider the man clearly, he thought he could recall almost every feature of his face. Yet if he had tried to describe him out loud he might have been speechless. His very averageness brought him anonymity. No one would remember much about him.

Trentworthy was cunning, though he had sounded like a blowhard when he sold Sybil to Cedric. He had rubbed at his jaw, hooked his fingers in his waistcoat, rocked on his heels and toes, just like thousands of men. He could talk a good line, gab with you, laugh and pat your shoulder, act as though he was taking you into his confidence. Whisper a tip with authority. But melt into the crowd and disappear at will. If he changed his waistcoat and hat, no one would recognize him.

When the two potential buyers rode into the yard, Cedric watched them from a distance, ready to move behind the house if Trentworthy was there.

He was not, though the two men were almost as indiscernable as Trentworthy, unmemorable fellows who looked entirely ordinary.

One wore a straw hat, bent and battered. The other had a red kerchief with which he mopped his face again and again. When Cedric strolled over to join them, they seemed to dismiss him. Cedric had taken the precaution of donning a castoff peasant's smock, had combed his hair flat with pomade, and kept his hands out of sight. He tried to look as unremarkable as Trentworthy. Seeing the pair of buyers, Cedric realized that the one thing that tied all of them together, the men of the gang and the horses they handled, was their anonymous character. All were forgettable, with no identifying characteristics that would make them stand out from the crowd.

Straw Hat took the lead in the conversation. "So where is that colt, the bay?"

Farmer Poynton followed Cedric's advice to the letter. "I turned him out in the field. But you might want to look at the filly, a better prospect altogether, in my opinion."

The horse he spoke of was a red chestnut, with two rear stockings and a wide blaze that ran to a point between her nostrils. Not a horse that could easily be confused with others if one catalogued her coloring and markings.

"Well," Straw Hat drawled, "had my heart set on the bay colt."

"He's feeling poorly, I reckon. Off his feed and sorta' slow these days. Don't have much get up and go, for some reason. Had to isolate him in case he caught something that would infect the other horses."

Straw Hat feigned disappointment. "That's too bad. He looked fine a few hours ago. I took a liking to that one. Off his feed, you say?"

"Just don't look too good," Poynton said. "Glassy-eyed. Can't figger what has come over him. Sweat runs off him. You won't have any more interest in him if you see him."

"That's a shame."

Red Kerchief poked his comrade. "But you know that man who has a magic touch with horses, Simpson. If the colt is sick, maybe that fella could fix him up."

"Yeah, I could take that sick colt off yer hands, Poynton, if the price is right. And then if he don't turn around, I haven't got a lot in him, but yer rid of him."

The conversation went just as Cedric had expected and warned Poynton to expect. No variation from what the other farmers had experienced.

"Well, that would be kind of you. I don't want him infecting my other horses. Let me go out and see if I kin find him."

Poynton left to saddle a horse and ride out in the fields, pretending to search for the colt. Cedric sat and talked to Straw Hat and Red Kerchief while Poynton was gone. The conversation, punctuated by long silences, was limited to weather once the men had brushed off Cedric's questions about where they came from.

Eventually, to Cedric's relief, Poynton came back, sniffling into his handkerchief. His performance rivaled the finest work Kean had done on the London stage. "He was way off in that hollow, dead as a stone. Covered with flies, poor nag."

They all traded long-faced sympathy. But Cedric thought they seemed less than shocked. When Poynton talked of sending men to bury the horse where he lay, Straw Hat and Red Kerchief took their leave. "P'rhaps we'll come by again next year, Poynton. Look at how your yearlings are running."

When the pair rounded the far bend in the road, Poynton turned to Cedric and shrugged. "Was that what you wanted?"

"Yes, exactly. You might have a great future on the stage, my man. Unless I have entirely misjudged the situation, your colt will be fine in a few days, when all the effects of the drug are out of his organs. That was what happened to my filly."

"I hope you are right."

"Your colt will bring a fine price if you decide to sell him, or he'll run well if you decide to race him. No one will ever know that the horse was drugged once."

Cedric accompanied farmer Poynton to look at his mares and their foals. He admired them effusively and took his leave.

***

"My dear, please come in and close the door behind you. Sit down by me on the sofa."

Jane smoothed her gray skirt over her knees when she sat.

"Now, tell me, Jane, my dear, how are you getting on with my nephew?"

"Mr. Williamson is a most polite gentleman."

"Do not gammon me! Cedric is a rascal. He was a rascal as a boy and he has only begun to grow up."

Jane was inclined to agree, but did not wish to cast aspersions. Or reveal her most ambivalent feelings. "I find him most polite, quite well-mannered."

"You don't mean to tell me he is actually helping you?"

"He has read and summarized some of the earliest letters in the collection. From what I have seen, his work has been quite satisfactory."

Lady Stockdale's face revealed her skepticism. "Humfph. Satisfactory is a poor way of saying he is barely competent."

"Not at all. I have examined those letters and they are difficult to read. The handwriting is old-fashioned, and the spelling inconsistent."

"Yes, that much I know. I tried myself, once. Are you saying he truly made them out?"

"I think so, yes."

Lady Stockdale pondered for a moment, tapping a finger against her cheek. "Then we have a very different situation than I expected."

"Are you not pleased that he has shown some ability?"

Lady Stockdale ignored the question. "Has he shown perseverance? Has he sat still for more than a quarter hour at a time?"

"Why yes, he has."

"I am intrigued." She waved a hand in the air as if dismissing the subject of Cedric. "Well, tell me, Jane, have you had many eligible young men seeking your company in Bath?"

"As you well know, if there were any eligible young men in

Bath at all, there are far more attractive and wealthy young women they would attend upon."

"I see your point. But certainly you have suitors."

"None at the moment."

"But in the past, you have had gentlemen seeking your company."

"Not to any extent. My experience with men has been rather limited in the past few years." And what there was, I would not repeat, she thought.

"You are how old now, twenty-three?"

"Twenty-four, Lady Stockdale."

"Humfph. A mere child, but you should be making an alliance soon, my dear. Waiting too long is not wise."

Jane sat mute, unwilling to confide her doubts about confining her future to a man of any sort. Nor did she think this the right moment to discuss writing the book.

Lady Stockdale went on. "But I should not be surprised. Your mother, one of the dearest ladies I know, married very young and has long been without your father." She almost seemed to be talking to herself, expressing out loud her interior thoughts. "She has few good contacts among families with eligible sons who would be good prospects for you."

Jane nodded.

"Well, I feel I should give you the benefit of my experience for I consider you almost like my own daughter. I shall be frank with you, my dear Jane. I think you should marry. And soon. I will find you an eligible connection. At the Sewell wedding next month, you should be able to enchant a certain suitable gentleman I have in mind."

"Please, Lady Stockdale. I am in no way looking for a match."

"You must marry, my dear. Your mother is not destitute, but when she is gone there will be nothing to sustain you."

"I hope, Lady Stockdale, to earn money myself."

"But my dear, there is very little chance of that."

Jane wanted to object, but she held her tongue. When she was ready to discuss the authorship of the book. . . .

Lady Stockdale rubbed her hands together. "I have a dressmaker coming this afternoon, and we are going to outfit you for this wedding."

"I cannot allow—"

"Do not try to resist me, Jane. I have known you since your infancy, and I understand you have your pride. However, I think I have the right to decide how to spend my money. I will brook no defiance. You will be here with me for a while longer and I want you to look better. Now stand up and let me see you."

Jane stood and turned around slowly, as Lady Stockdale waved her hand in the air.

"You have a very nice figure, perhaps a bit too thin, but you have quite a nice bosom. The other evening, that dress was sadly out of date, though it showed off your lovely shoulders."

"But—"

"Now go back to your work in the library, and I will call you when the dressmaker arrives. Think about the colors you like and what kind of bonnets are most becoming."

Jane left in a daze and trudged back to her pile of letters. A marriage arranged by Lady Stockdale? Heavens, no! A suitor was precisely the opposite of what she hoped for from her mother's dearest friend. Oh, things were far too complicated already, and now, the forecast was worse.

It would be a lie to say she did not wish for some new clothes, though certainly not to attract a gentleman's attention. What was she thinking? Her mother would balk at allowing Lady Stockdale to buy them new clothing, thank heavens.

Later in the afternoon, summoned by a servant to Lady Stockdale's boudoir, she was surprised to find her mother already being measured by the modiste's assistant.

When Jane came into the room, Mrs. Gabriel gave a helpless gesture. "Lady Stockdale insists."

Lady Stockdale looked on with a little smirk. "I do not understand your reticence, Winnie. If you had the money and I was wearing gowns more than five years old, you would want to outfit me, would you not?" Without waiting for a reply, she went on. "And you want your daughter settled. That I know! Jane is perfect for the young man I have in mind, but she needs to look her best."

Mrs. Gabriel did not meet her daughter's gaze. "I know you have our best interests at heart, Amelia, but I . . . I really wish it was not necessary for you to . . ."

Lady Stockdale made a dismissive gesture. "But it is necessary. Essential."

Jane slumped in her chair. There was no sense in petitioning Lady Stockdale to let her try to write the book until she had this wedding and her matchmaking schemes over and done with.

"Yes," Lady Stockdale continued. "I have an excellent young man in mind for Jane. And I think I know someone who would suit my nephew too. Cedric needs the right kind of wife and I intend to see him settled also."

Jane almost gasped aloud. Cedric would be livid to know what his aunt planned. And if he refused her wishes, what would happen? Oh, it did not bear thinking about!

If he was in his aunt's ill graces, he would be of no use whatsoever in convincing her to give Jane a chance to write the family history.

The shadows lengthened as Cedric rode away from the farm after sharing supper with the Poyntons. He sincerely hoped he had not misled Poynton and that his colt would soon be healthy once more. The farmer had been convincing when he told Straw Hat and Red Kerchief that the colt was dead.

The darkness came quickly under the leafy branches that blotted out the last rays of the setting sun. What was their tie to Trentworthy? Or whatever name he used with his friends.

Was Trentworthy counting on that colt for an upcoming meet, or would he have kept the horse for a later run?

Cedric heard a crashing in the nearby bushes. Atlas stopped suddenly, tossing him forward and nearly off. The black stallion snorted and danced sideways.

"Just some squirrel, boy. Steady."

Atlas gave a double snort, shaking his head and backing away from the side of the road.

Cedric tried to quiet him. "Don't be such a nuisance, Atlas."

Two figures on horseback smashed through the shrubs. In a blur, Cedric thought he saw a pistol and waited for the crack of a bullet. Instead, both horses rammed into Atlas. One of the men gave Cedric a quick punch and a great shove, almost out of the saddle. The stallion plunged away, rearing and throwing Cedric to the ground.

"Catch that horse," a man shouted.

Cedric, pitched flat on his back, could not breathe, could not drag air into his lungs. Darkness descended. At a great distance, he heard Atlas snorting and the sound of hooves pounding away.

Damn rogue horse, taking off when he was most needed. Worthless beast. Thoughts skimmed through his head, but Cedric felt nothing, could not even gasp. A man kicked at him, but he was too stunned to strike back. A jolt in the ribs. He was numb to everything. Another punch to the stomach.

Suddenly, his muscles thawed, his lungs cleared. His own deafening gasp rang in his ears. His head throbbed with pain, but at last air filled his lungs.

He regretted the return of feeling when another boot slammed into his side. He struggled to rise, but the men pinned him down. Overwhelmed by the stench of their sweat, he tried to twist away. They struck his head against the ground once, twice. Behind his closed eyelids, flashes of crimson and blue sped back and forth in brilliant flashes.

He fought to stay conscious, pushing himself against the

weight of the men, thrashing his arms and legs. But darkness grew and he choked, faded, dropped off to oblivion.

For a moment, he felt at peace. He stretched, flinched, then heard a moan from his own voice and squeezed his eyes shut.

"Is he awake?" It sounded like Straw Hat.

Cedric heard the rustle of feet stepping close, could smell their rank odor.

"Naw, still out. Still dreaming."

"Ya hit 'im too hard, Cawl, too hard."

"If he hadn't fought back, I wouldn'ta hit him. Thought he'd go down fast and we coulda' jest left 'im and took the horse."

"Where'd that damn beast get to, anyway?"

Cedric's head pounded, his pulse throbbed. They sounded like the same two who'd been at Poynton's farm, but without seeing them he was not certain.

"Since we don't have that colt, thought that black 'd bring a purty penny. But now we got nothin'."

"The guv'nor wouldn't like this. That black's a mean 'un. I'm not sorry he's gone. Don't think I'd like to feel his teeth or get in range of his kicks."

"So whadda we do with 'im? Jest leave 'im?"

"S'pose we could. He don't look hurt too bad."

"Shud we go after the horse?"

"Where'd you start lookin'? Reckon he'd be across two counties by now?"

"All the way to Lincolnshire?"

"Aw, Cawl, I don't mean exact."

They'd been after Atlas, Cedric thought, trying to listen as they walked away.

When he heard them mount and ride off, he tried to sit up. His head rang and his right arm ached. When he opened one eye and brought his hand close to his face, he saw a trace of blood on his knuckles.

Cedric sank back on the ground. His head hurt too much to try to stand. He closed his eyes again and hoped he'd fall back into oblivion. It was dark. He had no horse. He could go nowhere.

But instead his mind whirled with questions. Why had the men attacked him? Just to get Atlas? Or did it have something to do with Poynton's colt? They said something about their guv'nor, but who could that be? Trentworthy?

He tried moving his head again, lifting it and rising on an elbow. Lights flashed and swam before his eyes, but he stayed in that position until his vision cleared. He could see little in the darkness. Could he just lie here until dawn?

He pushed himself to a sitting position. Again the pricks of light, the scream of sore muscles, the urge to drop back and sleep again.

But if he stayed here, just off the road, he'd be vulnerable to anyone. Not that he had anything to steal. His money, his clothes, his notes from Coke's lectures, everything was gone, in the bags secured to Atlas's saddle.

Cedric wished he had the gumption to move father from the road, even if he had to crawl. Slowly the pain and misery were beginning to concentrate on a few points—on his shoulder, where he'd landed, his ribs, his thighs. He hated to think of what the bruises would look like. He lay back and closed his eyes. It hurt too much to move.

Atlas. Where had he gone? His loose reins could easily have snarled in the underbrush. The horse could have been injured, hurt trying to get untangled. Would he ever see Altas again? Even though he'd always thought the horse bad-tempered and bothersome, now Cedric hoped he was safe. And he wanted Atlas back.

He lay on his back, stomach aching and chest creaking with every breath. The sound of hooves broke into his pain. Were they coming back? His heartbeat skidded into rapid thumping.

He shut his eyes again, then heard a familiar snort. Atlas? Oh, if it was really Atlas, Cedric promised never to say another bad thing about the ornery animal.

He rolled to his side, stopped to let the throbbing subside, then raised up on one elbow and cautiously opened his eyes. Atlas snorted again. And Cedric managed to locate him a few feet away, reins dangling but saddle and bags intact.

He dragged himself to a sitting position. Would Red Kerchief and Straw Hat come back for him later, or had they simply meant to leave him to stagger back to the road by himself? He needed to put many miles between this place and himself as soon as possible. Slowly he shoved himself to his feet, staggering a little before he gained his balance. Atlas backed away, blowing and shaking his head.

"I know, old boy, you just came back to laugh at me, but I do not care how hard you guffaw, I am very glad to see you."

He walked forward and reached for the reins. Atlas backed again, just out of reach. "Oh, so you just came to tease me, you silly beast? Now come along."

Slowly he moved, step by step until he stood at the black's head. He took the reins and smoothed his hand across the stallion's muzzle and down his neck, picked the twigs out of his mane. "You are a proper mess, old boy."

He checked the bridle: bit pulled crooked but no damage done to the horse's mouth. Cedric cinched the saddle tighter and lengthened a stirrup. He did not see any rocks or logs suitable to use as a mounting block, and his body was in no condition to climb aboard with his usual smoothness and pride of form. Instead he dragged himself up, across Atlas's back, and slowly maneuvered himself into position, clenching his teeth against the pain. He sat in the saddle while Atlas sidled and danced, just letting his bones get used to being shaken. Nothing was broken and he had no serious muscle tears either, just the ache of bruises from pummeling fists and a body stiff with chill from the hard ground.

Atlas seemed in no doubt about where to head and within minutes they were on a well-traveled road, though no one was in sight at the moment. He urged Atlas to a ground-eating trot, enduring the pain by concentrating on the thought of getting back to Uphaven.

He stopped at a crossroads to look at the signs. He needed an inn that catered to a better class than Straw Hat and Red Kerchief. He did not want to meet up with them again.

His body felt like a bag of bones knocking together. His head rattled like dice in a cup. Not a single area seemed free of aches, aches so deep it was difficult to draw a breath. He was thirsty and dirty, but when he reached the Horse and Groom in Swaffham, he took time to see that Atlas was thoroughly rubbed down and fed an extra measure of oats before he drained a pint of ale and called for his own bath.

When he awoke to the sound of cocks crowing outside, he groaned with every move. His head was better, but his back, his shoulders, every inch of his torso ached.

A ride of a day and a half would return him to Uphaven, so he moved slowly to check on Atlas before he ate breakfast. The horse seemed entirely sound, unaffected by the dust-up. Blessed Atlas, without whom he might be sleeping in some pest-filled haystack behind a rural barn. Later, he limped down High Street to find a barber and men to mend his coat and polish his boots. Aunt Amelia need never know of his misadventures. Nor would he tell Jane. She did not need to know how dangerous his game had become.

One thing was sure. His beating only solidified his determination to bring Trentworthy down.

CHAPTER TWELVE

As he rode, Cedric countered the effects of his aches and pains by thinking of the times he had been happiest recently, the times he had spent with Jane. He relived their kisses. Each one of them—and there had been far too few—had seared itself into his head and heart.

The first kisses in the garden, between the rows of yews, had been perfect. Eager, yet tentative. Warm, yet unskilled. Innocent, yet carrying an undercurrent of excitement. The rush of a first encounter, the initial step toward passion. She had not pushed him away or ordered him to stop. Perhaps it had been mostly curiosity on her part, for her inexperience was obvious.

Just a few days later, on the dark path, their heated embrace had only whetted his appetite for more. The very thought of it brought him a glow inside. For the first time since the attack, he felt a different kind of throbbing, feelings that competed with his pain and made him smile. If he could have carried a tune, he would have been singing. He was heading home to her, to Jane, and his heart was full.

Then he remembered his words to her. You have time to forget this ever happened, he had said. Forget it? How he hoped she had not. In fact, he hoped she had lain awake and found it impossible to forget. He hoped she had thought of little else as she lay in her bed. No! Better to think of her at her table reading! He wished he could run into the library and snatch her up from her chair and smother her with kisses.

But giving in to such impulses would be foolish, perhaps even fatal to his purpose.

Purpose? What purpose? Certainly he could not entice her back to the yews and take her virtue. He wanted more, much more than a physical possession. He wanted her heart, longed to hear her words declaring her feelings for him.

To think that dreaded thought? To think of joining their lives in . . . in marriage? Was that really the purpose he sought? Or had he hit his head too hard when he fell?

No, his brainbox seemed in working order. But marriage? Was that what he wanted?

If the trembling of his hands and the palpitations of his heart were any measure, perhaps it was. The feelings were new, different. Was this how Matt yearned for Corrie? And Alfred for Sophy? Did Charles ache like this for the young lady he was to wed next week?

The realization of where his thoughts led only intensified the desire he felt. If this was what love did, then he had not known what he was missing.

But how did Jane feel about him? What if she had followed his suggestion to forget about those kisses? The thought brought stabs of pain. The aches intensified in his ribs, sharp twinges in his hip, but mostly hurt in his head. Without the hope for Jane's renewed kisses, he had nothing left but the agony of hanging in the saddle for the rest of the day.

Worse yet to imagine, she would not have the slightest interest in having him. He was entirely good for nothing. His prospects were few, unless Aunt Amelia came through and left him Uphaven. Anyway, Jane did not want to marry at all. She had said so quite emphatically.

But she had not kissed like a woman who wished to remain a spinster. The warmth of her body pressed to his was not the action of a woman who yearned to be forever alone.

Now all he had to do was convince her.

***

Refreshed by a second restful night's sleep, and only mildly bothered by his remaining aches, Cedric rode Atlas back to Uphaven by early afternoon. His dreams had been lovely ones, full of Jane and entirely free of Trentworthy and his minions.

He had to tread carefully with Jane. She had stated her aversion to marriage. Perhaps he ought to find out why the wedded state was so unpalatable to her.

At the stable, he left the stallion to Johnny, who immediately called for assistance from another undergroom.

"How is the filly, Johnny," Cedric asked. "Working well?"

Johnny had a wide grin. "Yessir. I hold 'er back, but she wants to run, she does."

"I'll come back to look her over in an hour or so. Do you like to ride her?"

"Yessir. Smooth as satin she goes."

"Watch out for Atlas now. He ought to be tired enough to settle in, but don't forget his teeth."

"No, sir."

Chuckling, Cedric walked toward the house, slowly overcoming his desire to favor the more injured side. He wondered if Johnny rode well enough to act as a jockey. He was certainly small and lightweight.

When Cedric stepped inside, he heard the pianoforte from the music room, but it was not music. One note, hit again and again, then the next note, over and over; then a chord, then back to notes, in octaves. Obviously a piano tuner at work.

Cedric stood in the entrance hall for a few moments, listening. He was torn between getting out of his travel clothes immediately or first just having a glimpse of Jane. Her smile might tell him all he needed to know.

He could hear the faint sound of voices, then a few runs and more octaves. He ambled toward the music room and paused outside the door.

"Mr. Gordon, it is sounding much better."

Jane's voice.

"Let me listen while you play for a moment, Miss Gabriel."

The high-pitched but masculine voice must be the piano tuner.

Cedric did not move. A sprightly tune began, a song he had heard many times but had no idea what the name was. It sounded like something he had once danced to. Was that Jane playing? It must be, since the man's voice had said he would listen.

After a few moments, the music stopped.

"How does that sound?" Jane's voice again.

"I think a few of those strings need a bit more work." The tuner.

Again the repetitive striking of notes, One, two, three, ten times, the later versions having a slightly changed pitch.

More notes, a chord or two. Then more.

Cedric stood as if transfixed, waiting for her to play again. Eventually, she must have taken a seat, for the same tune began once more. Very nicely, she played. Like everything else she did, graceful and efficient. The precise qualities one might desire in a wife. As long as they were combined with that dash of passion he found in her.

"Cedric, when did you return?" From behind him, Aunt Amelia spoke.

He turned and bowed to her. "I just came in. Please excuse my dirt." He could not admit he had been standing there listening to a piano tuner strike the same notes over and over for a half hour.

"I am having the pianoforte fixed. It was sadly out of tune. Jane did not want to play it. I insisted she favor us with a ditty last evening. But even I, without a dollop of musical ability, could hear it was off. How were the proceedings at Mr. Coke's?"

"Edifying, Aunt Amelia. A most august assembly with some very elaborate ceremonies and many long lectures."

She nodded her approval. "They say he has more dukes and earls every year."

"I renewed a number of acquaintances and made many new friends."

Her eyes had a faraway look. "Lord Stockdale went to many of them in years past, and I accompanied him once or twice. Now it has almost become a national institution. I am glad you found it worthwhile."

"Indeed I did, Aunt Amelia, and I appreciate it that you secured me an invitation."

"How did it compare with our modest celebration here at Uphaven?"

"Your festival, while smaller, may mean more to your tenants and the villagers. I tried to slip away from some of the more formal events. I thought the tenants of Mr. Coke were hard-pressed to entertain the many who come just to see what all the excitement is about. The workers don't have much to celebrate, at least until everybody else has left."

"Is that so? I must say I think our workers deserve the celebrations, not just the local gentry."

Cedric nodded. "If I weren't so fragrant of horse, Aunt Amelia, I would give you a big hug. I think you are exactly right."

She beamed. "I will have that hug later, perhaps, my boy. Now tell me more about Coke's."

"I heard several papers given on subjects like crop rotation and listened in on many discussions of various breeds of sheep. I came to the conclusion that Uphaven's flocks and operations are quite up to the latest standards."

"I am glad to hear you say that. I have relied on Mr. Sutton and Mr. Richards for some years. I trust their judgment, but it is always good to stay open to experiment."

Cedric tried to listen to the music with one ear and to his aunt with the other, but soon the music ceased and within moments Jane preceded a short man with wispy white hair and watery blue eyes into the hall.

Jane's eyes widened when she saw Cedric, and he felt a rush of satisfaction when her eyes lit up and she smiled at him.

The tuner bowed deeply. "Lady Stockdale, I replaced a few

strings, and I believe your instrument is back to its original capacities. But I would suggest you not wait so long the next time to call me."

Cedric waited to see how the tuner's words of caution would sit with his aunt.

But her mood was good, and she simply giggled a bit. In fact, there was almost a hint of flirtation in her manner. "Now, Mr. Gordon, well you should chide me for being careless in my attention to the pianoforte's care. I deserve your censure. I suppose I did not realize it would go out of tune if it was not played."

Cedric looked at Jane, who was watching the exchange with a half smile on her face. She was really quite pretty, he thought. Beautiful in her own way, clear eyes and pink cheeks, the way she tilted her head, and her direct look. He shook off his admiration after a few moments. This was not yet the time to go all mushy.

Aunt Amelia accompanied Mr. Gordon to the door, leaving Cedric and Jane alone.

Cedric clasped his hands behind his back to keep from reaching for her. "From what little I heard, you play very nicely, Miss Gabriel."

She shook her head humbly. "Not really, Mr. Williamson. I have no real talent, but I have attempted to play for many years, many years of lessons at home as a child and later at school. After all that I am no more than adequate for a few tunes."

"I would not want to think you were fishing for compliments—"

"Not at all." Her voice held a touch of shock. "Not at all. On the contrary, I am all too aware of my limitations as a musician. Lady Stockdale has insisted that I play later, after dinner. Then the meagerness of my capacities will become all too evident. So please reserve your judgment until later. Tell me about your journey. Was it useful?"

"Oh, quite." Of course he would not tell her about his

beating, but he could confide in her a little. "If you will meet me in a half hour, after I go upstairs for a few moments, we can walk together to the stables to see how Sybil is doing. I left Atlas and came directly inside."

"I shall await you in the rose garden."

Jane sat in the rose garden, looking very prim in her gray gown. Yet the expression on her face when she heard his approach made Cedric very happy.

"Miss Gabriel."

She stood and took the arm he offered. "Mr. Williamson. How was your journey?"

"Very useful. In many ways. Have you made progress on your tasks?" He wanted to ask if she had missed him.

"Yes, I have."

"But you have left a little for me, I hope."

She gave a little laugh. "Oh, I assure you there is a great deal more to do."

"Perhaps you can show me your accomplishments later."

She nodded.

"What other things have occupied your time?"

"Would you not rather tell me about the great gathering at Holkham?"

"As a matter of fact I would much rather hear what is happening at Uphaven."

"A comparatively dull subject, I am sure. Your aunt has been most generous to Mama and me. We have had a dressmaker come to ready us for traveling to the wedding. We are quite in Lady Stockdale's debt."

"Knowing Aunt Amelia, I am certain she does not feel that way about it."

"Perhaps not, but I am sorry Mama and I have so little in the way of means to set ourselves up in a reasonable manner. We shall certainly repay her when we can."

Cedric knew exactly how she felt. He had no right, being almost without means himself, even to consider courting her.

They saw the filly grazing in a paddock beside the stable and walked over to the fence to watch her. She lifted her head and looked at them, then trotted in their direction, ears pricked forward, black mane waving in the breeze. She was a handsome sight.

Cedric took a carrot from his pocket and handed it to Jane. "Sybil, you pretty thing, come here."

The bay slowed to a walk and proceeded to them cautiously, extending her head and snuffling softly. Jane held out the carrot. The filly's soft black lips took it, and with one sharp crunch, it was gone.

So, Cedric thought, could a dose of opium go down her throat.

Jane rubbed the horse's ears, patted her muzzle and cooed at her, straightening her forelock and smoothing a hand down the filly's neck. Cedric moved close to Jane and put an arm about her shoulders.

He wished he could speak to Jane about his feelings for her, but the words he spoke were about the horse instead. "If she works well this week, I might enter her in the next meet at Newmarket."

"You think she could do better this time?"

"Yes. I am not certain why she did so poorly before. I suspect the man who sold her to me made sure she would not win."

"How?"

"I am not entirely positive I know how. But believe me, there are ways. Probably as many ways as there are scoundrels who want to fix the outcome of a race."

She scratched the base of the filly's ears. "Men who do not want to play fair?"

Cedric wished he could bring her fingers to caress him rather than the horse. "Uh, yes. Even men who would not know what fairness or honesty mean."

"How very sad."

"Yes. Sad. But not unusual in this world of ours."

"Are you going to ride her this evening?"

He winced at the thought, still feeling enough of the beating's effects to make another minute in the saddle quite distasteful. "No, she has already had a workout today."

They gave her a last pat and began ambling back toward the house.

"Then I should try to do a little more work in the library. Lady Stockdale asked me to attend the pianoforte tuner, so I fear I did not accomplish much yet today."

"I will come with you. I need to get back into our routine of regular work."

"But we will be leaving in a few days anyway. Why do you not use the remainder of the afternoon to rest? You do look tired, Mr Williamson."

She picked up her pace, and he hastened to stay beside her.

"I thought we had progressed to the stage of 'Cedric' and 'Jane.'"

She stared at her hands for a moment. "Perhaps we have moved a bit too quickly. If Lady Stockdale and my mother hear us calling each other by our given names, they will be after the vicar to start calling the banns."

"Would that be so terrible, Jane?"

She stopped and tilted her head, looking at him in surprise. "You cannot be serious, Mr. Williamson. You need to find a young lady who has all the proper qualifications to be the wife of a great landowner, not an aspiring bluestocking like me." She resumed her brisk walking.

Cedric strode along beside her. "I think I am the best judge of the right match for myself. I am growing quite fond of ladies of the bluestocking persuasion."

She gave a little sniff. "Your aunt seems to have a preferred candidate for you."

"What are you talking about?"

"Lady Stockdale says she thinks we will both find amiable attachments among the guests at the wedding."

What had the old girl been up to, he wondered. Meddling with his future? And Jane's as well? "As I told you, I will choose the person with whom I spend the rest of my life."

"So you *are* looking for a partner?"

How had he lost control of the conversation? "That is not what I meant."

"I do hope you take your aunt's advice. Because I am afraid I will disappoint her. I have no intention whatsoever of betrothing myself to anyone. I doubt I shall ever marry."

"But you—" He was at a loss for words. Never marry?

They reached the house, and she paused for a moment. "Mr. Williamson, I am coming to the conclusion that everyone underestimates you, particularly yourself."

She favored him with a little smile, then went inside.

He stood on the gravel path for a moment, trying to glean the meaning of her words.

Underestimate himself? Ha! Here he had hoped she would welcome him back and welcome his more serious attentions. Instead she had him almost leg-shackled to some chit his Aunt Amelia chose. And she had declared her intention to be a spinster forever.

He kicked at the pebbles. The blasted wedding complicated everything. Obviously he would have to talk with Aunt Amelia before he could make Jane a serious offer. If she had a bee in her bonnet about some other gel for him, he probably should wait until after Charlie's nuptials. A nap was sounding more and more inviting. He could pull the pillows over his ears and drown out the sound of his little dreams, just barely born and already shattering to pieces like a wine goblet hurled into the fireplace.

CHAPTER THIRTEEN

Jane tried to fend off the cloud of misery that hung over her. Ever since she had her talk with Lady Stockdale, she felt glum. She would indeed be all that was polite to whomever her ladyship had chosen for her, but unless he was something far beyond her expectations, she would meet him for the first and last time at Patience's wedding. That brief encounter would make no difference to the plan for her life. She would continue with her biographical project and hope that if Lady Stockdale hired another writer, he would approve of her work enough to direct her inquiries for another organizational project, sorting some other family's papers and records. She had to keep trying.

But for Cedric, she thought, things were different. If he did not follow his aunt's wishes, he would not have Uphaven. Jane could not help thinking that if she agreed to marry him and he continued in his defiance of his aunt, they would be very poor, living on his family's allowance, an amount he already more than used up each quarter. If Lady Stockdale chose to deride Jane's efforts on the family history project, Jane would have a hard time earning any money, too.

She and Cedric had no future. She pinned on her hat and frowned at her image in the mirror. If he had not been stuck here in Suffolk, away from his usual haunts in town, he would not have looked twice at her. She might look quite elegant in the new clothes Lady Stockdale had insisted on acquiring for her, but she assumed her appearance would pale in comparison to that of the wealthy relatives and friends of Patience's family.

Nevertheless, all her arguments to herself could not prevent the little skip in her heartbeat when she met Cedric at the stable. He was so handsome, his smile so inviting.

How could any young lady not fall in love with him, especially if he pursued her eagerly? That young lady would probably never know he had been told to woo her. By an aunt who had a fine inheritance to bestow. Not that the young lady would care, once he turned his charm on her.

"You are particularly quiet this morning, Jane," he said as they rode along.

"Am I? I was just thinking how beautifully Sybil moves," she lied. "Unless I am mistaken, she has filled out a little."

"Oh, you are right. Whatever it is you have put in her food, it has been good for her."

He stopped to speak to a pair of workers in a nearby field. Jane watched, her feelings bittersweet. A few weeks ago, he would have paid little attention to those men. Now he knew them by name and cared for their welfare. He had fulfilled Lady Stockdale's requirements, but now she had added another: to marry the gel she chose for him.

An hour later, Jane read over the two chapters she had written while Cedric was away. She made a few changes, crossing out a word here and there, replacing a sentence or two. But generally, she was satisfied.

The best chapter dealt with three of the finest paintings in the collection, including the self-portrait by Judith Leyster. The other chapter dealt with the fourth baron. She could have begun at the beginning, but that would have meant revealing the fact that she had only given work to Cedric that she had already done. Somehow she worried that he might not take kindly to such a revelation.

As before, when he came to the library, he was admirably turned out. If it had not been for his damp hair, one would have assumed he had spent hours perfecting his ensemble. She felt a twinge of contentment when he set a vase of roses on the table. But he had words only for the filly.

"Sybil has never been faster. I was far too mild in my praise a while ago. Whatever you are putting in her feed seems to grow wings on her heels."

"Just a few herbs, and a little garlic."

"Garlic? Why garlic?"

"Oh, garlic is said to have all sorts of qualities, for strength, for general good health."

Cedric shrugged. "And you believe that?"

"It has not seemed to hurt her. And I daresay there is a clove of garlic in every pot of soup the cook stirs up. It has not seemed to harm you or me."

Cedric repeated his shrug. "I cannot dispute that. The filly seems quite lively. Whether it is the garlic or just her natural talents hardly matters. I think I shall take her over to the Walkers' tomorrow and match her against one of their runners. Oswald brags about their many winners, so I can get a better feel for how she measures up."

"That is an excellent idea."

Cedric turned the full force of his engaging smile on her and Jane sat down quickly, her knees suddenly made of jelly.

"Thank you for the flowers. I have missed them."

"Now what have you been accomplishing while I have been riding across the counties, besides missing your roses?"

"I have two chapters completed. But I may be overrating them. If you do not think they are—"

"Do not denigrate your work, Jane. I will give you my honest opinion. Are you ready to show them to Aunt Amelia?"

"I do not know. I feel—"

"You spoke to me about underestimating myself, and now you are doing the same thing."

"I am? I suppose that is true. I think we should wait to show any chapters of the book to her until after we return from the wedding. I believe she is preoccupied right now with getting ready. We all have more fittings later today."

"You are right. She will not have time to read them now. Did you say you knew the bride in school?"

"Yes. At Miss Dulwich's Seminary in Bath. We both had an interest in art. And you are an old friend of the groom?"

"We were together at Eton, though he was not among my closest companions. But I am almost the last of my set left single. Charles must think he can tempt me into following the rest of them into matrimony if he has me as his attendant."

"Of the girls I knew at school, those I still hear about anyway, most are married."

"So whom do you think Aunt Amelia has unearthed for us? Perhaps the sister or brother of the bride?"

Jane waved away the thought. "No, she is an only child, which is why, I believe, the family is having such a large gathering."

Cedric seated himself in his usual place. "Then it is a mystery to me. Whom has Aunt Amelia contrived to find for us?"

"I, too, am at a loss to know from whence they will turn up."

He picked up her manuscript and looked at the first chapter. "Now why have you begun with the second baron? Will there not be several chapters before that, on the early years of the family?"

"Those are the letters you are still working on." She kept what she hoped was an innocent expression on her face.

He laid the pages on the table and gave her a mischievous look. "You mean you had not already finished with those letters you gave me?"

Her heart leaped to her throat. "What?"

"Now, Jane, I feel quite certain you already read and summarized those first letters."

She felt as if the floor was sinking beneath her. "Oh, dear, I am so—"

He wore a wide grin. "Do not be upset. I cannot fault you for giving me material to work on that you had finished. After all, I was rather forced onto this task and you had no way of knowing what I could or could not do."

Jane pressed her hands to her burning cheeks and covered her eyes. What was the use of pretending? "I feel terrible, Mr. Williamson. I should not have been so quick to assume—"

"But what did you know of me? A London Corinthian, as you yourself said. A nodcock who had just lost everything on an asinine caper at the Newmarket racecourse, as I admit of myself. You would have been a complete henwit to have given me any work that had importance."

She peeped out between her fingers to see a big grin on his face, and she felt a bubble of laughter well up. "Truly, do you think so?"

He leaned back and nodded. "I do."

She allowed herself a little giggle, then a full-fledged laugh.

He joined her, and eventually they laughed so hard, they both had to wipe their eyes.

Cedric continued to beam at her. "The joke is truly on you. I have quite enjoyed reading those letters. I know you—and probably Aunt Amelia as well—thought I would give up. But instead, I find I really want to read the rest of them."

"Your summaries were first-rate, in my opinion. And so I told Lady Stockdale."

"I imagine she was shocked beyond belief."

Jane laughed again. "I would characterize her reaction as mild surprise."

He nodded. "It is kind of you to say so. But now, if there is anything I can do to be of real service to you, you need only show me what you want me to do."

No matter what he said, Jane still felt a little sheepish about her deception, or more accurately, about her attempted deception. "There is a set of letters, from the first baron, that I have not read and summarized. Many of them date from before he was given his title, others from much later."

"That would be the period of Cromwell and the Civil War?"

"Yes. I assume I will need to fill in a great many facts about the late years of Charles I, the battles, the restoration, and the reign of Charles II. If that would interest you—"

"If you trust me to work on those letters, I will be flattered to assist."

She reached for a box on the shelves behind her and pushed it towards him. "Oh, yes, Cedric. I know you will do an excellent job."

"I shall begin immediately." He placed a blank sheet in front of him, and opened the box.

Only when she watched him lift out the first of the letters did she realize what she had done. Their time together in the library would last for at least another month after the wedding next week. Or more.

What was she doing to her heart?

Cedric watched as Oswald's groom settled the borrowed racing saddle on Sybil's back and cinched the girth. She looked every bit the eager filly ready for a run. Her head high, eyes bright and ears pricked. No longer the sad young mare of a few weeks ago, with exhaustion in her posture.

He placed his foot in the groom's cupped hands and let himself be tossed into the saddle, fitting his toes into the light stirrups. He was unused to this kind of saddle. Although he had often watched jockeys ride in workouts and races, he had never done so himself. But he was anxious to try.

Oswald sat aboard one of his favorite racehorses, Lionheart, a chestnut with a noble arch to his neck and long legs. Oswald had been touting his pedigree for the last quarter hour as they prepared for their match. "He's won three of his five starts. Got boxed in halfway 'round the course in one and ended up fifth. His first race was a disaster, a jockey who had no idea what a young horse needed. But Lionheart learned fast."

Cedric hoped his filly was not too tired from the several-mile journey to the Walkers' place. At least she was good and warmed up for her contest.

The Walkers had a fenced oval of about half a mile on which they trained their horses, a far cry from the pasture Cedric rode Sybil around. He'd had the sheep moved into another field, but the circuit on which he had ridden on Atlas had a narrow grass-free path, well-trampled by his black stallion. It was not smooth like a racecourse, but it was the best he had found on Aunt Amelia's estate. This course of Walker's would be infinitely better, and they would do one circuit of it, running all out.

Cedric walked the filly down the course, then took her to a trot and into a canter. She felt loose and alert, ready to stretch out to a gallop. He turned her head onto the makeshift track and brought her to a stop. Then he spoke softly, "This is your first run, my girl. Let us see what you are made of." Walker brought his chestnut up beside her and the groom dropped his arm, signaling the start.

Cedric kicked Sybil forward, and her take-off almost pulled his arms out of their sockets. He struggled to hold on, grabbing a handful of her mane and righting himself on the tiny saddle. As her strides smoothed, he found his seat and let his hands on the reins move with the bobbing of her neck, gaining speed with every stride. Lionheart was a length or two ahead, but Cedric was sure Sybil had not reached her limit. Faster and faster she sped, leaning into the curve and slowly narrowing the distance to the chestnut. Cedric moved with her, her mane whipping in his face, silently exhorting her to speed up just another notch, catch the chestnut, pass him. And as if she heard him, Sybil stretched out her head and caught Lionheart, then passed him, moving into a half-length lead.

Cedric dared a quick glance at Oswald, who looked a little

surprised. They sped by the groom, finishing where they had started, with the filly still in the lead. Cedric felt a swell of pride, as he slowed her to a canter and turned her back to the start. If Lionheart was truly a winner—and Oswald had no cause to stretch the truth in this little match—then Sybil was truly as fast as he had imagined.

She was not quite ready to stop, it seemed, as she pranced and sidled around the groom. Lionheart was dancing too, both of them ready for more.

Oswald sat his chestnut effortlessly. "Neither of us are jockeys, Williamson, but I'd say you gave that filly a fine ride. I may not have ridden Lionheart as well, but I know this. You have a fast horse on your hands, despite what happened to her last time."

"I think you are correct. If Lionheart ran all out."

"As I say, he might do better with a jockey, lighter weight and all that, but I thought he was doing well. She beat him fair and square."

Cedric could not help grinning from ear to ear. Now he had to figure out what to do with her abilities.

Jane set her teacup in its saucer. This was the fourth visit of the dressmaker and his assistant to Lady Stockdale's Chinese boudoir. She sincerely hoped it would be the last time they had to assemble here. Lady Stockdale laughed about the situation, calling it her hen party invaded by the rooster. But, to Jane's way of thinking, Mr. Percival was not much of a rooster. Certainly he preened a great deal, dressed in bright hues, and could be said to crow about his abilities to suit the ladies with the very latest in Parisian fashions. But, as a masculine ideal, nothing else about him was particularly appealing.

Behind a screen, her mother donned a ball gown and now stepped into view to take her place between two cheval mirrors. Jane had to admit the gray silk was lovely, blending nicely with her mother's hair.

She listened to the conversation among her mother, Lady Stockdale and Mr. Percival with little interest, letting her mind wander back to the library where she had left Cedric, reading a voluminous history of the Stuarts.

He had worked hard since he arrived at Uphaven. He often seemed surprised himself to notice how diligently he had pursued his aunt's strictures.

"What do you say, Jane?" Lady Stockdale's voice pierced her musing.

Jane watched her mother turn slowly. "I think she looks very fine."

"I meant about putting a third row of ruching around the hem," Lady Stockdale said in a tone that clearly indicated she knew Jane had been paying no attention to their discussion.

"I think it might make Mama look shorter, less stately."

Mrs. Gabriel twisted to look at the rear view. "I think you could be right, Jane."

Mr. Percival launched into an explanation of how elaborate the latest designs were, how five and six tiers of decoration was the standard for the autumn gowns.

Jane let her thoughts prevail again over his chatter. Had Cedric not followed the steward around to the tenants, worked with Mr. Richards on the home farm, even had tried his hand at shearing? No one could have been more conscientious.

So now Lady Stockdale was about to suggest another qualification for him, to take a wife of her choosing. It seemed his aunt asked a great deal of him. On the other hand, she had every right to expect her heir to meet her requirements. If Cedric did not live up to her expectations, they all knew she had other nephews who might.

The clock chimed three. Already they had spent a half hour on one gown for her mother. At this rate they would not be finished until well beyond the dinner hour.

Jane stared at the hand-painted wallpaper. The branches that framed the repeated patterns of pagodas and bridges arching over ponds were cherry blossoms, Lady Stockdale had once explained, not apple blossoms as Jane had assumed. Whatever they were, they reminded her of the decorations at so many country churches for springtime weddings. She wondered if Cedric would wait until those blossoms returned next spring to wed the young lady with whom he would be paired at the wedding. The thought made her want to weep.

"Come now, Jane. It is your turn," her mother said.

Mr. Percival held up a frothy gown of pale blue silk. All Jane could think as she went behind the screen to put it on was, what a shame it would be to waste it on some numbskull Lady Stockdale had found for her.

Cedric hoped for an early start to their journey, but he could not prevent his aunt from remembering all sorts of last minute details that caused one delay after another. When at last the baggage was secured in the coach that would bring two maids and the butler, who had agreed to act as Cedric's valet for the journey, they set out on the road east. Lady Stockdale rode in her carriage with Mrs. Gabriel and Jane. Cedric rode Atlas, ever so glad that all his bruises and strained muscles had healed since his last cross-country day in the saddle. Without much traffic, Cedric had plenty of time to think about how his life had changed in the past few months and how it might change dramatically in the near future.

He wondered if his admiration for Jane's ambition, fortitude and hard work had rubbed off on him or whether he had truly had a change of character.

What had made him realize that he truly wished to amount to something in this world, that his carefree days of planning nothing more than the next caper no longer appealed to him? He was still rather shocked to find he enjoyed many of the duties on the estate and even wanted to know about its history. Instead of trying to figure a way to avoid sitting through some very long lectures at Coke's, he had relished the opportunity.

He was beginning to think he might accomplish something with his life after all.

Was this change due to Jane's example? She had achieved a great deal, starting with so much less. She had accomplished the beginning of her dream, and if he could help her complete the rest of it, he intended to do so.

He probably owed her the credit for helping him find what he wanted to do. Though now, looking back, he realized he had always wanted to belong to Uphaven. Not because it would bring him money; he wanted the estate because it would bring a purpose to his life, something he had long avoided. Yet it had been there, that need to belong, deep down inside.

Funny how it had taken a female to show him the way. His three best friends had settled down with their wives to productive lives. He had been the only hold-out, maybe, because he was afraid to sit down and ask what he wanted of life. Or what life wanted of him.

Why had no one ever told him about the satisfaction one felt in a job well done? How agreeable it was to earn the esteem and approbation of others? Apparently he had been too thick to figure it out until Jane's good opinion mattered to him.

How this would all turn out was anyone's guess. Aunt Amelia seemed to be feeling more favorably toward him lately. But he did not like her quest to find him a wife. He knew exactly whom he wanted to wed, if he could convince her.

But he also had to find a way to secure enough money for them to set up an establishment of their own. Aunt Amelia might send him on his way and give the estate to someone more amenable to her dictates.

Eventually they reached the inn where they planned to spend the night. Alderton was only a half-day's ride further east.

He hoped he could find some more hopeful thoughts with which to occupy his mind tomorrow.

Cedric took his dinner in the taproom while the ladies ate in their bedchamber. He let the boring buzz of local affairs lull him into an early bedtime. For the next few days, he needed to put his own affairs from his mind. His responsibility was to assist Charles with whatever the bridegroom needed and he meant to fulfill his duties without gloomily moping, worrying about Aunt Amelia's matchmaking. Either for Jane or for himself.

CHAPTER FOURTEEN

The tall towers of Alderton Castle dominated the flat Suffolk marshes, silhouetted against the vast blue of the sky for a long distance before Jane could see the other buildings clustered around its base.

"What you are looking at," Lady Stockdale commented, "is only the gatehouse. The rest of it was pulled down centuries ago."

Mrs. Gabriel peered out of the carriage, wide-eyed. "My heavens, it is enormous."

Jane remembered the few times Patience had talked of her home. Patience thought it was much too far away from anything interesting. On that score, Jane thought, she was probably correct. But it was certainly grand.

They were staying in the Dower House with Lady Stockdale's good friend, the bride's aunt, Miss Augusta Sewell, a plump lady of late middle age, who welcomed them with enthusiasm.

"Winnie, I have not seen you for years, my dear. You have not changed a bit."

"Nor have you, Gussie," Mrs. Gabriel responded.

That was a real bouncer, Jane thought, looking at the two of them. Even she and Patience would have changed considerably from their time at school just six or seven years ago. But leave the ladies to their fictions, she thought.

Miss Augusta was bursting with eagerness to recite all the events of the next three days. This evening would be a quiet dinner for the arriving guests; tomorrow a tour of the farms and stables, *al fresco* luncheon, and later after resting time, a grand dinner and ball to honor the bride and groom. The next day, the wedding, followed by the wedding breakfast and farewell to the bride and groom who were off to the continent.

Many guests would not arrive until the following morning. Regardless, Jane stayed close to her mother and Lady Stockdale for the afternoon, chatting, meeting other female guests, and admiring their ensembles. Though she watched carefully for any sign of Lady Stockdale's partiality for one of the un-attached young ladies, no one as yet appeared to fill that role. By staying close to the ladies, she might also avoid encountering the young man she was intended to meet for as long as possible.

After the first meal was over, Patience extracted Sophy and Jane from the drawing room and spirited them away to her boudoir for a good coze. Once the preliminary greetings were behind them, Patience acceded to their wishes and showed them her bride clothes.

Jane particularly admired the lovely satin cases, almost like pillow slips, in which Patience packed her gloves, stockings and stays. Each was a slightly different pastel shade, embroidered with silk roses and tiny pearls.

Patience laid the three cases on the counterpane. "They were gifts from my dressmaker and her stitchers. Can you imagine the time and work that went into making them? They were so sweet when they presented them to me. I had tears in my eyes."

Sophy leaned over to take a closer look. "You are very fortunate to have the esteem of your modistes. My mother was such a dragon that I shivered in fear that she would dismiss them before my bride clothes were finished. Nothing they did met her approval, though I was quite satisfied."

Jane remembered Cedric's story about the fearsome Countess of Lodesham, Lady Sophronia's mother. This morning, he had enlivened their breakfast at the inn by entertaining them with many tales of his friends and their capers. The stories had not relieved Jane's anxiety about the upcoming meetings, but they made her mother and Lady Stockdale laugh.

Patience looked at the clothing spread on the bed with a touch of melancholy in her expression. "I was not pleased that my mother wanted to have this big celebration. I wanted a quiet little wedding with no fuss, but Mama would not hear of it. Now my nerves are on edge, and I fear that Charles's are too."

Sophy took Patience's hand. "All of this will be over in a few days and you will be alone with Charles. At first you may feel strange but before long, you will love married life."

"So my cousins have told me."

"My husband and I are happiest when we are alone, without other family or friends. We read together or walk in the garden. Sometimes we study and take trips to distant ruined castles or Roman sites recently uncovered."

Jane found Sophy's words very touching. Such a marriage might appeal to her, after all.

Patience sighed. "Have you traveled to France? I am nervous about the sea trip, but looking forward to Paris."

"We were hoping to go last winter, but I was unwell for a while."

"Unwell? Shame on you, Sophy, for not telling me."

Sophy made a shy smile. "Perhaps unwell is not quite the correct term. I thought I was, ah, increasing, but I was simply off my regular schedule."

Jane noticed the pink beginning to tint Lady Sophronia's cheeks. "Were you disappointed or relieved?"

"Both. But here it is only a few months later, and I . . . I . . ."

Both Jane and Patience threw their arms around Sophy. "You are in a family way?"

"It is not confirmed, but so I suspect."

Patience gasped. "But you should have stayed home and cared for yourself, not traveled three days to be here at my wedding! You *must* take care of yourself."

"On the contrary, I think ladies of our class may coddle themselves too much. Many country women have several children, care for them while keeping the house, cooking, tending their hens, and Lord knows what else. I think it does them more good to be active and moving than to take to one's bed."

"Oh, I long to have a baby," Patience said. "Do you not want children, Jane?"

"I quite like little ones, but before they arrive, one needs a husband. I do not see myself marrying in the near future."

Sophy looked surprised. "Why not? Lady Stockdale's nephew is perfect for you."

Patience nodded her agreement. "Mr. Williamson is one of the best-looking fellows I've ever seen."

Jane shrugged. "I agree that he is excessively handsome. But he is also a rake, not at all the kind of match I would want. And he certainly would not want me."

"Why not? You are pretty and amiable, and intelligent, clearly a good prospect for any discerning gentleman."

But completely without any funds, hardly a penny to my name, she thought, unlike both Patience and Sophy, whose fathers were plump in the pocket. Aloud, she kept to the problems of Cedric's proclivities. "I do not think I would want to marry a rake."

Sophy's laugh was truly heartfelt. "Reformed rakes make the very best of husbands. That is a well-known truth."

"So I have heard." Jane did not wish to reveal the truth of the matter: Cedric was intended for someone else. "I think the maxim rests on a very, very important point."

Sophy and Patience spoke as one. "And that is?"

"The rake must be reformed! It would be quite unpleasant to marry a rake who continued his ways, would it not?"

"But what rake would want to marry without reforming himself?" Patience asked.

Sophy wagged a finger at Jane. "I have it on very good authority—from their wives—that the other two members of the Quorn Quartet, besides my husband and Mr. Williamson, are very happy in their marriages and have taken on all the responsibilities of their maturity."

Jane made one last try. "But Mr. Williamson could be an exception." Of course, she knew he was not, that he, too, was learning to discharge his duties cheerfully.

"It is possible, but unlikely," Patience said. "I heard from Charles that Cedric was quite knowledgeable on the subject of sheep."

Jane said nothing. It was indeed true.

Sophy took Jane's hand. "The men have all been very well behaved here, particularly Cedric."

Jane felt tears threatening. "To be honest, Sophy, he must stay in his aunt's favor or he will be penniless again. Lady Stockdale will choose his bride."

Cedric had known he would have to suffer through the retelling of his recent embarrassment, but the inevitable moment arrived well before he had expected it. Not, as he had anticipated, after dinner over the port when at least twenty would be sitting around the table, but on the first afternoon when just a handful of men sat in the billiards room, shut away from the ladies. Cedric tried to get his equanimity and be prepared to laugh away the others' teasing. Either that or sink again into utter humiliation.

"You should have seen her!" Charles illustrated his words with expansive gesturing. "At the first furlong, his filly slowed and dropped behind the leaders. By the third, she was in the middle of the pack, and by the end, you would have thought she was a plough horse plodding across a field."

"What was wrong with her jockey?" A burly man with a florid face, Lord Mountbasset clearly did not like the sound of the story.

Charles waved an arm in the air. "Jockey was yelling in her ear and waving his whip, but she was tuckered out, without a bit of verve. We all lost a bundle."

While the others hooted about Cedric's foolish whim, Lord Mountbasset looked at Cedric with narrowed eyes. "What happened to her?"

Cedric spoke in an undertone. "I believe she was drugged, sir."

"The deuce! What makes you think so?"

"Just the way she acted, not like a horse that's tired from a hard run in the morning or has a stomach packed with hay or full of water."

"And did she recover?"

"Yes, sir, she did." Cedric directed his voice to all of them. "I am going to run her again at the next Newmarket meet."

A chorus of laughter did not stop him. "I'd advise all of you to put your money on her, because she flies like the wind, and I expect her to show her tail to every other entry."

Charles had the loudest of the guffaws that met the news. "You cannot be serious, Williamson. That filly was a miserable runner."

"Not any more, she's not!"

"This ought to be rare!" Charles gave Cedric a friendly slap on the back.

Sir Neil Lambert, a tall, rather gaunt gentleman who had come in on the end of the conversation, poured himself a glass of claret. "Charles, will you bring your bride to our place for the races? Emmaline always appreciates having a few females with her to watch the races. And Williamson, you come too, and bring your party of ladies, if you wish. We have sufficient accommodations for a regiment, just on the edge of Newmarket village."

After Cedric and Charles quickly made the arrangements with Sir Neil, Charles took Cedric aside. "You really are not counting on that nag to have a crack at winning, are you?"

"As I said, she runs sound and true. A beautiful sight, Charles. I suppose I run the risk of making an ass of myself again. But I rather fancy seeing that filly in the winner's circle."

"But if that seller was more than a slick talker with a

good-looking prospect he knew couldn't run a hundred yards, if he was really mixed up with serious criminals . . ." Charles went no farther, but his question was clear. "I think you are ready for Bedlam."

Cedric listened to the conversation range over the prospects of many other horses, then gradually drift into talk about shooting season next autumn. His thoughts remained with Sybil and her chances to win. Even her victory would not be quite enough. He wanted to put a stop to Trentworthy and his conspirators, make sure they would never drug a horse again, or cheat a farmer, or rook a gullible young man. But how could he do it? He needed some ideas. Perhaps Charles or Alfred might have some. Or, he could consult the most intelligent person he knew. He could ask Jane. Her affection for the filly might outweigh her disapproval of wagering.

Jane was delighted that instead of indulging in an afternoon rest during the appointed time before the grand ball, Cedric wanted to climb the castle tower with several of the other gentlemen and ladies. Sophy bid them enjoy the view but declined the climb.

Patience preferred to get her rest. "I have been up there far too many times already," she said.

Charles Venable, the bridegroom, was eager to lead the party. "Lord Alderton said it is quite safe, that the steps were recently patched."

Jane was not acquainted with the other young lady who came along, who was called Cassie, and just might be Aunt Amelia's candidate for Cedric.

When Jane asked him, he shook his head. "Not Cassie. She is spoken for. By George Jenneret."

Jane grinned. She had rather expected that George was the man Lady Stockdale had intended for her, but apparently she was mistaken. Perhaps all would be revealed that evening at the grand ball.

"Not so fast," someone called as they went up and up.

After stopping to catch their breath several times, they reached the top. In the distance to the east was the sea, shining with silver highlights, above which the sky was gray. The land stretched flat to the west, and to the south were the marshes and the river. "The view is certainly worth the effort."

Cedric came to her side. "How do you like it?"

"I think it is lovely. The sea is so close. I have not walked on a beach for many years."

"Then we shall find time to drive over there. It could not take more than half an hour."

"I would like that."

When she donned all her new finery, Jane hardly recognized herself. She could almost believe that some gentleman, encouraged by Lady Stockdale, might find her attractive. Her nerves tingled at the thought of facing a roomful of strangers, one of them a gentleman Lady Stockdale thought she should single out for special attention. In the same company would be the young lady Cedric was expected to court.

Why Lady Stockdale had not pointed them out, or even named them, was a mystery. When she had asked, Jane had received no information, only a lifted eyebrow and a little laugh from Lady Stockdale. "Why Jane," she had said, "I would not want to spoil the spontaneity of the evening!"

All Jane wanted was to endure the evening and get back here to this bedchamber, without offending Lady Stockdale.

"Not true," Jane whispered to herself in the mirror. What she truly feared was to see Cedric with his young lady, smiling at her, captivating her, earning the kind of mooncalf look she presumed he often received.

Drawing a deep breath, she went down to meet the others from the Dower House for the short ride to the castle.

The beauty of the scene lifted her internal gloom, if only temporarily. Two drawing rooms opened to each other to form a large area for dancing. Clouds of filmy white silk lined the walls. Every few feet, large bouquets of white roses adorned silver candelabra, perfuming the room with their sweet scent.

Dancing began immediately, and Cedric caught her hand to lead her out.

"You look bang up to the mark, Jane. Let us get our dancing done before you are tossed into the clutches of some ramshackle sprig of fashion, and I am dragged off to meet Aunt Amelia's vixen."

Despite her nerves, the time sped by. She was introduced to so many people she could not keep track of any of the names. After the first set with Cedric, she dance another with Sophy's husband, Alfred Collingwood, and a third set with Charles.

When she met some very amiable young man, she maintained a happy face and uttered a steady stream of compliments about the bridal couple, the estate, the beauty of the ladies tonight—the meaningless and forgettable topics with which an evening such as this was filled. If one of the gentlemen who solicited her hand for the next several sets was Lady Stockdale's choice for her, nothing he said or did gave away his purpose. She kept a polite smile on her face and did not find any of them memorable.

By the time the dancing was over, Lady Stockdale and her mother had retired for the night. Jane joined a party of young people for a moonlight stroll around the grounds that would deliver her back to the Dower House. Cedric linked her hand through his arm, pressing her fingers warmly. They lagged behind the others. "Are you having a good time?" he asked.

"I think I preferred the dancing at the village, with that Binsley fellow."

"If you had worn that delicious confection of a dress, just like a fairy princess, I doubt Binsley would have had the nerve to draw you into the dance."

She looked down at her elaborately decorated gown, the

rows of frills and silk roses around the hem. "Yes, I am sure you are correct. It is overdone, to my taste."

"But it is the latest fashion, is it not?"

"So they say."

"It is also quite becoming. Now tell me if you like Lady Stockdale's prospect for you."

"I do not recall anyone singling me out especially. What about you?" She held her breath for a moment.

Cedric made a helpless gesture. "I kept one eye on Aunt Amelia for most of the evening. If she was giving me any special cues, I did not catch them."

She felt a wave of relief wash over her. "But what can we do?"

He gave a rueful laugh. "She told me that if I am too dense to ascertain her wishes, she would have to hold a house party before long. Make things so obvious that even a chucklehead like me would understand."

Jane could not help laughing. Cedric a chucklehead? Perhaps only from Lady Stockdale's blunt tongue!

At the door of the Dower House, she waved good night to the others and crept inside to keep from waking Lady Stockdale or Miss Augusta. The ball had not been half as bad as she had feared. Yet confusion clouded her thoughts and apprehension filled her restless dreams.

Late the next morning, the wedding guests filled the little church that stood in the shadow of the castle towers. When Patience and Charles repeated their vows, Jane observed to herself that the actual ceremony was the shortest, least elaborate part of the three-day celebration.

After the wedding breakfast, which lasted well into the afternoon, the bridal couple departed to spend a week at the estate of Charles's uncle near Cambridge before leaving for France.

Though a number of guests from the neighborhood departed soon afterwards, Lady Stockdale did not want to start for home until the next morning. If they left early and the weather favored them, they might be able to make it back to Uphaven by dusk.

Would the wedding celebration end without Jane ever discovering Lady Stockdale's choice for her and for Cedric? When she asked his opinion, he shook his head and suggested they use the time for a walk on the beach.

Only a quarter of an hour's ride away in a borrowed curricle, the landscape changed dramatically. The marsh grass gave way to sand and the road ended behind a rise of shingle high enough that they could not see the beach beyond. They left the curricle with the groom and carefully made their way over the shale to the sand.

Not another human being was in sight. Their only companions were the birds wading in the wash of the gentle surf.

Jane shaded her eyes against the glare from the sea. As far as one could see to the north and to the south, there was nothing but water, sand, shale, and the shore birds. "I always think one should know the names of different birds, but I do not seem to remember many of them."

Cedric stepped back from a wavelet. "Nor do I."

She squinted at a flock of tiny gray birds darting through the shallows. Their little black legs seemed to move in unison. "I have no idea what those are called."

"Nor do I. But I know a hawk when I see one."

"I think I would recognize an owl."

Cedric broke into his irresistible grin. "I saw a stuffed penguin once."

"I can tell a duck from a chicken and a swan from a goose."

They laughed, held hands, and ran down the beach. Anonymous birds both large and small fluttered out of their way.

When they ran out of breath, they slowed to a walk. A ridge of shingle marked the line of the high tide on the wide sand beach.

"The tide must be at about its low point," Jane said.

"Yes." Cedric pried a stone out of the sand and tossed it far out into the sea.

As close as they were to civilization, Jane thought, this lonely seafront had a wild quality as different from the polished ballroom and elaborate ceremonies of the past few days as one could imagine. It was elemental, real, and it gave her a magnificent sense of freedom.

She stopped for a moment and stared at the silvery sheen on the water, drawing in a deep breath of the briny air. The cry of the birds echoed in the wind. The sea sang with its own rhythm. The breezes blew from the Low Countries or perhaps even from Scandinavia.

Jane let the sound and smell of the shore sink into her. If only she could preserve this feeling, this sense of having no boundaries and no limits.

But this was not the reality of her life. Nor Cedric's.

She took his arm and they walked a little farther without speaking, until they had to step around a pile of weeds washed up by the waves.

"The beauty of this place makes me want to forget all our problems," Jane said.

"I agree. But I expect we will have no escape once we leave the shore behind."

Jane did not need to be reminded. "Did you learn anything more today about which young lady your aunt wants you to pursue?"

"Aunt Amelia acts as though I ought to know, but I must have missed something."

"Miss Lambert?"

"Possibly. But she told me she has a *tendré* for a fellow in Newmarket."

"Perhaps your aunt did not know about him."

Cedric heaved another stone into the sea. "That may be why her father invited us all to stay with them for the race meet."

"I am glad I will be able to see Sybil win her race."

He kicked at a rock half-buried in the sand. "If she wins, I will have my moment of triumph, but it will be a Pyrrhic victory. What I really want to do is crush Trentworthy and his gang of scoundrels."

"You want revenge."

"Yes, exactly." Cedric scooped up a handful of pebbles and hurled them into the water. "Merely seeing Sybil win a race will hardly bother them. Where the gang makes most of their money is through betting on a race. They know which horse is favored to win so they nobble it with a dose of opium and it comes in last. The bookmaker keeps all the losers' money."

"Opium? They give the horses opium?" So Sam's words were true.

Cedric tightened his hands into fists. "According to the apothecary, no one can predict exactly how opium will affect a horse. I suspect they had to experiment and may even have killed an animal or two."

"How could anyone do such a thing?" Alarm coursed through Jane's entire body. Sybil could have died!

"That is why I want more than just a comeuppance for Trentworthy. I want him to see that filly win a race after he abused her. But that is not enough. I want to destroy him. He should never be allowed on a racecourse again. I want him transported."

Jane wiped away a tear, but tried to keep her voice light. "Have some pity for the poor people who live in the Antipodes, Cedric."

"Truthfully, I'd like him hung, but endangering the lives of horses is not yet a capital crime. And it cannot be proved. To others, it looks like he's found sick horses, taken them off the farmer's hands, nursed them to health and sold them to fools like me. The fact they break down again in a race is no surprise. People buy and sell horses all the time. There is nothing illegal in the sales whether on the farm or in the hours before a race."

Jane felt sick inside. It seemed Cedric's cause was hopeless.

He hammered one fist against his palm. "That is why he can get away with it. The wealthy men who control the rules of the races, the Jockey Club members and their friends, would be shocked and horrified at what he has done to the horses, giving them drugs. But they would say the others, the sellers and the buyers, were just foolish. Or unlucky."

"And you cannot prove they drugged Sybil?" Jane asked.

"I have no evidence. Sybil seemed fully recovered in a few days. How can I prove she was dosed with something? Horses get tired for many reasons. Perhaps they have been run full out in the hours before a race, and they cannot finish. Perhaps they have been given a pail or two of water, which would slow them down. Just because a horse gets excessively tired and can hardly cross the finish line—well, the Jockey Club would need verification a horse was drugged and not just exhausted. I need proof."

"Who does the drugging and how?"

"From what I have learned, I believe they take some granules of undiluted opium, cut an apple in half, scoop out the center, and put in the opium. An apothecary told me just a teaspoonful or two could make a great deal of difference."

"You mean like laudanum?"

"Laudanum is greatly diluted. Pure opium would have the effect of many doses of laudanum. Timing is crucial. They want people to think the horse is going to win. It should be alert in the saddling ring. If the horse was dosed too long before the race, it could not even make it to the starting line, much less to the finish. The worst effects of the drug came well after the race."

Jane pondered the problem, gazing at the silver sea. "Could you get someone to confess? Or catch them in the act? Does Trentworthy do the deed himself or does he have someone else, who might be part of the gang or entirely innocent, give the drug to the horse just before saddling?"

Cedric shrugged. "Unless we watched every horse in every race, we would not have a chance—and that is impossible."

They resumed walking in silence for a few moments.

Jane stopped again and stared down at the sand. "Did you

not say that hundreds of guineas sometimes change hands in one race?"

"Indeed."

"How does Trentworthy and his gang make money, besides what they get for selling the horses? That does not seem like enough to buy horses and train them, hire grooms and lads to care for them. Where does the money come from? Betting?"

"I suppose they work with a bookmaker who could give long odds, very attractive to impetuous gulls like my friends and me. The bookmaker would know the horse would not win, so he could afford to offer a king's ransom to the bettors."

Jane took his hands in hers. "To beat him at his own game, you must gull him in return. Make his partner, the book-maker, think that Sybil could not possibly win, that she will be drugged again. Get all your friends to bet, lots and lots of money. Then, when she wins the race, the bookmaker, and Trentworthy too, will be ruined."

"But what if she does not win?"

"Did you not say that she was fit and very fast?"

"Yes, but there are so many things that could happen in a race. There are no guarantees. And we cannot break them unless we have a great deal of money. I have little to bet."

"You need a syndicate of your own, Cedric. Besides your friends, get those Trentworthy has cheated, those farmers and Oswald's friends. But you have to make Trentworthy and that bookmaker think Sybil cannot win so they give the long odds. Let them think they can drug her again, that you will never notice."

"Act the fool again?"

"Well, yes, I suppose so, but only temporarily. Then guard her carefully so they cannot do it. When she wins, the book-maker will lose a bundle."

Cedric rubbed his jaw. "Your idea depends on three things. First that Trentworthy thinks he can drug the filly again."

"Yes. You tell him you're going to win this time. If the right bookmaker is giving good odds, you will know they will try to drug her."

"The second thing is that she wins," Cedric said. "And the third is that I can talk people into betting. All three of those things will be difficult."

Jane nodded emphatically. "Yes, if the solution came easily, someone would have already done them in. The bookmaker is probably the key to the whole scheme."

Cedric looked at her with a grin. "You are the last person I would have expected to come up with such a devious plan."

She tilted her head to one side. "I can be a bit underhanded from time to time."

"It is risky, but worth it if we can ruin the bookmaker forever."

She spoke with sudden zeal. "Ordinarily, I deplore wagering in large amounts. But sometimes it is justified, as in this case. The only way those evil men can be defeated is to cause them financial ruin. They do not care for the victims, the horses, the sport of racing. They are selfish, greedy and I despise them!

He pulled her into his arms and kissed her.

She shoved him away. "Do not do that, please, Cedric."

"But I love you, Jane, and I want you to be my wife."

She backed away. "Do not talk nonsense. Your aunt has a plan for you." Jane could not allow herself to listen to him, no matter how fervently she wanted his words to be true.

"She is not an unreasonable woman. I feel quite sure she will welcome my feelings for you."

Jane kicked at the sand. "I am not so sure, Cedric. If you try to change her mind, you will be risking everything. Wait for a while, until after the Newmarket race meeting."

"My dearest Jane, your wisdom is overwhelming. Almost as splendid as your lovely face."

She shook her head, feeling tears threaten. "Please do not say such things to me, Cedric." She would not, could not meet his gaze.

"Then give me one more kiss, Jane."

Against her good sense, she stole a glance at him. He smiled, his lips parted and eyes soft. The breeze ruffled his hair. He held his arms out to her, and she could not help moving to him. "Oh, Cedric, this is foolish of us."

He wrapped his arms around her and drew her close. "I am getting used to being foolish. And I am enjoying this foolishness very much."

CHAPTER FIFTEEN

All the way back from Alderton Castle to Uphaven, Cedric's mind spun with the opportunities and risks inherent in Jane's ideas. He liked her plan, aimed at the money, which had to be the driving force behind the gang.

He did not know how Trentworthy operated his band of scoundrels, not even how many were involved. But he intended to find out.

Could he convince enough men to place bets on Sybil? They would not have to be large bets if the odds were long. At ten to one, for example, a bet of one hundred guineas would bring a return of one thousand.

He drew a shuddering breath. Assuming, that is, that Sybil won the race. She was certainly fast, but he was not a horse trainer, did not know the tricks of the trade. All he knew was he ran her every day, alternating an all-out gallop with several days of lighter work, just as Oswald said to do.

Another unknown was whether Trentworthy would try again to drug the filly. Could he come across as naïve enough to tempt Trentworthy to act? He had played the fool before, however unwittingly. He hoped he could do it again.

He had to contact all the possible players in the scheme to stop Trentworthy, talk to Snelling the blacksmith, and contact Sam.

If any part of the plan was not working out, he would stop everyone from betting. They would not make their wagers with the bookmaker until just before the race began.

Cedric grinned to himself. If he had started out to create a flimsy web of complicated deceptions that all depended upon his skill—if he had tried to make it difficult, he could not have done a better job.

But he was prepared to do his damnedest. In every fiber of his being, he burned to see this plot succeed. He would crush Trentworthy and his gang of scoundrels if it was the last thing he did.

At sundown, after leaving the ladies at the great house, Cedric went to the stables with the coachman.

At Sybil's stall, Sam stood beside Johnny, watching the filly.

Cedric slapped his shoulder. "Sam! You are back!"

"Yessir. And I got plenty of tales for you."

"I am eager to hear every single story you have."

They went into the room where the tack was stored and sat on bales of straw.

Sam drew a deep breath. "After I got to Newmarket, didn't take me long to find the alehouse where the stable lads spent their nights. I listened to all the talkin', and the second night, I got lucky. A fellow, name of Burt, was talking about his work fer a man who gave 'im lots of tips on races. I said the name Trentworthy and he just laughed. Said that might be one of the monikers the cove used. He couldn't remember, 'cause sometimes he had a different name."

Cedric nodded. "Treadwell, for one."

"Always has a couple of horses come to Newmarket, ran one or two and often won. Maiden or novice races, for young horses without much experience. Then usually he had a horse or two he'd offer for sale. Burt sez nobody could make a horse sound finer. Course he said, if you pardon me, Mr. Williamson, he picked the most obvious marks, ones he could easily convince."

"Yes, Sam, that would have been me."

"Well, sir, Burt jest laughed and laughed about how this fellow could sell his horse, then fix it so it couldn't win, then buy it back at less than half the price."

"How did he nobble the horse? Did Burt say?"

"I had to get him devilish foxed, but he finally spilled it. 'Bout the third night, I talked him into some gin and that sure loosened his tongue. Said it was some brown grains, sometimes lumps, put inside an apple."

"Just as I suspected. Does he expect Trentworthy or whatever he is calling himself to be at the meet in a few weeks?"

"He does. And I can be there too, Burt says. They always need an extra lad or two. He'll help me find work sweeping out the stalls where they stable all the horses that come from far off for the meet."

"After he told you how the fiddle operates, maybe he wants you in the game."

"Sir, I don't think Burt remembered much about our talk the next morning. He had a powerful bad head. I told him yesterday I had to go home for a few days, but I'd be back. That is, I will go if it will help you, sir. I didn't like this Burt much. Don't like what he said that fellow did to the horses. And what I saw of poor Sybil when you first brung her here— well, I would fancy helping to put those men to the gibbet, I would."

Cedric clasped Sam's shoulder. "I appreciate all you have done, Sam. Now, with the filly ready, I am figuring out how to stop the scoundrels. Get enough on them to take to the Jockey Club, at least."

"That's another thing, sir. Burt sez he once had a helper called Snare, who tried to get Burt to help him take the fellow to the authorities. Burt was going to do it, but somehow the fellow found out about Snare and he disappeared. Never heard from again. Burt was pretty worried about that, or else that blue ruin had him deeper than I thought. I think these be dangerous men, and not just to horses."

How well he knew, Cedric thought. "Sam, I appreciate your time, more than I can tell you."

"Should I go back to Newmarket?"

"By all means, in a few days. You can be a great help.

I'll be bringing the ladies to Newmarket. Let's say three days before the next meet, I'll be at the Lucky Horseshoe at seven. We'll meet there and you can fill me in on the latest developments."

"And you will give me a part in your plan, sir?"

"Yes, I will need you, Sam. Just stick to Burt and try to get wind of what they are up to. I especially need to know if there is one special bookmaker with whom they connive."

"I knowt that already, sir. Name of Gridley. Burt pointed him out. Said he and Trentworthy were thick as thieves." Sam chuckled at his own little joke.

Cedric grinned and shook his hand. "Sam, you are the best!"

When Sam left him, Cedric sat for a long time staring at the assortment of saddles, bridles and harnesses that hung in the tack room, Jane's plan taking full form in his mind.

Jane slipped into the library and noiselessly closed the door behind her.

"Where have you been all day?" Cedric asked, putting down his quill.

"Your aunt wanted me to drop everything else and help her choose readings for Lord Stockdale's memorial service."

Cedric frowned. "But that is hardly urgent, is it?

"Another month, I believe."

"But you did not ride this morning."

"I know. She wanted to begin early, have everything arranged before we go to Newmarket."

"I am surprised—"

"Cedric, she has lived a very quiet life for the last few years. I think the activity, the traveling, has upset her usual way of life. She says she loves it, yet she fusses."

"Poor dear lady. I shall have to reassure her."

Jane sat in her usual place. "I just snuck away to see what you are doing."

"I have written to most of the people who might wish to come to Newmarket and participate in our great caper."

"Good. I hope they are all favorable."

He reached across the table and took her hand, caressing her palm with his thumb. "What have you been doing for Aunt Amelia?"

"I have been reading Shakespeare's sonnets and some Milton. And John Donne, to find suitable selections." She shivered at his touch, but kept talking to cover her discomfiture. "We will visit the church tomorrow to see what refurbishing is needed."

"I hope I did not contribute to her burden when I gave her those chapters."

Jane felt a sudden stab of fear clutch her stomach. "When did you do that?"

"Yesterday. I suggested she might like to see what we have been doing. She said she would look at them before bed."

Jane's heart thumped as though she were about to step off a precipice. "Thinking of the baron's family probably reminded her of the memorial service."

"Probably. But her preoccupation with the service will probably postpone her perusal of your material."

Jane felt a bit of calmness returning.

Cedric continued. "I received a letter from Charles thanking me for my services at the wedding. He says he and Patience will take a bit of time from their honeymoon to attend the race meet. They will also stay with the Lamberts. He writes that Alfred and Sophy will be there too."

"I declare, Cedric, I do not know what bothers my nerves the most, the thought of Sybil's race or the vision of Lady Stockdale reading my chapters."

"You are no longer bothered by the specter of Aunt Amelia's gentleman offering for you?"

Jane was much more bothered by the thought of how his aunt might require Cedric to offer for a young lady, perhaps for Miss Constance Lambert. But she held her tongue on that subject. "I must go now, Cedric, before Lady Stockdale comes looking for me."

He stood and kept hold of her hand as she came around the table, raising it to his lips. "Until dinner, Jane."

She nodded, the sudden lump in her throat blocking words.

Cedric led the filly into the stable near the Newmarket racecourse three days before the meet. He gave his name to the groom in charge and took the filly to an assigned stall. As he turned her loose inside the box, two men stopped outside to take a look at her. One of them was Sam. Cedric did not acknowledge him, just fiddled with Sybil's halter.

The other man must be Burt. Cedric stepped to the other side of the horse so he could get a better look at the rascal.

"Nice looking filly," Sam said to Burt in a low voice.

Burt nodded. "Aye. Good long legs."

They stood for a moment, then moved on.

Cedric noted Burt's hair, his nose, the nasal quality of his voice, the way he stared through slitted eyes, squinting as though he badly needed spectacles. Cedric tried to recall if he'd seen the man before, if he'd been on hand when he first bought Sybil. Someone had been holding her, leading her around while he and Charles had watched and listened to Trentworthy. It could have been Burt, but Cedric did not have any memory of the face.

Cedric curried the filly, then repeated the job. Eventually, as he expected, Trentworthy opened the door of the stall and leaned against it. Cedric reminded himself to act naïve, make it seem easy for Trentworthy to dupe him again. "Good afternoon."

The man wore a nondescript gray coat with a waistcoat of dull green. His face was so commonplace as to be almost unidentifiable. "Seems to me you owe me the rest of the price for that there filly, Mister. Or should I go for the constable?"

Cedric acted surprised. "Whoa now, you would not want to

do that, Trentworthy. She is running nice as can be. If she wins her race, you can have your blunt."

"Izzat so?" He rocked back on his heels and hooked a thumb through the edge of his waistcoat. "So you admit you owe me?"

"That I do," Cedric said. "I would have paid you if she'd won the last time, but what could I do when she fell apart like that? I lost every farthing I had. Still owe more fellows than just you. Only way I have to settle up is to run her. I expect to bring home a bundle on her."

"Well, now. And here I thought you were a slippery one, taking off in the middle of the night."

"I did not like to do it, but I had to. Say, what do you think happened to her in that race?"

"I was as surprised as anyone."

Even when he was reciting such a brazen lie, his voice sounded as mundane as the drone of a fly.

Trentworthy rocked once more. "Poor thing just broke down."

And I am St. George home from slaying the dragon, Cedric thought. "Let's hope for a better outcome this time."

"I'll do that. I'm glad to hear she's running fast. Whether she wins or loses, don't run off like you did before. You get my meaning?"

"I do." Very clearly!

Cedric watched the man stroll away without closing the stall door. He shut it, wiped a cloth over the filly's shining coat, then sat on a bale of straw. Just another hour or two, to see if he comes back, Cedric thought. Then he felt it was safe to leave Sybil alone.

Later he waited at the Lucky Horseshoe until long past the appointed hour for his meeting with Sam, indulging in nightmarish fantasies about what might have happened to the groom. If anyone had found out he worked for Cedric, what would they have done with him?

When Sam arrived, he took a mug of ale and went into the darker back room. Cedric followed and sat down beside him on a rough bench.

"Sorry I am late, sir," he whispered. "I hung around at the stable 'cause the fellow I think you're looking for showed up. He 'n Burt were laughing about having another horse to nobble."

"Was it Trentworthy, a stocky fellow in a gray jacket and green waistcoat?"

"Yes, that's 'im. I assumed that new horse to fix is Sybil."

"Probably. But if they follow their usual pattern, they won't do anything until just before the race. So you keep watch and I will be there well in advance, before they act. But, Sam, if they do try anything, do not challenge them. A horse race is not worth getting hurt over."

"Yessir."

The next morning, before riding back to Uphaven to escort the ladies to Lambert House, he stopped at the blacksmith's forge near the racecourse, introduced himself to Mr. Snelling's cousin, Rusty, and explained his need.

"I hope you and Snelling will do me a great favor."

The blacksmith, whose forearms were as big around as the average man's thighs, paused in his shaping of thin horseshoes. "He told me you were onto some scheme to nobble horses here. I don't take kindly to chicanery of no kind, 'specially nobbling horses. I'll do what I can and me cousin will, too, when he gets here tomorrow."

"You can be a great help if you listen for information about several men. Trentworthy, sometimes called Treadwell. And a bookmaker called Gridley."

"I know of 'em both, and t'wouldn't surprise me to hear either one'd been up to no good."

"And I need to know if there are any special favorites for the first race. In order to stop those two men, I need to know the competition for my horse."

"Yessir, I'll do my best."

Cedric went back to his room at the Silver Fox and found a letter waiting for him from Mr. Easton. He would come for the race and had set aside a sum to bet on Williamson's filly. Getting back at the gang was going to bring him great satisfaction.

CHAPTER SIXTEEN

With each day that passed, Jane felt more and more tense, catching herself with a wrinkled forehead in every mirror she passed. Some days dragged by so slowly she felt the hourly chimes had surely broken down. At other times, she feared all the pieces of their plan could not be assembled in time. She worried about everything, whether it would rain, or a strong wind would sweep across the heath.

When she brought her fears about the race under control, there were a hundred other worries to take their place. What would Lady Stockdale think of her chapters? Or, indeed, would she find the time to read them?

Then the matter of those matches Lady Stockdale still dangled before her. And in front of Cedric as well. Lady Stockdale rarely mentioned them outright, but made remarks about what Jane should take in order to look her loveliest at the Lambert House race week festivities.

Cedric had taken the filly to Newmarket several days early so that she would be well rested before her race, the first race on the first day, for the youngest, least experienced horses. Jane had actually cried when Cedric rode off to Newmarket on the cob Sandy, leading Sybil behind him. It was only her nerves, she thought, smoothing out the handkerchief she had almost shredded in her distress.

By the time Cedric returned to accompany his aunt, her mother and Jane to the Lamberts', she was as nervous as a hen facing a fox. "How is Sybil adjusting?"

He patted her hand. "She is fine. Her jockey has galloped her around the racecourse several times and says she feels good."

"Is he a good man?"

"I am assured he is honest and will ride to win."

"I pray he does his job."

Once they arrived at the spacious Lambert estate, Jane promised herself she would keep her fears and emotions under control for Cedric's sake.

But she felt almost in a trance as they strolled the grounds, toured the town and countryside, dined and played cards. Cedric and the other gentlemen spent a good deal of time watching the horses work out on the heath and spoke of little but their chances in various races during the meet.

On the evening before Sybil's fateful race, Jane and Cedric stole a few moments alone in the moonlight beyond the terrace where most of the men had gathered to drink wine and smoke cigars in the late summer warmth.

Cedric waited for her at the side door with an open champagne bottle and two glasses. They quickly sought the privacy of the darkened garden, and found a bench near the fragrant, moon-tipped roses.

He poured her a glass of champagne and filled one for himself. "I have hardly seen you in the past days."

"You do not know how difficult it has been for me, sitting with the ladies, wondering how our plans are going."

"I think everything is in readiness. Quite a few of those I wrote to are here, ready to make their bets on Sybil with the bookmaker Gridley, just before the race."

"I wish I could be there."

He gave a little laugh and refilled their glasses. "You know that is impossible, Jane."

She nodded and took a swallow of the wine, letting it tickle her throat as it went down.

"The blacksmiths have reported on Sybil's competition, such as it is. These maiden races are difficult to predict."

As he continued to outline the status of their plan, Jane felt a little rebellion growing in the back of her mind. But she pushed it away, listening to Cedric instead.

"Sam will be nearby in the barn, keeping his eye on things, and I will go there early and stay in Sybil's stall. If I am there, at her head, I do not see how they can try to give her anything at the last minute. I will lead her to the saddling ring myself."

Jane nodded again, unwilling to express the anxiety that kept her heart racing. Instead, she drained her glass again and held it out for more.

A bright half moon glowed in the sky, casting a silvery sheen over the shrubbery and flowers. Water splashed in a nearby fountain, and from a distance came the sound of hearty laughter. She did not know whether to join in or cry, instead.

Cedric pulled her into his arms and pressed her head against his shoulder.

"Whatever happens tomorrow, Jane, my feelings for you are deep and lasting. After the race is over, I intend to speak to Aunt Amelia and tell her I want to marry you."

"But no, Cedric. You cannot."

"Yes, I can. I have heard quite enough of this matchmaking scheme of hers."

"Please do not go against her wishes."

"She will come around to seeing our marriage as best for all of us."

With all her heart, Jane wanted to agree with him. But her head spoke differently.

"Just promise me to wait a little longer, Cedric. Please."

"If that is your desire, Jane, I will honor it. But—" He reached out to take her in his arms.

Quickly she stood and handed him the glass. "I must go now, before you—before I . . ."

She whirled and dashed toward the house, running away from her heart again.

***

The next morning, Jane waited beside Cedric's borrowed pony trap.

Cedric was adamant. "Jane, you simply cannot come along with me. You must go later, in the barouche with the other ladies."

"No, Cedric, I want to go to the stables and be with Sybil."

"Ladies do not frequent the racecourse except to watch from their carriages. There are people with whom you would not wish to mix. And you would become a subject of gossip."

"Do not be a thick-skulled widgeon, Cedric. I do not care what people say. I want to be with Sybil."

"Sybil does not need you. She has me. And she even has Sam."

"That does not matter. I must be with her."

Cedric heaved a great sigh. Anyone would think she was the most compliant and biddable of young ladies. Her gray eyes looked entirely innocent beneath her straw bonnet tied with a wide blue ribbon; she looked like a perfect French doll in her blue pelisse with its matching parasol. But Jane was clearly not cooperative this morning.

"My dear, what if you get in the way?" he asked.

"Cedric Williamson, I am quite able to take care of myself."

"I cannot watch over you. I have to keep myself at the filly's head every moment to be sure no one gives her anything to eat or drink in the stable or before the race when the crowds will be looking over the horses and making their final bets. No ladies come to the barns."

"So this will be the first time."

"Really, Jane, there will be nothing for you to do, just stand there while I keep watch in her stall."

"I will keep you company."

"But we cannot talk. I will be listening for any bit of conversation I can pick up. And ladies simply do not—"

"Pooh. You have said yourself that from time to time the wife of a trainer might be with him."

"But I am not a trainer and you are not . . ."

"Why not the betrothed of the horse's owner? Who will object to that?"

Cedric almost jumped out of his skin. "What? Betrothed? But I thought you said you would not . . ." His voice failed him.

"I would not say yes last night, Cedric, because I feared my answer would be coming from the champagne." She cast her eyes downward. "Or because when you kiss me, I cannot think. Anyway, you promised me on the beach that we would wait until after the race meeting. But now I have changed my mind. If you ask me again in the light of day, and without coming an inch closer, I will give you my answer."

Even though she had just called herself his betrothed, he found his mouth had gone dry and his brain had emptied. When he opened his mouth, nothing came forth.

Jane frowned.

Abruptly the words gushed out. "Jane Gabriel, will you marry me? I know I am not a good catch, that I have some ways to go—"

She placed two fingers on his lips, pressing them shut. "It is a simple question, is it not? And I answer simply. Yes."

Her parasol fell to the ground as he swept her into his arms.

When she pulled back from his kiss, she had a mischievous light in her eye. "So now you cannot keep me from coming with you."

He sighed. "I know when to give up, Jane. You win."

Jane accepted Cedric's help into his trap and clamped her teeth onto her lower lip to keep it from trembling. What had she done, agreeing so blithely to marry him? Would he hold her to her promise later, or would he see the match as fool-hardy once the filly had won her race and he was the darling of his fashionable friends, the victorious owner of a victorious racehorse?

He took up the reins and nodded to the groom, who hopped up behind them.

She settled back against the backrest and tried to calm her pounding pulse. She hoped she could help, be at his side when he led Sybil out, and see his grin as he watched the filly win her contest.

Anything still could happen. If Cedric's expectations of how the events of the day would unfold were fulfilled, he would lead the filly to the saddling ring himself, without the attendance of that wicked groom Burt. Once Sybil was saddled and the jockey was up, there would no longer be a chance for anyone to give Sybil a drug or do anything else that could spoil her chances.

At the large racecourse barn, she climbed down and took Cedric's arm to enter. Contrary to what she had expected, the structure was alive with activity. Grooms, stable lads, jockeys, and many, many others milled about in the aisles, and she caught a number of faces surprised to see a lady walking among them. On second thought, she mused, they probably did not think she was a lady.

At Sybil's stall she looked carefully at the filly, who appeared to be entirely calm. In the next stall she sighted Sam, slowly grooming another horse, but watching them from the corner of his eye. She caught the quick nod he gave to Cedric.

"Well, my lovely girl," Cedric said to the filly. "I hope you are ready for your big day."

She nickered softly and leaned into his hand tickling her ears.

Jane looked about her but could not identify anyone who met the description Cedric had given of the wicked Burt. Or rather, any of a half dozen men within view could be the one.

She pressed herself against the door of the stall, trying to be as inconspicuous as possible and closed her ears to the chatter around her. Cedric had been correct, of course. She really did not belong here in this man's world. She concentrated on thinking about Sybil, of how game she was to recover from the drugs forced on her, to run again without fear. She tried to will her strength to Sybil, though the filly probably had plenty of her own. Especially with the good mash Jane had added to her feed.

Slowly the time passed, as they waited for the first race to be called. Sybil seemed just as usual, alert but not excited. Another quarter hour crawled by. Jane was determined not to flinch from the job at hand, protecting the horse. But Cedric was right. There was nothing to do but let her imagination go wild. What if a gang of men burst in and overpowered Cedric? But in the bustle of the stable where so many horses were being prepared for the day's races, how could that happen? She chided herself for being too fanciful. With Cedric—and her— at the horse's side, no one, not even a gang, would dare to approach them in the presence of so many other people.

Cedric motioned to her. "Come give a last pat to our girl before we get her outside to be saddled."

When she stood near him, he lowered his voice to a whisper. "I think we have thwarted any plans they had to drug her, because it would have to have been within the last few moments. Soon, I'll take her out to be saddled. Once out there in the crowd, I do not see what they could do to her."

Jane took off her glove and slid her hand down Sybil's glossy neck. "Good. My darling girl. I expect you to run your very best. Will you do that?"

The filly blinked her bright eyes and pawed at the straw.

The first horses were led out of the barn to the saddling area, each followed by a group of men. Within minutes, the barn was nearly empty. Cedric buckled on Sybil's bridle and opened the door of the stall.

There stood Trentworthy, rocking back on his heels, hands in his pockets. "She is looking fit, my friend," he said.

Cedric stopped in his tracks. "What are you doing here?"

"Just looking after my money, don't ye know?"

And suddenly another man, a dark fellow, tried to snatch the lead line from Cedric.

Cedric elbowed him away. "Watch out, Burt. I will do this myself."

Almost too fast for Cedric to catch, Burt had his hand out of his pocket and stuck an apple toward Sybil's mouth.

Jane gave a little scream. Cedric knocked the apple to the floor.

"We'll have none of that," Cedric snarled.

Jane kicked the fruit into the straw.

Burt hesitated just a moment too long, and Cedric punched him hard in the stomach. As Burt began to double over, Cedric drove his fist into the groom's jaw with an audible crunch. Burt crumpled to the floor and lay without moving.

"Fool!" Trentworthy spat.

"Go, fast," Jane hissed at Cedric.

Cedric started to lead out the filly, then paused, looking back at her.

Instead of reaching down to help his man, Trentworthy backed away to avoid the horse.

"Go, quickly," she said, giving Cedric a push.

Jane started to follow him, then realized Trentworthy might scramble for that apple, the evidence they could use to end his evil deeds forever. She did the only thing she could think of. She flung herself at Trentworthy.

"Oh, I think I shall faint. Please, sir, please." She caught his waistcoat as she fell against him and clawed at it. "Help me, please."

He grabbed her around the shoulders, and tried to push her away, but she reached up to hold onto his neck.

She had to get him away from the stall and trust that Burt was out for a long time. "Water," she moaned. "I need water."

"Here, sir." She recognized Sam's voice. "You must carry her outside."

"You take her," Trentworthy said.

But Sam was already trotting down the long walkway between the stalls, holding open the door, motioning to them.

Jane staggered against Trentworthy, letting most of her

weight pull on his neck and grasping his waistcoat as tightly as she could. She let her feet drag, hoping to slow his progress. Once he got her outside, he could put her on the grass and run back to the stall. If he got hold of that apple and somehow got it to Sybil before the race began, all their efforts would be for naught.

Slowly he hauled her toward the door. Trentworthy puffed with the effort. "Here now, miss, let go."

Her answer was a long moan, and she tightened her grip on his collar.

He gave her a heave, but she held on. "Here, man, give me a hand."

But Sam had disappeared.

Trentworthy managed to get her outside, just beyond the door. "Let go of me, woman," he gasped. He thrust his hands against her shoulders, and she feared she would have to let go.

She tried to kick his shin but her pelisse was too tight to get a good swing at him. As she felt herself begin to slide down, she put all her strength into shoving an elbow into his ribs. But it hit lower, squarely between his legs.

For a fraction of a second he did not cry out, and she fell in a heap at his feet. Then his wail began with a rumble in his throat rising higher to a gurgle that twanged like a broken hurdy-gurdy. He clutched at himself, sank to his knees, and rolled onto his side, groaning, curling himself into a circle.

"How dare you simply drop me, Mr. Trentworthy?" She was certain he did not hear, could not hear. She thought she ought to be ashamed of herself for committing such an unladylike assault. But since she knew very well how he'd been cheating folks for a long time, she felt rather proud of herself.

Sam ran up with a length of cord and a shovel. "What did you do to 'im, Miss Gabriel?"

"I think I hurt him rather badly, Sam."

"Oh!" Sam took a second look and let out a guffaw. "One thing's sure, miss, he won't be running to his bookmaker to change his odds at the last moment. I was fixing to slam him over the head with this spade."

Jane brushed the dust from her pelisse and readjusted her bonnet. "That might have killed him. He will not die from my blow, but I predict he will be uncomfortable for a long time."

"I wouldn't be surprised, Miss."

Cedric led the filly to the saddling ring. She seemed unaffected by the scuffle, her head high, looking toward the other horses.

He glanced behind him, expecting to see Jane hurrying after them. He wanted to hustle back to see where she was, but he had no one to hold Sybil. He never should have left Jane.

Before he could give it any more thought, the jockey, Bobby Chambers, carried the saddle to him. Together, they set it on Sybil's back and did up the girth.

Cedric looked back again, but did not see her yet. And where was Sam? His nerves stretched even tauter, Cedric led the filly around the ring. She pranced a little, lively and ready to run.

It had all happened so fast. As long as he was there, Cedric believed Sybil was safe. They would not dare to interfere. As long as he was protecting the horse, he had not imagined that Trentworthy and his gang would try anything so brazen as to feed the apple to the filly right in front of him. But he had not counted on such a simple, quick skirmish.

Jane watched Trentworthy groan. He did not look as though he was about to leap to his feet. Not for a very long time. "Come, Sam, let's go find that apple. Then we may go and watch Sybil win her race."

But finding the apple took longer than she had imagined. First, Sam had to tie up Burt, who was beginning to stir. Then he raked carefully and slowly through the straw. Jane wished she could take the rake herself, but Sam insisted on keeping her at a distance from Burt, even though he was still too groggy to speak. Eventually Sam found both halves of the apple, not far from one another.

"Be very careful picking them up, Sam. There could be some drugs there."

"Yes, Miss Gabriel, there is something, all right."

Sam handed her the first half, clearly holding brown granules. The other half, too, had grains of a brown substance stuck to it.

Jane took it gently, pressed the two halves together and wrapped the apple in a handkerchief. She put it into her reticule. "I think Cedric will want to see this. And show it to the Jockey Club."

Cedric felt wound as tight as a spring run clock. If Jane had been hurt, he would never forgive himself.

"Is she eager to run, sir?" the jockey asked.

"I hope so, Bobby. She has had only a few races, and the last one was a disaster. So let her set her own pace. Just don't let her fall too far back."

"I will do my best."

"I have every expectation of a win. She bested Mr. Walker's Lionheart two weeks ago in a little test race."

Cedric looked toward the stable again. Still no sign of Jane.

Bobby squinted at the filly. "Then she should do well."

Cedric searched for a familiar face in the crowd watching the parade of runners. Everything might be riding on Sybil, but he had to get back to the stable and see what was keeping Jane. Surely she had been able to get away from Trentworthy. Sam must be helping her. Devil take it, he never should have left her.

At last, he saw Charles and Alfred waving from across the ring.

He headed straight for them. "Charles, Al, can you give me a hand?"

They ducked under the rope and Cedric handed Sybil's reins to Alfred. "You two and Bobby know what to do. I have to get back to the stables. Get her out there to win."

"But what are you—"

"Where are you going?"

Cedric did not wait to answer but pushed his way through the thickening crowd and broke into a run.

There was no sign of Jane or Sam outside the stable, but he dashed inside and found them in Sybil's stall. Jane stood holding a spade and watching Sam retie a cord around Burt's feet. Trentworthy was curled up in a corner, moaning.

Cedric felt a wave of relief wash over him. Jane was safe.

She grabbed Cedric's arm. "What happened in the race?"

"It is just starting now."

"But where is—" she began.

"Alfred and Charles are leading the filly."

"Is she all right?"

"I think so."

"What about the money, Cedric? All your friends and all those farmers, everyone who joined us. Did they all bet with Gridley?"

"I think so. And you kept Trentworthy from getting to Gridley and telling him. He could not have done much in the last minutes, but he could have laid off some of those bets with other bookmakers."

Trentworthy let out a deep moan, this time not all from his pain, it seemed.

"You must want to see the race, Cedric. Go back and watch."

"Here, now, what's this." A man strode into the stable and peered into the stall. "I'm Bartholomew, from the Jockey Club. Someone said there was a ruckus over here."

Cedric pointed at Trentworthy. "That man tried to fix this race." He waved at the form of Burt, who was struggling to pull his wrists from the cord. "That man, under orders, tried to feed drugs to my horse."

"I didn't do nothing," Burt growled.

Jane stepped forward. "He tried to give our horse an apple full of opium to make her sick."

"He made me do it," Burt sniveled, motioning his head toward Trentworthy.

Bartholomew looked from one to the other. "I had better get the constables to take these men into custody."

Burt spat out his words. "I didn't do nothing but what he told me to do."

Bartholomew stepped closer to Trentworthy. "What's wrong with him?"

"He had a little accident," Cedric said.

Trentworthy gargled a few words, but they made no sense.

Two more men in the black coats of the Jockey Club came into the stable.

Bartholomew gestured to them. "Here's Mr. Grant. He's a constable." He turned to Grant. "These people accuse the two men in this stall of trying to fix the race."

"I been hoping to get the goods on that fellow," Grant said, gesturing to Trentworthy.

The other man in Jockey Club garb hauled Burt to his feet.

Cedric could not keep the satisfaction for his voice. "Take them away. We will provide the proof as soon as you have them secured."

Jane pulled on Cedric's arm. "Let them settle things here," she whispered. "If we run we might be able to see the end of the race."

Cedric turned back as Jane drew him away. "I will talk to you after the race."

"Yessir," Bartholomew said. "We'll see to these bounders."

Cedric heard shouts from the racecourse, and they hurried in that direction. As the noise grew, his pulse sped faster.

Jane panted as she spoke. "You run, Cedric. I'll come as fast as I can."

"No, I must stay with you." He would never let her out of his sight again. Ever.

"I am fine, just hurry or you will miss the whole thing."

The cheering crescendoed. Cedric was sure he could hear Alfred's voice above the roar.

Cedric kept hold of Jane's arm though she tried to push him away. "Please hurry."

"No. I am staying with you. Permanently."

At last they reached the back of the crowd and tried to edge forward. By the time they pushed through to the rail, the race was over.

Cedric squinted toward the chalkboard where they would post the number of the winner. He felt his heart was pounding at the very back of his throat.

Jane looked toward the carriages farther down the course, where the groups of ladies sat. "Patience is standing and applauding, Cedric. I think Sybil must have won."

Cedric stopped still and watched the sweating horses returning to the finish line, the jockey in a red cap leading the pack. Sybil indeed seemed to be heading for the winner's circle.

He wrapped his arms around Jane. "I think we have done it!"

Lambert House had never seen a more uproarious victory celebration. Gridley's accounts were empty long before he paid out all the winning wagers, but no one seemed to mind.

One after another, they told the story of the race from every angle of the course, stride by stride, as the gallant filly outran the entire field. Cedric and Jane repeated their versions of the arrest of Trentworthy and Burt, with evidence enough to convince any magistrate in the land. Several members of the Jockey Club related tales of how the two criminals, along with Gridley, were busily blaming each other and implicating several other men.

Mr. Poynton and Mr. Easton said little, but drank and ate with vigor as they rejoiced. Ben Frey and Oswald Walker were deliriously foxed.

Cedric and Jane visited the kitchen where Sam had the maids in awe of his heroism. He patted his pocket, full of the winnings he would take back to many of the servants at Uphaven, for he had brought their bets to Gridley and had been among the first to claim his spoils, before the constable closed Gridley down.

But the loudest cheers and cries of excitement came when Cedric stood on the stairs and hushed the crowd in the hall.

"After our great victory today, I have more good news to share. Miss Gabriel has consented to become my wife."

Jane was nearly crushed in a flurry of hugs from Sophy, Patience and all the ladies.

Not for half an hour after Cedric's announcement did Jane find a moment to speak to Lady Stockdale.

"Lady Stockdale, I hope I am not upsetting your plans for your nephew. I know you had a match in mind for him at Alderton Castle . . ."

"And I had a match in mind for you too. As clever as you are, Jane, sometimes you can be very thick. As for Cedric, I thought he would adopt my plan, jump at the chance to follow my wishes immediately."

Jane's heart fell to the tips of her toes. Poor Cedric, after all his efforts, he would lose everything.

But Lady Stockdale wore a wise half-smile, a strange expression for a formidable lady whose wishes had been contradicted. "You still do not catch on, do you, Jane?"

"No, ma'am."

"The match I had in mind was yours. Yours and Cedric's. Now come to me and give me a kiss. I wish to have the banns called as soon as we return home."

Jane pressed her lips to Lady Stockdale's soft cheek. "I am glad you approve. Can I ask you one more little question?" Jane's pulse raced faster than when she had confronted Trentworthy.

"What is that, my dear?"

"Have you read the chapters of the Stockdale story that Cedric gave to you?"

"Yes, and I thought they were exceedingly good. You did an excellent job."

"What?" Jane felt thoroughly bewildered.

"Oh, come now, Jane. Did you think I could not tell whose scholarly work and spirited prose style they were? I think Cedric is becoming quite a remarkable young man, has made more progress than I expected. But to think he could write like that? No, my dear, I recognized your work almost immediately."

Jane sat amazed, without knowing how to react.

"I suspected you wanted to write the whole book. You have almost asked me several times, have you not?"

"Yes, almost."

"If your husband will let you continue, I cannot think of a better person to complete the project."

Jane felt the tears rolling down her cheeks. "Thank you."

Cedric sat down beside her. "Why are you crying, Jane? Aunt Amelia, what has happened?"

Lady Stockdale lifted an eyebrow. "She has rather a lot to tell you, Cedric. And I think you are going to like what you hear."

Author's Note

Newmarket has been a center of English racing for centuries. For a few pictures, go to *www.victoriahinshaw.com* and click on "England," then "Autumn 2003" on the left-hand menu.

<u>BOOK YOUR PLACE ON OUR WEBSITE</u>
<u>AND MAKE THE</u>
<u>READING CONNECTION!</u>

We've created a customized website just for our very special readers, where you can get the inside scoop on everything that's going on with Zebra, Pinnacle and Kensington books.

When you come online, you'll have the exciting opportunity to:

- View covers of upcoming books
- Read sample chapters
- Learn about our future publishing schedule (listed by publication month *and author*)
- Find out when your favorite authors will be visiting a city near you
- Search for and order backlist books from our online catalog
- Check out author bios and background information
- Send e-mail to your favorite authors
- Meet the Kensington staff online
- Join us in weekly chats with authors, readers and other guests
- Get writing guidelines
- AND MUCH MORE!

**Visit our website at
http://www.kensingtonbooks.com**

More Regency Romance
From Zebra

__**A Daring Courtship**   0-8217-7483-2   **$4.99**US/**$6.99**CAN
  by Valerie King

__**A Proper Mistress**   0-8217-7410-7   **$4.99**US/**$6.99**CAN
  by Shannon Donnelly

__**A Viscount for Christmas**   0-8217-7552-9   **$4.99**US/**$6.99**CAN
  by Catherine Blair

__**Lady Caraway's Cloak**   0-8217-7554-5   **$4.99**US/**$6.99**CAN
  by Hayley Ann Solomon

__**Lord Sandhurst's Surprise**   0-8217-7524-3   **$4.99**US/**$6.99**CAN
  by Maria Greene

__**Mr. Jeffries and the Jilt**   0-8217-7477-8   **$4.99**US/**$6.99**CAN
  by Joy Reed

__**My Darling Coquette**   0-8217-7484-0   **$4.99**US/**$6.99**CAN
  by Valerie King

__**The Artful Miss Irvine**   0-8217-7460-3   **$4.99**US/**$6.99**CAN
  by Jennifer Malin

__**The Reluctant Rake**   0-8217-7567-7   **$4.99**US/**$6.99**CAN
  by Jeanne Savery

Available Wherever Books Are Sold!

Visit our website at **www.kensingtonbooks.com**.

More Historical Romance From
Jo Ann Ferguson

__A Christmas Bride   0-8217-6760-7   **$4.99US/$6.99CAN**

__His Lady Midnight   0-8217-6863-8   **$4.99US/$6.99CAN**

__A Guardian's Angel   0-8217-7174-4   **$4.99US/$6.99CAN**

__His Unexpected Bride   0-8217-7175-2   **$4.99US/$6.99CAN**

__A Rather Necessary End   0-8217-7176-0   **$4.99US/$6.99CAN**

__Grave Intentions   0-8217-7520-0   **$4.99US/$6.99CAN**

__Faire Game   0-8217-7521-9   **$4.99US/$6.99CAN**

__A Sister's Quest   0-8217-6788-7   **$5.50US/$7.50CAN**

__Moonlight on Water   0-8217-7310-0   **$5.99US/$7.99CAN**

Available Wherever Books Are Sold!

Visit our website at **www.kensingtonbooks.com**.